Last Request

The man Longarm had shot came after the rifle. He pitched forward and fell end over end down the stairs, finally coming to rest with a big crash at the bottom. Longarm kept his Colt trained on the man and got a toe under his shoulder, then rolled him over onto his back

"Patch McCurdy." Longarm's voice echoed slightly in the dusty, deserted rear foyer.

Patch McCurdy opened his one good eye and glared up at Longarm. He had both hands pressed to his midsection. Bright red blood welled between the splayed fingers.

"Kill . . . me . . ."

"Make the dyin' easier for you, you mean? No, I think I'll just stand here and watch while your guts come oozin' outta that big hole in your belly."

"You . . . bastard!"

McCurdy flopped onto his side, then rolled onto his stomach and started crawling across the foyer toward his rifle, leaving a crimson smear of blood in his wake. Longarm waited until the would-be killer got his hands on the Winchester and tried to swing the barrel around toward him.

"Well, if you insist . . ."

The Colt blasted again, and McCurdy dropped back to the floor, a bullet hole in the middle of his forehead and his brains splashed across the linoleum under him.

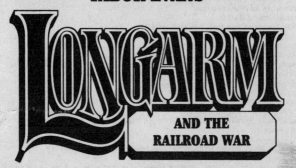

LONGARM

AND THE
RAILROAD WAR

—◆ TABOR EVANS ◆—

J

JOVE BOOKS, NEW YORK

THE BERKLEY PUBLISHING GROUP
Published by the Penguin Group
Penguin Group (USA) Inc.
375 Hudson Street, New York, New York 10014, USA

Penguin Group (Canada), 90 Eglinton Avenue East, Suite 700, Toronto, Ontario M4P 2Y3, Canada
(a division of Pearson Penguin Canada Inc.)
Penguin Books Ltd., 80 Strand, London WC2R 0RL, England
Penguin Group Ireland, 25 St. Stephen's Green, Dublin 2, Ireland (a division of Penguin Books Ltd.)
Penguin Group (Australia), 250 Camberwell Road, Camberwell, Victoria 3124, Australia
(a division of Pearson Australia Group Pty. Ltd.)
Penguin Books India Pvt. Ltd., 11 Community Centre, Panchsheel Park, New Delhi—110 017, India
Penguin Group (NZ), 67 Apollo Drive, Rosedale, North Shore 0632, New Zealand
(a division of Pearson New Zealand Ltd.)
Penguin Books (South Africa) (Pty.) Ltd., 24 Sturdee Avenue, Rosebank, Johannesburg 2196,
South Africa

Penguin Books Ltd., Registered Offices: 80 Strand, London WC2R 0RL, England

LONGARM AND THE RAILROAD WAR

A Jove Book / published by arrangement with the author

PRINTING HISTORY
Jove edition / October 2010

Copyright © 2010 by Penguin Group (USA) Inc.
Cover illustration by Milo Sinovcic.

ISBN: 978-0-515-14846-6

JOVE®
Jove Books are published by The Berkley Publishing Group,
a division of Penguin Group (USA) Inc.,
375 Hudson Street, New York, New York 10014.
JOVE® is a registered trademark of Penguin Group (USA) Inc.
The "J" design is a trademark of Penguin Group (USA) Inc.

PRINTED IN THE UNITED STATES OF AMERICA

10   9   8   7   6   5   4   3   2   1

Chapter 1

Longarm was whistling cheerfully as he started up the steps of the Federal Building in Denver. It was a beautiful morning, and for a change, he wasn't late for a meeting with Chief Marshal Billy Vail. As a matter of fact, he was a little early.

That was because Billy was going to tell him to take the next two weeks off from his job as a deputy United States marshal. Peace had plumb broke out across the West. Billy had alluded to the vacation when he was talking to Longarm the day before, and today he would make it official.

Longarm was only halfway up the steps when shouts and screams erupted behind him.

He stopped, wheeled around, and saw a wagon loaded with barrels careening down Colfax Avenue. The six big, sturdy draft horses pulling it were racing along as if something had plunged them into a state of sheer terror. The man perched on the high seat at the front of the wagon sawed at the reins but couldn't slow the stampeding team.

Pedestrians scattered in front of the wagon, running for dear life to get out of the way. Most of them made it, but a woman with a young child suddenly tripped as she tried to scoop the little girl up into her arms. The woman sprawled on the cobblestones. The girl stood beside her, screaming as the runaway bore down on both of them.

Instinct took over and sent Longarm bounding down the steps in long leaps. Just as he took off, he felt as much as heard something buzz past his ear. He paid no attention to it. Everything in his being was focused on reaching the woman and the little girl before the horses and the wagon crushed them.

Other people were closer, but none of them moved with the blinding speed of the big lawman. In fact, none of them moved at all, because they were transfixed by the horror of what was about to happen. It was like watching a train wreck. They couldn't take their eyes off it.

Longarm reached the street. The horses loomed up close on his left as he darted across the cobblestones. The woman had managed to get to one knee, but obviously she was shaken up by her fall and wasn't going to be able to get out of the way in time, much less carry her daughter with her.

Without slowing his headlong plunge, Longarm reached down, wrapped an arm around each of them, and then launched himself forward in a desperate dive that carried all three of them out of the way of the team, although the horses' hooves pounded the cobblestones no more than a foot away from where Longarm landed.

He kept his arms wrapped tightly around the woman and the little girl and rolled over. The wagon swerved a little and the rear left wheel almost got them. Again the miss was only by inches.

At that moment, the leather strap holding the barrels on the wagon snapped under the strain. The barrels began to roll backward off the wagon. Longarm didn't know what was in them, but whatever it was, he didn't want them landing on him. He got a foot under him, surged up, and leaped out of the way yet again. The barrels shattered under the impact, strewing rocks of some sort across Colfax Avenue.

Longarm had the little girl cradled in his left arm. His right arm was around the woman's trim waist, and her feet swung off the ground as Longarm carried both of them onto the sidewalk. Down the street, the runaway wagon kept going.

Longarm set the woman and the little girl on the sidewalk, and even though he was breathless from the swift action that had just taken place, he managed to say, "If you ladies will excuse me . . ."

Then he turned, drew the Colt .44 from the crossdraw rig on his left hip, and raised the revolver. Squinting slightly, he drew a bead and fired.

On the seat of the runaway wagon, the driver yelped as Longarm's bullet shattered his left shoulder. The man dropped the reins and grabbed at the wound. As he did, the wagon gave another lurch, this one violent enough to throw the driver right off the seat. He sailed through the air, crashed to the ground, rolled over, and then lay there motionless, obviously stunned.

With no hand on the reins, the team swerved wildly back and forth, making the wagon sway until it turned over. Wood flew in the air as sideboards splintered and wheel spokes snapped. A screeching sound filled the air as the horses dragged the wagon on its side for several yards before its weight forced them to stop.

Longarm looked at the man he had shot and decided that the hombre wasn't going anywhere for a few minutes. Still gripping the Colt, he ran toward a building across the street from the Federal Building. He was scraped and bruised from diving and landing on the cobblestones, but he ignored those aches and pains for the moment. He had more important things to do than worry about a few minor injuries.

The building was three stories tall and housed assorted offices: lawyers, bookkeepers, sales firms, a doctor, and a dentist who claimed he was painless. Inside, Longarm headed for the rear of the building because he was interested in the service stairs. He pounded across the lobby, down a hallway, and through a door that opened into a small rear foyer. Rapid footsteps sounded on the narrow staircase that ascended to his right.

As he turned and looked up at the landing, a man appeared there, his left hand grabbing the lintel on the railing to steady himself as he took the turn fast. His right hand held a Winchester.

When the man saw Longarm at the bottom of the stairs, he tried to stop, but his momentum carried him into the wall with a solid thud. He bounced off and started to raise the rifle to his shoulder, but he never had a chance.

The .44 in Longarm's hand roared twice. Both slugs punched into the man's guts and doubled him over. The rifle slipped from his fingers and tumbled down the stairs. Longarm stepped back quickly, trying to get out of the line of fire in case the Winchester discharged on its way down.

The man Longarm had shot came after the rifle. He pitched forward and fell end over end down the stairs, finally coming to rest with a big crash at the bottom. Longarm stepped forward and used a booted foot to slide the rifle across the foyer where it would be out of reach of the man who had dropped it. He kept his Colt trained on the man as he got a toe under his shoulder and rolled him over onto his back.

"Patch McCurdy." Longarm's voice echoed slightly in the dusty, deserted rear foyer. The man on the floor had a black patch over his left eye. "I thought that was Little Ike on the wagon."

Patch McCurdy opened his one good eye and glared up at Longarm. He had both hands pressed to his midsection. Bright red blood welled between the splayed fingers.

"You . . . you killed me . . . you son of a bitch!"

A grimace tugged at one corner of Longarm's mouth under the sweeping longhorn mustache.

"Seems like you were tryin' to do the same to me a few minutes ago. Little Ike was supposed to distract everybody on the street with that phony runaway while you plugged me from a third-floor window. Nobody would've seen where the shot came from because they were all looking at the wagon. That was the plan, wasn't it?"

McCurdy opened his mouth, but the only thing that came out was a groan. Longarm didn't really need the confirmation. He knew what had happened and why.

"You figured I'd stand there and stare, too, while you ventilated me, but you didn't know that woman and her kid were gonna get caught right in the path of the runaway. When I took off to try to get to them in time, it made you miss and fouled up your whole scheme. Ike tried to run me down then, but he didn't quite make it. Then I reckon he probably cut the strap holding those barrels on, hoping that'd do the trick, but I managed to avoid them, too. The two of you just had bad luck all the way around. Reckon you got the worst of it, though, Patch. Ike's got a busted shoulder, but you're gutshot."

This time, McCurdy managed to get a couple of words out.

"Kill . . . me . . ."

"Make the dyin' easier for you, you mean?" Longarm used his left hand to slide a cheroot from his vest pocket and stuck it between his teeth. He didn't bother to light it.

"I might've considered that, old son, if you two inconsiderate bastards hadn't come so damn close to killin' a woman and a little girl, too. No, I think I'll just stand here and watch while your guts come oozin' outta that big hole in your belly."

"You . . . bastard!"

McCurdy flopped onto his side, then rolled onto his stomach and started crawling across the foyer toward his rifle, leaving a crimson smear of blood in his wake. Longarm waited until the would-be killer got his hands on the Winchester and tried to swing the barrel around toward him.

"Well, if you insist . . ."

The Colt blasted again, and McCurdy dropped back to the floor, a bullet hole in the middle of his forehead and his brains splashed across the linoleum under him.

Longarm thumbed fresh cartridges into the revolver's cylinder to replace the ones he had fired, then kept the gun in his hand as he walked back along the hallway toward the building's lobby. Quite a crowd had gathered, but they parted quickly at the sight of the tall, grim-faced lawman.

As he left the building, he saw several uniformed police officers standing around Little Ike McCurdy, Patch's brother, who had regained consciousness and was sitting up in the street. Longarm heard the diminutive outlaw's whining, high-pitched voice as he approached.

"You gotta get me to a sawbones, I tell you. I'm gonna bleed to death!" Then Little Ike caught sight of Longarm walking toward him and cringed like a whipped puppy. "There he is! Don't let him shoot me again! Don't let that loco bastard kill me! He didn't have to shoot me! I didn't mean to let them horses get away from me!"

Longarm smiled down at him. "You didn't let 'em get away from you, Little Ike. I reckon when we take a look, we'll find some burrs or something else to irritate them tucked up under their harness. It don't really matter, though. Patch is dead, but before he died, he told me the whole thing."

That was stretching the truth a little, but it wouldn't be the first time.

"You and your brother were trying to kill me because I had to kill your pa last year when I went to bring him in for those stagecoach robberies."

Little Ike began to sob. "You didn't have to shoot him."

"No, I suppose I could've let him chop my head in two with that ax, but I just didn't feel like it at the time."

One of the uniformed officers spoke up. "You want us to arrest this fella, Marshal Long?"

Longarm nodded. "That'd be a good idea. Charge is attempted murder. Make it three counts. His brother took a shot at me from that window up yonder"—Longarm pointed to it—"and Ike here came within a whisker of runnin' down a poor defenseless woman and her little girl."

"We'll tend to it." The officers reached down to take hold of Little Ike and haul him to his feet. "You say there's another one who's dead?"

Longarm jerked a thumb over his shoulder toward the building across the street. "Back in the rear foyer. There's a pretty good mess back there, too. I'm afraid it'll take some cleanin'."

With that taken care of, he turned toward the Federal Building again. He slipped his turnip watch from a vest pocket and flipped it open, and scowled as he saw that he was going to be late for his appointment with Billy Vail after all.

"Road to hell, good intentions, all that shit." Longarm snapped the watch closed and replaced it in his pocket.

The woman and little girl he had saved were waiting for him at the bottom of the steps leading up to the Federal Building's impressive entrance. The woman had blond curls under her hat and a perky, pretty face that still looked a little pale and shaken from what had happened. She smiled as Longarm came up to her.

"Thank you, sir. You saved my life and that of my daughter, and for that I simply cannot express my gratitude adequately."

Looking at her, Longarm could think of a way she might be able to express her gratitude adequately, but when he glanced at her left hand, he saw the wedding ring and knew he couldn't suggest that, even if the little girl hadn't been standing right there. His upbringing in West-by-God Virginia had instilled just enough chivalry in him that he didn't pursue married women or allow them to seduce him, except on very rare occasions.

Instead, he smiled, nodded, and tugged on the brim of his hat. "No thanks necessary, ma'am. I just did what any other fella would do."

"But none of the dozens of other men who were standing around actually did *anything*. That's what makes your actions so remarkable, Mr. . . . ?"

"Long, ma'am. Custis Long." He didn't add that he was a deputy U.S. marshal.

"Well, Mr. Long, at the very least, you have to come to dinner at my home Sunday. I'm an excellent cook, if I do say so myself, and I'm sure my husband would want to meet you and thank you as well."

"Sunday, eh?" Longarm scraped his thumbnail along his jawline and frowned. "I'm sorry, ma'am, but I'm going to be out of town on business."

She looked disappointed. "Some other time, then?"

"We'll see." Longarm just smiled and didn't make any promises. He reached down and tickled the little girl under her chin, prompting a giggle from her. "Take good care of your mama now, sweetheart."

He tipped his hat as the woman walked away, leading

the little girl by the hand. She looked back over her shoulder and giggled at him again. It was almost enough to lift Longarm's spirits back to the point they had been earlier, before he'd nearly been run over and shot on what was supposed to be a good morning.

On his way up the steps, he saw the place on the granite where Patch McCurdy's bullet had left an ugly mark after narrowly missing his head.

It wasn't such a beautiful day anymore, and even though Longarm wasn't superstitious, he suddenly had a premonition that he might not like what Billy Vail had to tell him after all.

Chapter 2

"You said I was gonna have a couple of weeks off, Billy."

An annoyed expression appeared on the round pink face of Chief Marshal Billy Vail. He might look a little like a cherub now because years of riding a desk had softened him a mite, but in his prime, which had included a stint in the Texas Rangers, Vail had been a hell-roaring lawman the equal of any star packer west of the Mississippi. At times, such as now, that toughness was visible in him again.

"Things come up unexpectedly, Custis. You ought to know that, seeing as how you were nearly murdered in the street outside just now."

Longarm had explained to Vail about the elaborate attempt on his life by the late Patch McCurdy and his brother Little Ike. Vail had not been surprised. He had even commented as to how the moment he heard gunshots outside, he figured that Longarm was mixed up in the ruckus somehow.

Now Longarm shifted the unlit cheroot from one side

of his mouth to the other, took out a match, snapped it to life with an iron-hard thumbnail, and set fire to the gasper. The procedure consumed a few seconds and gave him a chance to bring his own irritation under control. He didn't say anything until after he had blown a perfect smoke ring toward the banjo clock on the wall of Vail's office.

"All right, Billy. Tell me about this chore that's come up unexpected-like."

Vail pushed some papers across his desk toward Longarm, who sat in a comfortable chair covered in red Morocco leather. Longarm's theory was that Vail had a secret streak of perversity that enjoyed the idea of his deputies getting good and comfortable before he dropped another load of horse apples on them.

"I'm sure you remember Clayton Abernathy."

Longarm's teeth clenched harder on the cheroot. He controlled the reaction in time to keep from biting the end off it.

"Damn right I remember him. He was one of those blasted railroad barons who had that secret meeting down in Texas at Blanco Verde a while back. That whole business played a part in almost gettin' me killed, along with Jessie Starbuck and some other folks."

Vail nodded. "The Railroad Ring, I believe you called them. They didn't break any laws by getting together, Custis."

"Maybe not, but it don't seem right, the way they're planning on carving up the whole West amongst 'em, so that regular folks don't get a say." He paused. "Not that regular folks've ever had much of a say about anything, anyway."

Vail pointed at the documents. "Abernathy's having trouble with a railroad line he's building up in Wyoming. He asked one of his politician friends up in Washington for some help, the politico went to the Justice Department, and the Justice Department came to me. Now *I'm* turning to *you*."

"Aw, hell, Billy!" Longarm didn't bother trying to keep the disgust out of his voice. "Abernathy's the next thing to a crook. You don't want to assign this case to me. Give it to one of your more corrupt deputies."

Vail got that fire-and-brimstone look on his face again. His hand smacked down hard on the desk.

"I don't have any corrupt deputies, and the Justice Department said for me to be sure I put my best man on this. God help us all, that's you, Custis."

Longarm heaved a sigh as he flipped through the papers, skimming the report detailing the problems Clayton Abernathy had been having with the construction of his rail line.

"I suppose I could go talk to the man . . ."

"You'll do more than that. You'll find out exactly what he wants us to do, and then you'll do your best to accomplish it." Vail's expression softened slightly as he leaned back in his chair and laced his fingers together over his ample stomach. "I know I can count on you, Custis. You may bend the rules now and then . . . hell, you bust 'em all to pieces more than I'd like . . . and you may lie a mite when you figure I wouldn't want to hear the exact truth, but I never saw anybody better at getting the job done."

"I appreciate the kind words, Billy, but they don't make me any more enthusiastic about payin' a visit to Abernathy." Longarm squared up the papers by tapping them on Vail's desk. "Where do I find him?"

Vail told Longarm the name of the hotel where the railroad baron was staying—the best hostelry in Denver, of course—and then said, "He's expecting you at eleven o'clock."

Longarm glanced at the banjo clock again. The hands

stood at just past ten. That gave him plenty of time to get to the hotel. He considered stopping at one of his favorite saloons to fortify himself with a shot of Maryland rye, but if he showed up for the meeting with booze on his breath and Vail heard about it later from Clayton Abernathy, there'd be hell to pay.

"All right, Billy." Longarm reached for his flat-crowned, snuff-brown hat, which he'd dropped on the floor next to the red leather chair, and then stood up. "I'll let you know what Abernathy wants me to do, but I'd bet this hat of mine that I'll be heading to Wyoming."

"I know. That's why I took the liberty of telling Henry to go ahead and prepare your travel vouchers. You can pick 'em up on your way out."

"I'd say that I'm obliged . . . but I ain't."

Vail waved a pudgy hand toward the door. "Just go deal with the miscreants who're giving Mr. Abernathy so much trouble."

Longarm tugged his hat down tight, gave his boss a curt nod, and left the office.

In the outer office, the four-eyed young fella who played the typewriter smirked at Longarm. "Looks like your vacation was interrupted before it even got started."

Longarm propped a hip on the secretary's desk. "You know, Henry, Marshal Vail's talking about promotin' you to a full-fledged deputy marshal."

"He is?" Henry looked surprised and a little worried. "But he can't do that. I'm not, ah, qualified for such a job. My eyesight and all . . ."

"There are deputies who wear spectacles. As long as you can see well enough to shoot, it don't really matter."

Henry swallowed hard. "You're making this up."

"No, no, it's the truth. He's gonna partner you up with me and send you out in the field, so I can show you the ropes." Longarm leered an evil smile at the prissy young gent. "We'll make a tobacco-chawin', gunslingin' lawman out of you before you know it . . . if you don't get yourself killed first."

Henry picked up the stack of travel vouchers and slapped them against Longarm's chest in disgust. "Here. Take these and go. I know when I'm being made fun of."

"Finally figured it out, did you?"

Longarm tucked the vouchers into a coat pocket and gave Henry a wave as he left the office. He enjoyed his friendly feud with Vail's secretary. Sending a few verbal jabs in Henry's direction always livened up a trip to the office.

He had some time to kill before he walked over to the hotel to meet with Clayton Abernathy, so he bought a news-paper from the vendor in the lobby of the Federal Build-ing, found a bench in an out-of-the-way corner, and sat down to read for a little while first. The paper reported on the latest speech by President Rutherford B. Hayes and the latest comments by his wife Lucy, better known as Lemonade Lucy because of her opposition to alcoholic beverages. Longarm had never met the woman, but he ad-mired Lemonade Lucy for having opinions and being willing to express them. Of course, she was totally wrong about the liquor question, but Longarm didn't hold that against her.

He checked the time a little later, stood up, and left the folded paper on the bench for somebody else to peruse. A brisk walk took him to the hotel. It was a successful trip. Nobody shot at him or tried to run over him.

Longarm paused in a washroom off the lobby of the hotel to check his appearance. He knocked some dust off his hat, wiped the toes of his boots against his trouser legs, and straightened his coat, vest, and string tie. His brown tweed suit was a mite rumpled from rolling around in the street, but it would have to do. That was something he could thank Lemonade Lucy for, he thought with a wry grin. She was the one who'd insisted to her husband the President that all federal employees ought to dress with the proper dignity and decorum.

He went to the desk where a slick-haired clerk was on duty. "I'm Deputy Marshal Long. Mr. Abernathy is expecting me."

Obviously, the clerk had been filled in, because he didn't hesitate in his answer. "Yes, sir, of course. Mr. Abernathy is in Suite E. That's on the third floor."

"Much obliged."

Longarm started to turn away, but the clerk stopped him. "I'll have a bellboy take you up."

Longarm started to object that that wasn't necessary, but then he shrugged and nodded. The folks who ran these fancy hotels had their own way of doing things.

A bellboy dressed in an outfit that reminded Longarm a little of an organ grinder's monkey went with him to the third floor and knocked on the door of Suite E. He had an eager, hopeful expression on his young face, and when the door opened, Longarm understood why.

A woman pretty enough to take a man's breath away stood there, a faint smile on her lovely face.

"Yes? Can I help you?"

Longarm took off his hat and shouldered the bellboy aside. "Deputy U.S. Marshal Custis Long, ma'am. I'm supposed to see Mr. Clayton Abernathy."

"Of course, Marshal Long." The woman held out a hand to usher him inside. "Please come in."

Longarm paused long enough before entering to flip a coin to the disappointed bellboy, who'd obviously been looking forward to the opportunity to talk to the beautiful young woman. Then he followed her into the suite's sitting room. She closed the door behind him.

He still didn't much want to be here, but at least the

scenery was better than what he'd expected. She was in her early twenties, he judged. Thick auburn hair fell in waves around her face and spilled over her shoulders. Eyes as deeply green as a forest studied him. She wore a light gray gown that, judged solely by its style and cut, should have been conversative, even demure. The ripe young body sheathed within it made it anything but.

"I'm Danielle Abernathy, Marshal. I'll let my father know that you're here." She glanced at a clock on the wall. "And right on time, too. He'll like that. Railroad men are always punctual."

"Yes, ma'am."

"I like a man who's willing to take a little extra time if necessary, myself."

Those green eyes of hers sparkled with mischief as she spoke. She turned away, leaving Longarm to stifle a surprised but pleased chuckle.

Danielle Abernathy went to one of the doors on the other side of the room and knocked lightly on it. She didn't wait for a response. She opened it and went in, then reappeared a moment later followed by a man dressed in an expensive suit. He was in his late forties, with a mostly bald head and a beak of a nose. Some people might have called him hawk-faced. He reminded Longarm more of a turkey buzzard.

"Marshal Long." The man held out a hand. "I don't know if you remember me or not. Clayton Abernathy."

Longarm shook the man's hand. "Sure, I remember you, Mr. Abernathy. It'd be hard to forget what happened down there in Texas."

"That's the truth. I thought we were all doomed when those madmen captured us and held us hostage. How is Miss Starbuck?"

"I haven't seen her for a while, but the last I heard, she

was fine. I expect she still is. Jessie's a gal who can take care of herself."

"She most certainly is. I wish my friends and I could have persuaded her to join us in our business arrangement." Abernathy waved a hand. "But that's neither here nor there. Miss Starbuck doesn't have anything to do with my current difficulties. I assume that Marshal Vail filled you in?"

Longarm shrugged. "He didn't give me any details, just said that you've been having some problems with a railroad line you're building up in Wyoming."

"A spur line, actually, to a town called Rimfire. You've heard of it?"

"Yeah. It's a cattle town. There are some big, successful spreads in that area."

"Indeed, and there are coal mines nearby, too. The town is going to do nothing but grow and prosper, especially once my spur line reaches it and connects it by rail to the rest of the country."

Danielle stepped forward with her hands pressed together in front of her. "Father, we're not being very good hosts. Marshal Long, can we offer you something to drink? We have some excellent brandy."

"Well, it's a mite early in the day for that . . ." There he went, stretching the truth again. "But if there's any coffee left in that pot I see on the side table there, I wouldn't mind a cup."

"Of course. It should even still be warm."

Danielle poured the cup of coffee and brought it to him. Her fingers brushed his as she handed it to him, and he thought her touch lingered a shade longer than necessary. Abernathy asked him to have a seat. Longarm settled down carefully on a divan with legs that looked almost too spindly to support his weight. They seemed to hold up all right, though.

Abernathy took a seat in an armchair while Danielle poured coffee for herself and lingered near the side table. The railroad baron placed his hands on his knees and leaned forward slightly.

"Someone is trying to stop my rail line before it ever reaches Rimfire, Marshal. There have been several incidents of blatant sabotage. One night a wagonload of supplies was pushed over a cliff into a ravine. Another time, a load of railroad ties stacked on a flatcar attached to a work train was set on fire and destroyed. A partially constructed trestle was dynamited in the middle of the night."

"Anybody been hurt?"

Abernathy shook his head. "Fortunately, no. But the damage and the loss of supplies have caused continual delays in the construction schedule."

"I reckon that's pretty annoying and frustrating, all right. What is it you want me to do?"

"I want you to find the people responsible for this— actually I have a pretty good idea who they are—and bring them to justice." Abernathy smiled. "And if they won't surrender, Marshal, I want you to kill them. Kill them dead."

Chapter 3

Longarm sat there, the coffee cup in his hand forgotten, and stared at the railroad baron. Abernathy appeared to be completely sincere in what he had just said. Longarm took a deep breath and with an effort controlled the angry reaction that tried to well up in his throat. After a moment, he trusted himself to say something.

"You want me to kill folks over some petty vandalism?"

This day that had started out so promising was steadily getting worse.

"I want you to bring them to justice, as I said. If that means killing them, then so be it. Most importantly, though, I want their efforts to keep my spur line from being completed to stop."

"No offense, Mr. Abernathy, but I'm a federal lawman, not a hired assassin."

Abernathy's mouth tightened angrily. "I don't recall asking you to assassinate anyone, Marshal, only to do your job."

"My job is to enforce the law."

"There are laws against the sort of wanton destruction being carried out against my railroad."

"State laws, maybe. Not federal ones."

"Marshal Long ... did your superior tell you that I have requested aid in this matter from the Justice Department?"

Longarm nodded. "He did. I know you've got friends in high places, Mr. Abernathy."

"I also have a contract pending with the federal government to deliver mail to Rimfire once the spur line is complete and operating on a regular basis." Abernathy stabbed a skinny finger in Longarm's direction. "That makes this a federal matter, Marshal, and gives you jurisdiction over it."

A frown creased Longarm's forehead. He didn't like it, but Abernathy was right. You might have to squint your eyes and tilt your head a little, but when you looked at the case like that, it was Uncle Sam's business, and therefore Longarm didn't have any excuse for refusing to investigate Abernathy's problems.

But he was damned if he was going to just start shooting folks and hoping that would fix things.

Danielle must have been smart enough to sense the tension in the room. She set her coffee cup aside and stepped forward.

"Father, I'm sure Marshal Long will do his duty to the best of his ability ... which I suspect is quite competent indeed."

Abernathy made a harrumphing noise.

Danielle turned to Longarm. "And, Marshal, you have to understand how important this spur line is to my father. For years he's made it his mission in life to bring civilization to those out-of-the-way pockets of the West that don't have it. Rimfire will never grow and become the town it can be if the railroad doesn't reach it."

Longarm supposed she had a point. Sometimes he

thought that maybe civilization's expansion across the West wasn't necessarily a good thing, but it was too late to stop it now. Like a bear coming out of a long winter's hibernation, progress had an insatiable appetite, and it wouldn't stop until it had consumed everything in its path, whether for good or for ill.

"All right. Chief Marshal Vail said I was supposed to render you whatever aid I can, Mr. Abernathy, so I reckon that means I'll head for Wyoming and ferret out whoever's behind your troubles. I ain't promisin' to kill anybody, though."

Abernathy's look of irritation vanished, to be replaced by a satisfied smile. Longarm thought he looked more than ever like a buzzard contemplating a nice juicy corpse that had been rotting in the sun all day.

"That's excellent, Marshal. Thank you. And I'll be very surprised if the villains behind the sabotage will come along peacefully when you try to arrest them. For your own safety, I urge you to be prepared to take action."

Longarm nodded. "I always am."

Danielle's smile took in both men. "Now, see, isn't it better to get along?"

Longarm didn't figure the question needed an answer. Instead, he asked one of his own.

"Who do you think is behind the sabotage, Mr. Abernathy?"

"A man named Adam Warfield." The railroad baron's lips tightened in displeasure again, as if the name tasted bad in his mouth.

"Who might that be?"

"He operates a stagecoach line that's been running between Laramie and Rimfire for the past several years, just about the time Rimfire was founded. He was quite upset when he found out that I was going to build a spur line and wrote a letter to me, asking me to reconsider. He's afraid that the railroad will put his little two-bit stage line out of business . . . which, of course, it will."

Abernathy smirked as he added that last comment.

"It's a pretty big jump from writing a letter to blowing up trestles."

"Writing a letter isn't the only thing Warfield did. He came to see me when I was in Laramie a few months ago, just before construction got under way. He threatened me and said that the rails would never reach Rimfire. He said I would be sorry if I even tried to build the line." Abernathy waved a hand. "Of course, I paid no attention to his blustering and had him thrown out. I haven't achieved the success I have in business by being timid and listening to the ravings of madmen and naysayers."

Longarm was curious. "Who did the throwing out?"

"I always travel with several bodyguards. The West can be a dangerous place."

"Where are they now?"

Abernathy smiled. "One is in the next room. Well armed, I might add, and quite proficient with his weapons. The others are somewhere around, but not on duty at the moment. Actually, I assumed I wouldn't need any protection since I wasn't expecting anyone but you, Marshal."

"It's probably a good idea to keep somebody close by. If this fella Warfield is as upset as you say, there's no tellin' what he might do. He might decide to strap on a gun and come after you."

"It wouldn't surprise me in the slightest. That's why I said I think you'll have to kill him if you try to arrest him, and probably the men who work for him as well." Abernathy frowned. "In fact, now that I think about it, perhaps one man isn't enough for this job. It might be better if you took several more deputies with you, Marshal Long."

Longarm shook his head. "I'm not gonna organize a

posse until I've gotten the lay of the land for myself. If I need somebody to lend a hand, I can send a wire to Billy Vail later on."

Abernathy's narrow shoulders rose and fell in a shrug. "Whatever suits you best, Marshal. I told everyone involved that I wanted the best man possible for this job, and I'm going to give you the benefit of the doubt and assume you're that man."

Danielle spoke up again. "I can tell by looking at him that Marshal Long is the best man for the job, Father." She smiled at Longarm.

He returned the smile warily. Danielle obviously enjoyed flirting with men right in front of her father, where the object of her mischief couldn't do much about it. Whether that made her daring and audacious, or just a tease, he didn't know.

"Where will I find Warfield?"

"His stage line is headquartered in Rimfire. I assume that he's there most of the time."

"How far are the rails from the settlement?"

"At least twenty miles. Progress has been slow because of all the trouble we've had. And if something's not done about it, I'm certain that we'll continue to have trouble, every foot of the way."

"More than likely." Longarm had balanced his hat on his knee when he sat down on the fragile-looking divan. He reached for it now. "There's a train bound for Cheyenne leaving in the morning. I'll be on it. It may take me a day or two after that to get to Rimfire, but I'll be there as soon as I can."

Abernathy nodded. "Excellent. If you stop along the way at end-of-track, the construction boss is Earl Fenton, and the engineer in charge of the project is a young man named Morgan Delahunt. They know that I was going to see about having a federal marshal assigned to the case, so if you need any assistance from them, don't hesitate to ask. They'll do anything they can to help you."

"Much obliged." Longarm stood up and looked at Danielle. "And thanks for the coffee, Miss Abernathy. It was mighty good."

"You say that you're not leaving until tomorrow morning, Marshal Long?"

"That's right, ma'am. That's when the next northbound train comes through. I keep the schedule in my head, since I never know when I'll have to leave town in a hurry on a case."

"Then you'll be free this evening?"

Longarm frowned slightly. "Free for what, if you don't mind me askin'?"

"To have dinner with us, of course."

The idea of sitting down to dinner with Buzzard-face Abernathy didn't really appeal to Longarm, but he reminded himself that he would have a chance to see Danielle again, too. That was enough for him to make up his mind.

"It would be my pleasure, Miss Abernathy."

"Please, call me Danielle. And you said your given name is Custis?"

"That's right, ma'am."

"Very well, Custis. We'll expect you here at seven o'clock."

"You want to meet down in the hotel dining room?"

"No, *here*. I'll make arrangements for the hotel to serve our meal in the suite."

Abernathy stood up. "Excuse me, Marshal. I have some business documents I need to go over."

He left the sitting room. That left Longarm and Danielle alone, and from the way she'd been acting so far, he halfway expected her to throw her arms around his neck and stick her tongue in his mouth.

Instead she just smiled sweetly. "Good day, Custis."

"Ma'am." Longarm put his hat on. Maybe he was wrong about her. Maybe she was just being friendly and polite, rather than acting like she wanted to jump between the sheets with him for a session of slap-and-tickle. He considered himself a pretty good judge of folks' intentions—that was one reason he was still alive after so many years in a dangerous profession—but even he made a mistake every now and then.

She went to the door, opened it for him, and held it as he went out. She was all business now, which brought him right back to the possibility that she was just a tease.

It was enough to make him ponder whether or not he'd made the right decision by agreeing to have dinner with the two of them.

In the meantime, he hadn't even had lunch yet, so he left the hotel and walked several blocks to one of his favorite saloons, where he could get a roast beef sandwich as well as a mug of cold beer and a shot of Tom Moore. While he was there, he spent a pleasant couple of hours playing in a small-stakes poker game. He was a whole three dollars and fifty cents ahead when he cashed in his chips and started back to his rented room on the other side of Cherry Creek.

Once there, he packed his gear for the trip, then cleaned his Winchester, the Colt .44, and the little .41-caliber derringer that was welded to the other end of his watch chain like a deadly fob. When he was satisfied that he was ready to set off for the wilds of Wyoming first thing the next morning, he took off his boots and stretched out on the bed for a nap, relying on his instincts to wake him in time to go back to the hotel for that dinner with the Abernathys.

They did. He shaved, took a whore's bath using a cloth and the basin of water on the table, and then put on a clean shirt. He spit-shined his boots, brushed his coat and hat, and thought that he looked at least halfway respectable as he left to keep his dinner engagement.

The sun had dropped behind the Front Range to the west. Dusk was settling down over Denver. The evening was warm. Longarm smiled and tipped his hat to the ladies he passed as he walked toward the hotel. He still would have preferred that Billy Vail hadn't given him this job, but he would make the best of it. He always did.

When he reached the hotel, he didn't stop at the desk this time but went directly upstairs to the third floor. As he approached the door to Suite E, he took out his watch and opened it. Almost straight-up seven o'clock. If Abernathy valued punctuality, he ought to be pleased by Longarm's timing.

Longarm didn't know who would open the door to his knock. Either Danielle or one of those bodyguards the railroad baron had mentioned, he supposed. He was hoping for Danielle.

He got his wish. She smiled a greeting as she swung the door back.

"You're right on time, Custis. Come in."

As he entered the room and she closed the door behind him, he couldn't help but let his gaze play appreciatively over her. The conservative gray dress she had worn that morning was gone and had been replaced by a dark green gown that went well with her eyes. The short sleeves revealed her round, bare arms, and the neckline was low enough to leave her shoulders bare as well, plunging even lower in the middle so that he could see the top of the enticing cleft between her breasts.

She was bound to know that he was looking—women were nearly always aware of where men were looking, he had discovered—but she clearly didn't care. In fact, judging by the smile on her face, she enjoyed his scrutiny.

Because it was difficult to tear his eyes away from her,

several seconds went by after he entered the sitting room before he noticed that the table which had been set for dinner had only two places on it.

"Your father's not joining us for dinner?"

Danielle shook her head as she took his hat. "No. Some crisis came up in the St. Louis office, and he's burning up the telegraph wires between here and there. He told me to extend his apologies to you. I told him it was rude for him not to be here, but since he's already explained everything you need to know about your assignment, he didn't feel that his presence was necessary. Father's very devoted to his business, you know."

"I reckon that's how folks get ahead."

Danielle placed the Stetson on a small side table and turned back to him. "That's right. I think people really ought to devote more time and energy to their personal needs, though." She gestured gracefully toward the table with its snowy white tablecloth, its settings of fine china and crystal, and the covered dishes on silver trays. "Like a good meal, for example."

"I couldn't agree more, ma'am."

"You were supposed to call me Danielle, remember, Custis?"

"Yes, ma'am . . . I mean, Danielle."

She strolled toward the table and spoke over her shoulder. "I hope you're hungry."

It had been a long time since that roast beef sandwich in the middle of the day. "As a matter of fact, I am."

"Well, then, we can go ahead and eat . . ." She stopped beside the table and turned to smile at him again. "Or, if you're not actually *starving*, we could wait until after you've made love to me to have dinner."

Chapter 4

He wasn't sure at first if he had heard her correctly. The sultry smile on her face didn't leave much doubt, though, as she waited for his answer.

"I don't know if that would be a good idea, what with your father coming back and all."

Danielle shook her head. "He won't be back for a couple of hours. He left just a short while ago, and he told me it would take at least that long to clear up all the problems in the St. Louis office. I'm afraid some of the people there will be working late tonight." She laughed softly. "I know I said that I like a man who takes his time, Custis, but I think two hours will be long enough for us to at least start getting to know each other."

"If you figure I'm workin' for your father and you can tell me what to do—"

Her smile disappeared as she grew more serious and took a quick step toward him. "No, not at all! There's nothing . . . compulsory about it. I just think that you're a very attractive man, and I could tell that you're attracted to me as well, so I thought . . . well, it seemed like a logical conclusion . . ."

Longarm had been coming closer to her as she talked. Now he was within arm's reach, so that was exactly what he did. He reached out and took hold of her arms, urging her toward him. She smiled again as her head tipped back a little so she could look up into his face.

"So I was right."

"Don't get too smug about it." His voice was a menacing growl. "I could still turn around and walk out of here."

A look of alarm leaped into her eyes. "You wouldn't!"

"No . . . but I could. Or I could just do this."

He brought his mouth down hard on hers.

Her body surged against his. He felt the softness of her breasts against him. Her arms came up and around his neck, and her lips parted invitingly as his tongue prodded between them. The urgency of the kiss rose as their tongues swirled and danced together.

Longarm slid his hands up her bare arms to her shoulders. His fingers dug into her soft flesh, kneading and caressing. After a moment he slipped the dress from her shoulders and worked it down. Danielle had to move back a little to put some space between them. Her rounded breasts came free as Longarm pushed the dress down even more.

His right hand cupped her left breast as they continued to kiss. The firm, warm flesh filled his palm. His thumb found the erect nipple and stroked it, causing it to harden even more. While he was doing that, he reached around her with his left hand and deftly unfastened the buttons that ran up the back of the dress. That loosened the garment enough so that he was able to slide it over her hips. It fell to the floor, the dark green fabric puddling around her feet.

She was nude underneath it.

That left no doubt about her intentions, not that Longarm needed any extra confirmation. The bold way she kissed was evidence enough. She moaned deep in her throat as his hands roamed over her body, exploring the smooth curves of her breasts and hips.

Finally she pulled back, visibly breathless. Her breasts rose and fell rapidly from the excitement that gripped her.

"We need to get you out of those clothes."

Longarm smiled. "I was just thinkin' the same thing."

He shrugged out of his coat as Danielle began unbuttoning his shirt. He unbuckled his gunbelt and took it from around his waist, then fastened the buckle again and hung the belt and the holstered Colt from the back of one of the chairs. Danielle peeled the shirt off him.

"Sit down. I'll help you with your boots."

Longarm wasn't going to turn down an offer like that. He sat while Danielle turned her back to him, straddled each leg in turn, and bent over to pull his boots off his feet. The view in that position was intriguing, to say the least. He ran a finger down the lower part of her spine and saw a shiver go through her.

He had barely stood up again before her fingers were at the fly of his trousers, working the buttons through the buttonholes. He wore the bottom half of a pair of long underwear under the trousers. She rested a hand on his belly for a second, then slid it under the waistband of the underwear and started exploring. She gasped as she found his shaft, which had already hardened as much as it could in the confines of the balbriggans.

"Oh, Lord. If it's that big now, how big will it be when it's loose?"

Longarm chuckled. "Only one way to find out."

She practically tore the rest of the clothes off of him, freeing his cock so that she could wrap both hands around it and run them along its iron-hard length.

"I'm not sure how I'm going to get all of that inside me . . ." She laughed. "But it's sure going to be fun to try."

Something else had occurred to Longarm. He hated to bring up the subject of her father at a time like this, but he wanted to be sure of one thing.

"Your pa took all those bodyguards of his with him, didn't he?"

"The two who are on duty. The other two are probably out getting drunk or looking for a brothel. Don't worry, Custis, we're alone. We won't be interrupted."

"That's good." Longarm reached around her again, cupped his hands under her buttocks, and picked her up. She squealed in joy and wrapped her legs around his waist. He kissed her again, pressing his mouth to hers for a long moment before breaking the kiss to ask the question that was uppermost on his mind at the moment.

"Bedroom?"

She waved a hand frantically toward one of the doors. "There!"

The door was already open a couple of inches, for which Longarm was grateful. He kicked it open the rest of the way and carried her into a luxuriously furnished bedroom with a thick rug on the floor and a massive four-poster bed. The room was softly lit by a lamp turned low on an exquisitely carved nightstand next to the bed.

"Don't bother with the covers." Danielle's voice trembled with urgency and need. "On top of the spread is fine."

Longarm placed her on the fine silk spread. As she lay back, her legs spread wide, revealing the triangle of finespun auburn hair at the juncture of her thighs. Tiny droplets of moisture glistened on the hairs around the cleft of her sex, like morning dew on grass.

Longarm's manhood throbbed. He ached to plunge the long, thick rod of male flesh into her, and from the way

Danielle was panting and turning her head back and forth, she was just as eager for him to be inside her.

"Now, Custis! I can't wait. I need you in me now!"

Longarm always liked to oblige a lady whenever he could. He moved onto the bed and poised above her, positioning himself between the widespread thighs to answer their invitation. He brought the head of his cock to her already drenched opening and thrust with his hips. She was so wet he went easily into her, penetrating her depths with one smooth surge that left most of his shaft sheathed inside her.

She whimpered and bucked her hips up at him in an effort to take every last bit of him. She hadn't quite made it when Longarm hit bottom. She was filled to the brim, and the gates of her femininity were stretched wide around his thickness.

She closed her eyes and threw her head back. "Oh, God!" The words came out of her in a muffled groan. "I never . . . never knew . . . never dreamed . . ."

Longarm withdrew a couple of inches and then surged forward again. Danielle gasped. She raised her legs higher and locked the ankles together above his hips. Her arms went around his neck and hung on for dear life as she pulled his head down. Longarm drove his tongue into her mouth and worked his hips back and forth again. Danielle bucked underneath him, suddenly frantic. He felt the almost supernatural strength in her muscles as she clung to him and shuddered. He knew she was climaxing already.

He was far from finished, though. He held himself still as the spasms continued to run through her for a long moment. Then he lifted his mouth from hers and let her head loll to the side. She panted heavily in an attempt to catch her breath. He felt her heart slugging in her chest like it was trying to leap out.

The respite stretched out for several minutes. Longarm's

cock was still buried inside her and was as hard as ever. His own needs wouldn't be denied. Slowly, he withdrew until half of his length was out of her. She made a little moaning sound of disappointment.

She wasn't disappointed for long. He slammed back into her, thrusting forcefully as deep as he could go. She cried out in mingled pleasure and surprise, then clutched him and started pumping her hips.

"Give it to me! Give me all you've got!"

Longarm did, pistoning his shaft in and out of her in a steady, driving pace that became faster and more urgent as the seconds ticked by. He felt his climax beginning to boil up inside him, and he didn't try to hold it back. Danielle cried out softly as she began to spasm again. Longarm plunged into her as deeply as he could and this time held his manhood there as his juices exploded from him in a blistering flood.

The long, slow descent from the peak was almost as sweet as the climb. Longarm stayed hard long enough so that he was able to remain inside her as he wrapped his arms around her and rolled onto his back. Her smaller form lay sprawled on top of him. She kissed and licked at his chest while his hands slid over the sleek curves of her hips. He hated for the moment to end, as it inevitably did when he softened enough to slip out of her, and judging by the pout on her pretty face, she didn't like it, either.

"Let's do it again."

"That's an admirable sentiment, darlin', but not exactly reasonable."

"Oh, the hell with being reasonable!" She pushed herself up and slapped him lightly on the chest. "Was it reasonable for us to do this to start with?"

"Maybe not . . . but it sure was nice."

She smiled and snuggled against him, resting her head on his shoulder. "Oh, it was. It really was."

They rested there like that long enough that Longarm began to worry that they might go to sleep. He didn't figure Clayton Abernathy would be too happy if he got back to the suite and found his daughter sprawled buck naked on the silk bedspread with a deputy marshal whose only reasonable expectation was that he would wind up dead on some lonely hillside someday with outlaw lead in him.

That was a sobering thought, and it did away with any ideas of a second bout with Danielle.

"We've got dinner out there waitin' for us, and we don't want it to be completely ruined."

She sighed. "No, I suppose not. And it would probably be a good idea to get dressed, just in case Father gets finished with his work sooner than he thought he would." She leaned forward and gave him a peck on the cheek. "But I just want you to know, Custis, that was the best time I've had in . . . in, well, ever!"

Longarm grinned. "That's always good to know. I hate to disappoint a lady."

Three days later, Longarm still seemed to smell the fresh scent of Danielle's hair. It beat the smell of a sweaty horse and the bitter stink of the sulfurous spring he had passed a little ways back. He lifted the canteen to his mouth and took a swallow. The brackish water was a far cry from the brandy he and Danielle had drunk a few nights earlier, just like the jerky and stale biscuit from his saddlebags he'd had for lunch wasn't nearly as good as the dinner they had shared. Even cold, that meal had beaten the hell out of trail food.

But he could see end-of-track a couple of miles ahead of him as his gaze followed the twin lines of the steel rails. It was late in the afternoon, and he figured to spend the night there before pushing on to Rimfire the next day. Maybe the food in the railroad camp's mess tent wouldn't be too bad.

He had caught that train for Cheyenne early the next morning after his pleasant evening with Danielle Abernathy. In Cheyenne he had changed trains to a westbound that took him to Laramie, and there he had rented a horse and had it loaded onto the train. The journey had continued to the siding where Abernathy's spur line to Rimfire veered off to the north. The engineer had stopped the train there, Longarm had unloaded the horse, and he had spent the next day and a half riding north, following the rails of the spur line.

He wasn't wearing his Lemonade Lucy–mandated suit anymore. He had changed into denim trousers and a faded butternut shirt, the sort of range garb that was much more appropriate for spending days on the trail.

The stage road between Laramie and Rimfire was several miles to the east and ran at more of an angle than the spur line. Longarm had thought about following it, but he wanted to talk to Earl Fenton and Morgan Delahunt, the two men bossing the railroad construction, before he proceeded on to the settlement. Following the rails seemed like the easiest way to make sure he didn't get lost along the way.

Even from a distance, he heard the ringing of steel on steel as the workers swung heavy sledges and hammered home the spikes that held the rails in place on the wooden ties. A work train with several flatcars and a caboose attached to it sat parked about a hundred yards south of the spot where the men were working. Big tents were set up on both sides of the tracks. The men slept and ate in those tents. Longarm had seen plenty of railroad construction camps just like this one, from the Rio Grande on up into Canada.

He headed for the caboose, figuring that he might find one or both of the men in charge there. When he reached it, he reined in and was about to swing down from the saddle when the door at the back of the caboose opened and a man stepped out onto the rear platform. He was short, dark-haired, and wore gray woolen trousers, a white shirt, a black leather vest, and a string tie.

He also had an old Henry rifle in his hands, a rifle he lifted to his shoulder and pointed right at Longarm.

"Stay where you are, mister! If you try to get down from the horse, I'll blow you out of the saddle!"

Chapter 5

Longarm's first instinct whenever anybody pointed a gun at him was to draw his own Colt and ventilate the son of a bitch. Since he was supposed to be helping these railroaders, he decided that probably wouldn't be a good idea here. Instead he controlled the reaction and sat easy in the saddle, keeping his hands in plain sight so he wouldn't give the hombre on the platform any excuse for getting trigger-happy.

"Take it easy, old son. I'm not lookin' for trouble."

The man didn't lower the rifle. "Then what are you looking for?"

"Not what. Who. Earl Fenton and Morgan Delahunt."

The barrel of the Henry sagged a little. The man holding it looked surprised.

"Who are you?"

"Name's Custis Long. I'm a deputy U.S. marshal out of Denver. My boss sent me up here to look into the trouble you've been havin' on this spur line." Longarm made a guess. "Reckon you must be Delahunt, the engineer in charge of the project."

The man ignored that. "Do you have any proof that you're really who you say you are?"

"Well . . . if you'll let me reach into my pocket without gettin' nervous and shootin' me, I can show you my badge and bona fides."

The man made a little motion with the rifle barrel. "Go ahead."

As Longarm took the leather wallet containing his badge and identification papers from his pocket, he saw another man striding rapidly along the tracks toward them. The newcomer must have seen him riding up, and he was as cautious as the man who'd stepped out of the caboose. He had a holstered revolver on his hip and kept his hand on the gun as he approached.

"Who's this, Morgan?"

The second man's question confirmed Longarm's hunch about the identity of the first one. He pegged the second man, who was tall and broad-shouldered, with a pugnacious, sun-browned face, as Earl Fenton, the construction boss.

"He says he's a U.S. marshal from Denver."

The man on the platform still hadn't lowered the rifle, so Longarm tossed the leather wallet to the man on the ground. "Take a look for yourself."

Fenton, if that's who he was, opened the wallet and studied the badge pinned inside it. He unfolded the identification papers and read them. Then he nodded and visibly relaxed.

"I reckon he's the genuine article, Morgan. You can put that rifle down."

Delahunt was slow to do so, but after a moment he shrugged and lowered the weapon until it pointed toward the platform at his feet.

"After everything that's happened, I didn't think it would be a good idea to take any chances."

Fenton came closer to Longarm and handed the wallet back to him. "I can't blame you for that." He smiled. "Get off your horse and come on inside, Marshal. I'm Earl Fenton, and this is Morgan Delahunt. I expect we've got a lot to talk about."

Longarm swung down from the saddle. Fenton called one of the railroad workers over.

"Riley, take Marshal Long's horse and put it in the corral with the others."

Delahunt had already gone back into the caboose. Fenton ushered Longarm inside. The rear part of the car was fitted out as an office, as they usually were. Through an open door, Longarm could see into the front part of the car, where several bunks were built into the walls. The bunks were strictly functional and probably weren't very comfortable, but they would be better than sleeping on the ground or on a narrow cot in one of the tents.

A potbellied black stove sat in one corner of the office, with a round tin stovepipe running from the top of it up through the caboose's roof. Delahunt stood at it with the Henry tucked under his left arm. He had a tin coffee cup in his left hand and was using his right to pour coffee into it from a pot.

The engineer put the pot back on the stove, then turned and held out the cup toward Longarm. "Call it a peace offering, Marshal. I'm sorry we got off on the wrong foot there. I suppose I was a little too jumpy. But after everything that's happened, I just don't trust strangers."

Longarm took the coffee and sipped it appreciatively. "Can't blame you for that. When I talked to your boss Mr. Abernathy, he told me you've have several instances of sabotage up here."

"It's gotten worse." Delahunt's voice was grim. "The people trying to stop the railroad have stooped to murder now."

Longarm's fingers tightened on the cup. Abernathy hadn't said anything about murder. Of course, it was possible the railroad baron hadn't known about it at the time he was talking to Longarm in Denver.

"You'd better tell me about that. All I knew about was a supply wagon being pushed into a ravine, a load of ties being burned, and a trestle that got blown up."

Delahunt nodded. "Those things were bad enough, and there were other incidents similar to them, but now we've had a man killed. Yesterday he was scouting the survey up ahead when someone ambushed him. He was dead when we found him. He'd been shot in the head."

The young engineer's voice was flat and hard but held a slight quiver of strain, as if he were trying to control his emotions. Longarm didn't know how much experience Delahunt had. It was possible that the man had spent most of his career as an engineer behind a desk, which meant he wouldn't have seen very many dead men, if any. An hombre with his brains blown out was enough to spook anybody who wasn't used to it.

"So you don't know who actually shot him?"

"His body was found near where the stage road curves close to our right-of-way. That's enough to remove any doubt from my mind. Adam Warfield killed him."

Longarm frowned. "I thought Warfield was the owner of the stage line. Why would he be out on the trail instead of in the office in Rimfire?"

Fenton took up the explanation. "The Rimfire Stagecoach Company is already struggling, even before the railroad reaches Rimfire. Warfield's had to let most of his drivers and shotgun guards go. He handles some of the runs by himself, while his sister keeps the office going."

"Here's what I think happened, Marshal. Warfield was driving one of his stagecoaches along the road when he spotted our man Phil Jefferson. I believe that he stopped the stagecoach, drew a bead on Phil with a rifle, and killed him."

Delahunt's voice quivered with indignation now. The scout's death clearly disturbed him.

"But you don't have any proof of any of that. As a lawman, I've got to have more than just a hunch."

Which was not exactly true, of course, since Longarm had acted on hunches many times in his career . . . and been proven right a lot more often than not.

Fenton made a suggestion. "I can show you exactly where it happened. You can have a look around, maybe see if you can find anything that'll prove Warfield's the one who bushwhacked Phil. I know how to get a railroad built, but I'm no tracker or manhunter."

Longarm thought about it and nodded. "That's a good idea. We'll take a ride up there in the morning. It's gonna be dark too soon to do anything like that today."

"Yeah, that's right. You'll be staying here with us tonight, Marshal?"

"I'd be obliged."

Delahunt gestured toward the front part of the caboose. "There's a couple of extra bunks up there, and there's plenty of food. I'll tell the cook to send three meals over tonight instead of two."

"You fellas don't eat in the mess tent with the workers?"

"I've never thought that such fraternization was a good idea."

Fenton just shrugged, indicating that he didn't care all that much one way or the other. It was Delahunt's idea not to eat with the rest of the men, Longarm decided. There were two schools of thought on such matters, one holding that it was good for morale when the men in charge mixed with the ones who had to carry out the orders, the other saying that bosses ought to remain aloof in order to maintain discipline. Longarm didn't know which was right and which was wrong, but he'd always figured it was better to treat everybody just about the same. He would go along with whatever Delahunt and Fenton wanted, though.

But it might be a good idea if he could manage to talk to some of the workers while he was here in camp. Sometimes they knew what was really going on when the folks in charge didn't.

The fare at the railroad camp was simple: steak, potatoes, beans, biscuits, and canned peaches. But it was good and filling, and Longarm was glad to get it.

Over supper in the caboose, Longarm talked about the case and the people involved with Fenton and Delahunt.

"You say Warfield's got a sister who runs the stage line office?"

Delahunt nodded. "That's right. I think her name is Rose, or Rosa, something like that. I've never met her, but I saw her in Rimfire when I was up there completing the survey for the rail line several months ago. She's a rather attractive young woman. It's too bad she's stuck in such a bad situation, with a failing business and a murderous brother."

"Mr. Abernathy said that Warfield threatened him."

"I'm not surprised. He threatened me, too, when I was in Rimfire. If his sister hadn't been there, I think he might have tried to pull a gun and shoot me."

"That's why you don't need to be going to town by yourself, Morgan." Fenton pushed back his empty plate. "And it would be a good idea if you stopped riding ahead by yourself to check the route, too. Hell, it could've been you that Warfield shot, instead of Phil."

"From here on out, you'd better not let anybody leave camp by himself. If Warfield's behind the trouble, he'd be less likely to attack a group of men than if it was one hombre by himself."

Delahunt raised his eyebrows at Longarm's comment. "*If* Warfield's behind the trouble? You don't seriously think that someone else could be to blame for what's happened, do you, Marshal?"

"I don't know. There's still that pesky little matter of provin' it."

Delahunt's jaw tightened angrily. "There's no one else who could be behind it. No one stands to gain anything by stopping the railroad except Warfield. All the other citizens of Rimfire and the ranchers and mine owners from the surrounding area *want* the railroad to get there. They know their businesses will only grow once the spur line arrives."

What Delahunt was saying made sense. Longarm was going to have to talk to Adam Warfield for himself, though, before he decided whether or not the man was guilty. It probably wouldn't take much. If Warfield really had murdered the railroad scout, Phil Jefferson, then the arrival of a federal lawman asking questions about Jefferson's death might well spook him into trying to escape. Then it would be a question of whether or not he put up a fight when Longarm tried to arrest him. If he did . . .

If he did, then more than likely Longarm would have to kill him, and Clayton Abernathy would get his wish. That realization didn't make Longarm feel any better.

An apple could only be eaten one bite at a time, though, so there was no reason to worry about it tonight. After the three men had eaten, they stepped out onto the caboose's rear platform. Longarm fired up a cheroot while Fenton announced that he was going to take a walk around the camp and make sure everything was all right.

Longarm stood there, leaning against the railing and

smoking, as he listened to the sounds that filled the night. Men talked and laughed in the mess tent and the sleeping tents. Somebody played a squeeze box while several other men sang a bawdy Irish drinking song. From the other side of the camp, a lone, beautiful tenor sang about Galway Bay. Everything seemed peaceful.

That right there was enough to make Longarm worry. Too many times in his life he had seen all hell break loose in the middle of an equally tranquil setting without any warning.

Delahunt must have noticed the way he tensed. "Something wrong, Marshal?"

"No, not really. How far are we here from that stage road?"

Delahunt pointed off in the darkness toward the east. "It lies about three miles in that direction. The route passes through more rugged terrain, but it's slightly shorter than the route we're following with the railroad."

Longarm chewed on the cheroot and turned over some other thoughts in his head.

"I'll grant you that Warfield could've shot your man Jefferson, especially if there weren't any passengers on the stage. Even though I don't know him, I have a hard time believin' that he'd stop and bushwhack a man in front of witnesses."

"It wouldn't have been unusual for the stage to be empty. Warfield doesn't have many passengers anymore. He's scraping by on the mail contract ... a contract that Mr. Abernathy will take over as soon as the railroad arrives in Rimfire."

Longarm tugged on the lobe of his right ear, then scraped a thumbnail along the rugged line of his jaw. "I reckon he could've set those railroad ties on fire, too, but I doubt if a man could push a wagonload of supplies into a ravine by himself. He must've had some help to do that."

"He still has a few men working for him. I'm sure he just brought some of them along with him that night."

"You don't post guards at night?"

"We do now, of course." Delahunt's voice was sharp with annoyance. "In fact, we posted them after the first incident, which involved someone cutting the brake line on this work train. But there's only so much good that a few sentries can do. Someone who's stealthy enough can still slip past them to do his dirty work."

"Post more guards, then."

"We don't have the extra men. Earl says that if we have too many men losing sleep at night for guard duty, they won't be able to get enough work done the next day. Mr. Abernathy is already upset because construction is behind schedule."

Longarm blew smoke into the night sky. "Sounds to me like the ol' damned if you do, damned if you don't business."

"That's exactly what it is. The only real solution is to put Adam Warfield behind bars where he belongs . . . or in a grave."

Longarm smiled faintly in the darkness. These railroaders sure were a bloodthirsty bunch. He drew on the cheroot, causing the coal on the end to glow brightly for a second, like an orange eye winking in the night.

A heartbeat later, another orange eye winked out there in the shadows, but this was no cheroot. It was flame spurting from the muzzle of a rifle, and at the same instant Longarm saw it, he heard the sharp *spang!* of a bullet ricocheting off metal somewhere near his head.

Chapter 6

Acting instantly, Longarm clenched his teeth tighter on the cheroot, shoved Morgan Delahunt back through the open door of the caboose, and palmed his Colt from the crossdraw rig.

The range was too long for a handgun and he knew it, but his Winchester was still in its saddle sheath on the rented horse. He triggered three fast shots in the direction of the muzzle flash he had seen, aiming high because that would make the bullets carry farther. Chances were, he wouldn't hit anything, but maybe he could come close enough to spook the bushwhacker into fleeing.

Unfortunately, more than one rifleman lurked out there in the darkness. Like a flock of fireflies, several more flashes ripped the black fabric of the prairie night. Longarm heard more slugs thudding into the caboose and ricocheting from its metal fittings. He ducked inside before any of them could find him.

"Blow out those lamps! Where's that rifle of yours?"

Delahunt sprang to obey the order, answering the question between puffs as he blew out the lamps that lit up the inside of the car. "Over in . . . the corner!"

Longarm spotted the Henry just as the last lamp went out. He grabbed it and went to one of the windows, which stood open to let some evening breeze into the caboose. He knelt there and brought the Henry to his shoulder.

Outside, the camp was in an uproar. The shots had caused men to spill out of their tents and shout questions and curses. Then they cursed some more as flying lead forced them to dive frantically for cover.

The muzzle flashes that continued to wink in the gloom were scattered over a fairly broad area, telling Longarm that there really were multiple attackers out there, not one man running from place to place. He zeroed in on one of the flashes as he peered over the Henry's sights, and when another spurt of orange showed from that spot, he was ready. He pressed the trigger and sent a .44 slug whistling right back at it. Then he dropped down below the level of the window, figuring that his shot would draw some return fire.

Instead he heard the swift rataplan of hoofbeats outside, and shouts that held a renewed urgency. Longarm risked a glance and saw flames bobbing through the night. Colts banged and popped. Torches sailed through the air.

The sons of bitches were setting the tents on fire!

Longarm sprang outside to the platform again and saw that his hunch was correct. A group of riders swept in from the Wyoming prairie, some of them carrying torches while the others sprayed lead through the camp with six-guns. When the torch-wielders were close enough, they threw the blazing brands at the tents.

The canvas caught fire as the torches landed on them. As they began to burn, railroad workers who had taken shelter in the tents burst from them with yells of alarm.

Out in the open like that, they would be easy targets for the raiders.

Longarm brought the Henry to his shoulder and started shooting again, cranking off several rounds as fast as he could work the rifle's lever. He wanted to draw the raiders' attention to him, so that maybe they wouldn't massacre the workers.

It worked. The men on horseback surged in his direction and blasted shots at him. He threw himself onto the floor of the platform to make himself a smaller target.

Several of the tents were burning now. They cast a hellish glare over the camp as the flames consumed them, and by that flickering light, Longarm saw that the raiders were all masked, with bandannas tied over the lower halves of their faces and hats pulled low over their eyes. In addition, they all wore long dusters to conceal their clothes, not an uncommon practice for murderous varmints who struck out of the night like this. Longarm drew a bead on one of them and squeezed the trigger, and he was rewarded by the sight of the man rocking back in the saddle as the bullet punched into him.

The man didn't fall. He managed to stay mounted and swerved his horse away from the tracks. Several of the other riders went with him immediately, and then the others followed. They were breaking off the attack, Longarm realized. He wasn't sure why they were giving up, unless the man he had wounded was the leader and the others wanted to get him away from there so they could see how badly he was hurt.

The important thing was that the raiders were taking off for the tall and uncut, but not without leaving a broad swath of destruction behind them. The fire was spreading from tent to tent, as well as setting the grass on fire in places, and the men were too busy trying to contain the blazes to worry about anything else.

Longarm stood up and sent a couple of final shots in the direction of the fleeing raiders. Sensing movement behind him, he glanced over his shoulder to see that Morgan Delahunt had come out of the caboose. The young engineer looked shaken and scared.

"My God, Marshal, are you all right?"

Longarm nodded as he lowered the Henry. "Yeah. It was a regular hornets' nest out here for a minute, but thanks to El Señor Dios, I didn't get stung."

Delahunt gripped the platform's railing and stared at the burning tents. "Good Lord! What have they done? What have those bastards done now?"

Running footsteps pounded up to the caboose. Earl Fenton hauled himself hurriedly onto the platform. The construction boss gripped his revolver in his right hand.

"Morgan! Are you hurt? How about you, Marshal?"

"We're both fine, Earl. What about you?"

Fenton waved off Delahunt's concern. "I wasn't hit. But we've got to get that fire under control before all the tents are destroyed!"

Longarm handed the Henry back to Delahunt and turned to the construction boss. "We'll get a bucket brigade started. Didn't I see a bunch of water barrels on one of those flatcars?"

"Yeah, it's down here." Fenton leaped back to the ground. "Come on!"

He and Longarm left Delahunt there at the caboose and hurried to the flatcar where the water barrels were loaded. When they got there, they found that some of the other men had already had the same idea. A line was being formed to pass buckets back and forth. A couple of men had climbed onto the flatcar to knock lids off some of the barrels. The men on the ground tossed empty buckets up to them. They filled the buckets and handed them back down.

It was a tedious, time-consuming process, but it was the only way to get water on the flames. Luckily, the attackers had only struck at the tents on the eastern side of the rails. If the workers had had to fight fires on both sides of the right-of-way, it would have been a hopeless battle.

Longarm and Fenton joined the bucket brigade. They were at the end of the line, taking filled buckets from the other men and throwing the water onto the flames. They ran back and forth in an attempt to spread the water as much as possible and contain the blaze. Other men were doing the same thing, while still others took shovels and swatted out any place where flying sparks tried to start a new fire.

Gradually, their efforts began to pay off. The flames started to die down. Maybe that was because they had already burned up just about all there was to burn. That bitter thought went through Longarm's brain as he flung a bucket of water on what was left of a tent. The smell of ashes filled his nose. He hated it. Always had.

The men with shovels tamped out the last of the flames. The light now came from lanterns that men brought from the train and from the tents on the other side of the tracks. In that feeble glow, the wet, tired, grimy men looked at the devastation that had been wreaked on the eastern side of the camp.

"We lost the mess tent and most of our food." Fenton shook his head in disgust. "We'll all be on short rations until the train can get to Laramie and back."

Delahunt stalked back and forth in an agitated state, waving his hands around. "And we lost so many of the other supplies! What are we going to do, Earl?"

The construction boss heaved a sigh. "Make do as best we can, I reckon. You can take the train back to Laramie first thing in the morning, Morgan. Send a wire to the boss and let him know what happened. He can afford to replace everything that we lost." Fenton paused. "At least I hope so."

Longarm figured that replacing some tents and supplies were within Clayton Abernathy's means. But Abernathy might run out of patience before he ran out of funds. How long would he keep pouring money into this project?

Something else was on Longarm's mind as he turned to Fenton and Delahunt. "Was anybody hurt?"

"I don't know. With all that lead flying around, somebody must have been hit." Fenton called over one of the workers. "Roy, find out how many men were wounded."

"Sure, Boss." The man hurried off.

There was nothing else Longarm, Fenton, and Delahunt could do. They went back to the caboose. Once they were inside, Delahunt lit the lamps again, after Longarm told him it would probably be safe to do so.

"I don't think that bunch will be back. They've done enough damage for one night. Anyway, some of them were hit, too. I reckon they'll go off and lick their wounds for a while."

Delahunt made a fist and shook it in front of him, a pretty futile gesture as far as Longarm was concerned.

"That bastard Warfield! He's behind this."

Longarm frowned in thought. "You said he's only got a few men still working for him."

"That's right."

"There were at least a dozen hombres out there tonight, maybe more."

Delahunt frowned, too. "Are you saying that Warfield *isn't* responsible for this outrage?"

"I don't have a clue one way or the other. But according to what you told me earlier, he doesn't have that many men working for him."

"He hired more." Fenton made the suggestion as he opened a cabinet and took out a bottle of whiskey. "He recruited some hired killers."

"What did he use to pay them? His stage line is just barely scraping by."

Fenton shook his head. "I couldn't tell you. Maybe he promised them a share of the profits later on. All I know is that I want a drink. How about you boys?"

Delahunt nodded. "I could use one. All this trouble is more than my nerves can stand."

Longarm accepted a shot of the who-hit-John, too. Fenton splashed whiskey in coffee cups and handed them around. While they were drinking, the man Fenton had sent to check on injuries climbed onto the platform and came to the open door.

"We've got half a dozen men with bullet wounds, Boss."

Fenton grunted. "How many dead?"

"None. Nobody was killed."

Fenton looked surprised. "What do you know about that? I reckon we got off lucky."

"If you don't count all the supplies we lost." Delahunt added that gloomy note.

"Are any of the men hurt bad enough to need a regular sawbones? If there are, you can take them back to Laramie on the train in the morning, Morgan."

Delahunt nodded. "All right. Then I'll get back out here just as quickly as I can. By nightfall tomorrow, I hope."

Fenton looked over at Longarm. "You're still welcome to spend the night here, of course, Marshal. And thank you for what you did to help run those varmints off. But no matter how grateful we are to you, we won't be able to offer you a very fancy breakfast in the morning. A little coffee, maybe."

Longarm nodded in understanding. "It won't be the first

time I've ridden a hungry trail. At least I'll be in Rimfire tomorrow and can get something to eat there." A thought occurred to him. "Wouldn't it be easier to go there for supplies than going all the way back to Laramie?"

"It would if we had a wagon or two." Fenton shrugged. "But they were all parked on the east side of the camp . . ."

"And burned up with the tents." Longarm nodded. "Yeah, that would make it difficult, all right." He downed the rest of the whiskey in his cup. "Might be a good idea if you fellas avoided Rimfire anyway, until I've had a chance to figure out exactly what's goin' on."

"We all know what's going on." Delahunt drank the rest of his whiskey, too, and looked pale and angry as he lowered the cup. "Adam Warfield is trying to ruin us, and we're counting on you to put a stop to it, Marshal."

"Do my best," Longarm said.

In the morning he gave most of the jerky he had left to Fenton and Delahunt, keeping only a couple of strips to gnaw on as he rode toward Rimfire.

Luckily, the horses had been corralled on the western side of the tracks, so they were all right. While Longarm was saddling his rented mount, Fenton came over to him.

"I was going to show you the spot where Phil Jefferson was killed, but after what happened last night, I reckon I'd better stay here. We'll try to get a little work done while Morgan's gone with the train, but it won't be easy. I can tell you how to find the place, Marshal, if you want to take a look at it."

Longarm nodded. "Yeah, that's a good idea."

"You'll be able to see the stage road where it curves to the west and starts to run parallel to the right-of-way. The right-of-way's been graded all the way to Rimfire, so you'll be able to follow it. When you can see the road, look for three boulders set in a rough triangle, with about fifteen feet between each of them. Phil's body was found there beside those boulders."

"Who found him?"

"I did." Fenton's face and voice were grim as he answered. "When he didn't come back when he was supposed to, I took a couple of the boys and went looking for him."

Longarm nodded. "He was shot in the head, you said?"

"That's right."

It took a good marksman to hit a fella in the head, especially from a distance. Longarm filed that thought away for future reference.

He said his farewells to Fenton, mounted up, and headed north not long after first light, following the wide, graded right-of-way where the steel rails would run when the spur line was finished. He hadn't had a chance to really talk to any of the workers, but after what had happened the night before, he figured it was more important for him to get on to Rimfire and question Adam Warfield.

Behind him, the big Baldwin locomotive *chuffed* as it built up steam. Three of the wounded men had insisted that they were fine to stay and carry on with their work once they were patched up. The other three were hurt badly enough that they had been carried into the caboose and placed on the bunks so that Morgan Delahunt could take them back to Laramie with him and get medical attention for them.

The work train would have to back all the way to the siding where the spur line began, which meant it couldn't travel very fast. With luck, though, it would be back at the camp with a fresh load of supplies and tents before dark.

Longarm intended to reach Rimfire long before that.

The jerky was enough to keep his stomach from rumbling too much, although he was tempted from time to time, when he spotted a rabbit running across the prairie, to use his Winchester to knock down one of the furry critters and have him a roasted rabbit. He didn't want to take the time to do that, though. He pushed on, heading for a low range of mountains that loomed in front of him. He knew that the settlement was located at the edge of those mountains.

By midday, it seemed like the rounded peaks were just as far away as they had been when he started, but he knew that was just a trick of the eye, compounded by the clear high country air. He rode on, and a couple of hours later it was obvious that the mountains were closer.

Something off to the right caught his eye. When he looked closer, he saw that it was a road, a pair of ruts worn into the prairie, actually. That would be the stage road, he realized. He looked around for the three rocks Earl Fenton had told him about and found them a few minutes later.

That was where the scout, Phil Jefferson, had died, Longarm thought as he reined in and studied the ground. He didn't see anything out of the ordinary, just a welter of horse tracks that came as no surprise. Jefferson's mount would have left some of them, and the others came from the horses ridden by Fenton and the men he brought with him when he came looking for the scout.

Longarm turned his head and squinted toward the stage road several hundred yards away. After a moment, he turned his horse and trotted in that direction to take a closer look.

There wasn't much to see, of course, just those ruts he had noticed. But when he lifted his eyes and gazed along the road toward the mountains, he spotted dust rising in the distance. A thick column of it climbed into the sky, and from the size of it, he knew that it came from the hooves of a team of horses and the wheels of a vehicle.

The stagecoach was coming.

And judging by how fast the dust cloud was moving, it was in a hurry.

Chapter 7

Longarm sat there on his horse and watched as the stage came closer. After a couple of minutes, he could see the coach itself and the team pulling it at the base of the dust cloud. The vehicle rocked back and forth. Those ruts were pretty rough, and at that speed, if anybody was inside the coach, they were probably being bounced around all over the place.

The jehu's teeth might be about to be jolted out, too. Longarm wondered why the driver had whipped his team up into such a lather. Usually a stagecoach never went that fast unless . . .

Longarm's jaw tightened as he reached for his Winchester and pulled it from the saddle boot. A stagecoach usually didn't go that fast unless it was being pursued by owlhoots who were trying to stop it and rob it.

All the evidence in this case so far pointed to Adam Warfield as the man responsible for murder and destruction involving the railroad. But even if that turned out to be true, Longarm knew he couldn't sit by and watch while outlaws held up a stage. He would have to take cards in that game.

The coach was only about a hundred yards away now. Longarm moved his horse back from the road to give the vehicle plenty of room to pass him. He held the rifle ready as his eyes searched the trailing dust for signs of pursuit.

The problem with his theory, he realized a moment later, was that nobody seemed to be chasing the stagecoach. He didn't see any riders, and he didn't hear any gunshots. If outlaws were after the coach, they would be throwing lead. It was possible that the dust concealed the pursuers, but Longarm thought he would have spotted them by now despite that.

The stagecoach careened wildly past him. He got a fairly good look at the driver, who perched on the box and hauled back on the reins, evidently trying to get the team to stop. The horses ignored the driver's efforts and plunged on, running full-tilt along the road.

Just as the coach passed Longarm, the driver's hat flew off, caught by the wind. Long blond hair streamed out behind the driver's head.

Longarm had known some gents who grew their hair long. Commodore Perry Owens down in Arizona, for example. But not as long as the hair of the driver on that stagecoach, and as he turned his head to look after it, Longarm felt sure that the person handling the reins of that stampeding team was a woman.

He yanked his mount around and heeled it into a run. The horse pounded after the stagecoach.

Longarm was convinced now that he was looking at a runaway. The team had bolted for some reason, and once horses were spooked like that, they fed off one another's fear and kept running, making it very difficult to stop them.

At the rate that coach was going, if it hit a particularly bad bump it might overturn or break an axle, which would also cause it to crash. In that case, the woman on the driver's seat would be lucky to escape with her life. She would have some broken bones, at the very least. Longarm knew he had to stop the runaway team before that could happen.

He had gotten to know his rented horse fairly well over the past few days. The gray gelding had some speed, but Longarm wasn't sure it would be enough to catch the stagecoach. He urged the horse on, leaning forward in the saddle, and after a minute he could tell that his mount was narrowing the gap between him and the coach.

His plan was to race up alongside the team, lean over, and grab the harness of one of the leaders. If he could do that, he was confident that he could stop the team.

But as his horse drew even with the rear of the coach, he felt the animal began to falter. The gray had responded gallantly to his call for more speed, but now it was running out of steam. Longarm knew he wouldn't be able to overtake the horses pulling the stage.

That wasn't the only problem. The driver had slumped over to one side and now swayed back and forth loosely on the seat. Longarm figured she must have passed out. That meant she could topple off the seat at any time, and if she did, she might fall right under the hammering hooves of the horses.

He didn't have any time to waste.

While the gray was still able to keep pace momentarily, Longarm leaned over to his left and caught hold of the canvas that covered the baggage boot at the rear of the stage. He kicked his feet free of the stirrups and lunged out of the saddle, reaching for the cover with his other hand. He grabbed it and hung on tight.

His feet dragged the ground for a few seconds before he was able to start pulling himself up. Then, hand over hand, he climbed up the boot until he was able to get a foothold on it. He reached higher and closed his hand around the brass railing that ran around the roof of the coach. It took only a moment for him to haul himself onto the top of the swiftly moving vehicle.

Longarm started crawling toward the front of the coach. The driver was still slumped on the seat, and Longarm could see now that he had been right. She was definitely a woman, despite the fact that she wore a man's fringed buckskin jacket. As she swayed toward the edge of the seat, he lunged forward and grabbed her arm to hold her on the coach.

He bit back a curse as he looked down and saw the reins trailing loose on the ground between the horses in the team. The blonde must have dropped them when she passed out. That was going to make things more difficult.

First things first. He couldn't deal with trying to stop the runaway horses until he made sure that the woman wouldn't fall off the coach. As he slid down onto the driver's seat beside her, he saw that she wore denim trousers and had a belt around her waist. Holding her steady with one hand, he used the other to unbuckle her belt and pull it out of the loops on her trousers. Then he put the belt around her again, this time under her arms so that it passed across the upper slopes of the breasts that filled out the buckskin jacket. He looped the belt around the railing on top of the coach, pulled it tight, and buckled it. That way she couldn't fall off unless the belt broke, which was unlikely.

With that taken care of, Longarm turned his attention to the problem of stopping the team. He knelt on the floorboard of the driver's box and reached down, trying to snag the trailing reins. They were out of his reach.

Longarm grimaced. There was only one thing left for him to do, and he didn't like it. He had pulled off such stunts before, but the odds were that he would break his neck.

Of course, if he waited, there was an even greater chance

that the stagecoach would crash and kill both him and the blonde. He crouched at the front edge of the driver's box and took a deep breath, then leaped forward as hard as he could.

He thrust his arms out to the side as he fell between the galloping horses. He was able to grab the harnesses of the middle pair in the six-horse hitch. One foot hit the wooden tongue extending out from the front of the stagecoach; the other slipped down beside it. But he was able to hang on tightly enough with both hands so that he could pull that leg back up and plant that foot on the tongue as well.

Then, balanced precariously, he edged ahead a few inches at a time. He had to get hold of the leaders and stop them in order to halt the team. That meant eventually he would have to let go and make another grab.

When he judged that he was close enough, he made sure his feet were planted solidly—or at least as solidly as they could be under the circumstances—and released his grip on the harness. He leaned forward, reaching, and for a second it seemed that his fingers were going to slip off the harness of the leaders.

Then they closed around it firmly, and he hauled back as hard as he could, at the same time shouting, "Whoa! Whoa, you damn jugheads, whoa!"

Relief flooded through Longarm as the horses began to slow. Even in their panic-stricken state, they instinctively responded to a strong enough hand on the reins, or in this case, their harness. He kept his grip until the team came to a complete stop. Then, breathing hard from his exertions, he turned to look up at the driver's box and make sure the blonde was all right.

Not only was she all right, but she was awake again . . . and she had a Colt in her hand that was pointing right at Longarm.

"Don't move, mister! I'll shoot if you try anything. I swear I will."

Surprise and disgust welled up inside Longarm. He didn't know where she had gotten the gun, but that didn't matter. He was careful not to make any sudden moves, because the woman appeared to be as spooked as those horses had been a few moments earlier. Folks who were scared were always dangerous because they were also unpredictable.

"Take it easy, ma'am. I reckon you're too shaken up to have figured it out yet, but I'm the hombre who just stopped these runaways and saved you."

It seemed obvious to him that was what had happened, otherwise he wouldn't be perched out here on this tongue like a bird on a wire. But he didn't say that. She would likely see it for herself if he was patient.

After a moment, she began to frown. "Who are you?"

"Name's Custis . . ." He hesitated as a thought occurred to him. "Custis Parker, ma'am." It was a name he used sometimes when he didn't want people to know that he was a federal lawman. He didn't have any trouble remembering it, since Parker was actually his middle name. He might have more luck finding out the things he wanted to know if she wasn't aware of who he was.

"What are you doing here?"

"You mean besides stopping this team?"

She made an impatient little motion with the gun barrel. "Yes, you said that. How did you come to do that?"

"I was sitting my horse there by the road when you came barreling past on this stagecoach. The way you were goin' so fast, I figured there must be owlhoots after you, but then I saw that you were tryin' to stop the team and that you weren't being chased. So I came after you as fast as I could. My horse got me even with the back of the coach. I climbed on, came over the top, and saw that you had passed out. I fastened you on as best I could, so you wouldn't fall off, and then jumped down here to stop these horses."

"You *jumped* in the middle of a runaway team?" She sounded like she didn't believe him. "Nobody could do that without falling and getting killed."

Longarm shrugged. "I'm here, and I don't know how else I could've gotten here."

The gun in her hand wavered a little. "I guess that's true. When I came to, I . . . I saw you working your way up to the leaders. I didn't think you could do it, but you did. I suppose you saved my life."

Longarm smiled. "Seemed like the thing to do at the time."

"You're not one of the men who shot at me?" She shook her head before he could even answer the question. "What's the point of asking? If you were, you'd just lie about it, wouldn't you?"

"I don't know, because I'm not one of those hombres. I never saw you before until the stage passed me on the road, ma'am." He paused. "I reckon I'd remember if I had."

That was true enough. The woman was very pretty with that long blond hair tumbling down her back and a sweet figure in the buckskin jacket and tight denim pants. Longarm put her age at twenty-five or so. As understanding of what he meant by his last comment soaked in on her, she got even prettier as a blush spread across her lovely face.

She jerked the gun impatiently. "All right, I suppose there's no need for you to stand there like that. Climb down. And then climb up here and get me loose. I can't reach that blasted buckle."

Trying not to grin, Longarm joined her on the driver's box a moment later. He unfastened the buckle, but he still had hold of the belt when she suddenly let out a moan, dropped the gun onto the floorboards, and sagged forward. He caught her before she could fall off the box.

"Ma'am? Ma'am, are you all right?"

She didn't answer. Longarm stood up and carefully positioned her so that she was lying across the driver's seat. She seemed to be having trouble getting her breath, so he undid the top two buttons on the jacket and spread it open, revealing a frilly shirt. He smiled. She didn't dress completely in men's duds. He opened the top two buttons of the shirt as well.

Her eyelids fluttered and then came open as he did that. "What . . . what are you *doing*?" She grabbed at the shirt and tugged it together, then tried to sit up, only to groan and fall back again.

"You'd better just take it easy, ma'am. You don't seem to be wounded, but it's clear that you're pretty shaken up. You just rest for a minute." Longarm reached over and grasped the brake lever, pulling back hard on it to set the brake. "Don't worry, the coach isn't goin' anywhere. I'll get you some water."

"There's a canteen . . . in the coach."

Longarm had planned to fetch the canteen that was tied to his saddle—he had already spotted his horse standing about fifty yards behind the coach with reins trailing—but this was even better. He swung down from the box and opened the door on the side of the coach. As he had suspected, the vehicle wasn't carrying any passengers. The only things on the front seat of the coach were a mail pouch and a canteen.

He left the mail pouch where it was and took the canteen with him as he climbed back to the box. He pulled the cork, then slipped a hand behind the blonde's shoulders and helped her sit up a little. She took the canteen in both hands and drank. Her color seemed a little better.

"You know, I've got a flask in my saddlebags. A little nip of Maryland rye might brace you up even more."

She shook her head. "I don't drink. But thank you, Mr. . . . Parker, was it?"

"Yes, ma'am. You can call me Custis."

"I think I'll call you Mr. Parker. I'm Rose Warfield."

That information came as no surprise to Longarm. He had already decided there was a good chance that was who she was.

"I'm pleased to meet you, Miss Warfield. Just wish it had been under more pleasant circumstances."

She frowned slightly. "How do you know it's not Mrs. Warfield?"

Longarm gestured toward her left hand, which sported no jewelry. "I reckon you could be married, but most married ladies wear a wedding ring. So I just guessed."

"Well, you were right, as it happens. I'm not married." She lifted the canteen to her lips and took another drink.

Longarm waited until she was finished to ask her a question. "You said some men shot at you?"

"That's right." Anger crackled in her voice. "I was going through Fielder's Cut when they opened fire. I whipped up the team and got out of there as fast as I could."

"You think it was outlaws? Were they tryin' to steal that mail pouch I saw inside the coach?"

Rose Warfield shook her head. "No, they weren't outlaws, but I know exactly who they were. The men who shot at me were some of those hired killers who work for Clayton Abernathy and his damned railroad!"

Chapter 8

Now *that* was a surprise, but Longarm didn't show it on his face. He nodded toward the south.

"I passed a railroad construction camp back yonder a ways. Is that the railroad you're talkin' about?"

"That's right." Rose's fingers clutched the canteen tightly, a sign of the anger she was feeling. "They hate my brother and me. They'd do anything to ruin us."

Longarm played dumb. "Your brother?"

"Adam. We own the Rimfire Stagecoach Company."

That was something else Longarm hadn't known. Abernathy, Fenton, and Delahunt had all talked about Adam Warfield owning the stage line but hadn't said anything about Warfield's sister being a part-owner as well. Maybe they didn't know about that and thought that Rose just worked for her brother.

"I don't think I understand, Miss Warfield. If you own the line, what are you doin' drivin' one of the coaches?"

She blew out an angry sigh. "We don't have enough money to pay all our drivers anymore. We've had to take over most of the driving ourselves." She looked up at Longarm. "And I don't want to appear ungrateful, Mr. Parker, but what business is that of yours?"

"None at all, ma'am." He smiled. "Reckon I was just curious."

"I'm sorry. I don't mean to be rude."

He waved a hand and continued smiling. *"De nada."*

"What?"

"Spanish for don't mention it."

"Oh. All right. I'm glad I didn't offend you." She put the cork back in the canteen. "But I'm feeling better now, so I have to be going. Even though I don't have any passengers on this run, I like to keep to the schedule."

"You're going on, even though those fellas shot at you?"

"Of course."

"What if they make another try?"

"Then I suppose I'll have to outrun them again." Rose began to look impatient. "I really appreciate you helping me, and I'd pay you for what you did if I could, but unfortunately, I don't have any extra money."

Longarm pretended to huff up a little, since he knew that's what most cowboys would do in these circumstances. "No payment necessary, and no thanks, neither. I just did what any other fella would've done if he saw a gal in trouble. But I ain't sure you should be drivin' on by yourself."

"Are you volunteering to come with me to Laramie?"

Longarm hesitated. He wanted to find out more about some of the intriguing things Rose Warfield had said, and if somebody had already taken potshots at her, he really would worry about her traveling by herself.

But he was on his way to Rimfire to find out if her brother was behind the raid on the construction camp and all the rest of the railroad's troubles, and he didn't want to postpone that for the several days it would take to ride to Laramie and back. It was a dilemma, all right.

One that was solved by a sudden sharp crack as the stagecoach lurched slightly.

"Oh, my God!" Rose's eyes widened. "What was that?"

"I've got a pretty good idea. Let me take a look."

Longarm climbed down from the driver's box again and bent over to peer underneath the stagecoach for several seconds. Then he straightened and looked up at Rose.

"That's what I was afraid of. Front axle's busted. All that bouncing around while the horses were stampedin' was just too much for it."

"Oh, no! I can't fix that."

"Neither can I. Not out here on the road, anyway. You need a place where you can block it up and take the wheels off to replace the axle. I reckon your company's got a barn back in Rimfire?"

"Yes, of course, but what good does that do us here?"

Longarm bent and studied the axle again. "It ain't busted clean through. It's just got a good crack in it. If I tie it up real tight and you take it slow, you might be able to limp back to Rimfire. How far is it?"

"About four miles."

Longarm glanced up at the sky. "Probably won't make it by dark, but that's still your best chance. You sure can't make it all the way to Laramie, that's for sure."

"There's a way station four miles to the south."

"Any spare axles there?"

"Well . . . not that I know of. Just a change of horses and an old-timer who looks after them."

Longarm shook his head. "Then you'd still be better off turning around and headin' back to town."

"That means I'll be late delivering that mail pouch."

"Won't be the first time the mail's been late, I reckon."

"You don't understand—" Rose stopped short and shook her head. "Never mind. You're right, Mr. Parker. The only logical thing to do is turn around and go back to Rimfire."

He smiled. "And if you're doin' that, then I can ride along with you, just in case you run into any more trouble."

"That's right." She put a hand to her head. "Do you happen to know where my hat is? That sun is pretty bright."

Longarm jerked a thumb over his shoulder. "Yeah, it blew off back yonder, just like mine did when I climbed on top of the coach. I'll get my horse and go find both of them."

"Thank you."

"First, though, have you got some spare harness?"

"I think so. Look in the boot. What do you need it for?"

"I'll cut it into strips, then get it wet and tie it good and tight around the crack in that axle. The leather will draw up as it dries and hold even tighter."

Longarm set to work. It didn't take him long to bind up the axle. Cracking the way it had was a stroke of luck for him. If that hadn't happened, he might have had to reveal his true identity to Rose and order her to come back to Rimfire with him. This way he didn't have to tell her that he was a deputy U.S. marshal.

Once he was finished, he got his horse and retrieved their hats. Rose's was a battered old brown hat with the brim turned up in front. She didn't bother trying to tuck her hair into it when she put it on. Longarm thought she was even cuter wearing the hat.

Then he reminded himself that her brother might well be a murderer, and she might know that he was. After that, she didn't seem so cute.

But he wasn't going to jump to conclusions. He still had plenty of questions that needed answering before he made up his mind about anything.

"All right, turn the coach around. Take it slow and easy. Unless you'd rather I did it . . ."

Rose shook her head. "I can handle it. Just because the team got away from me when all that shooting started doesn't mean I can't drive this stagecoach."

Longarm waved a hand. "Have at it, then."

Rose managed to get the coach turned around. She started the team heading toward Rimfire at a slow walk. Longarm rode alongside. After several hundred yards, he dismounted and led the gray, leaning over to look under the coach and check the axle. As slow as the vehicle was going, he had no trouble keeping up.

When he swung into the saddle again, he nodded to Rose. "Looks good. I think it'll hold until we get there."

The look of worry on her face eased a little. "I hope so. I suppose if it breaks down completely, you could ride on into town and send help back out here to me, but my brother has enough on his mind right now. I don't want to heap any more troubles on him."

"How'd the two of you wind up running a stage line?" Longarm grinned. "Yeah, there I go, bein' curious again."

Rose surprised him a little by smiling back at him. "I suppose you've earned the right to ask a few questions. After all, I might be dead now if it weren't for you, Mr. Parker."

"Custis."

"All right, if you insist. Custis. The way that axle cracked, the stage definitely would have wrecked if the team had bolted much farther. So at the very least, you saved us a lot of damage that we can't really afford to have to deal with right now." She paused. "As for how we wound up running the stage line, that's simple. We inherited it. Our father started the line several years ago, not long after the town of Rimfire was founded."

That was news to Longarm. Clayton Abernathy had

told him that the stage line had been operating just about since the settlement began, but he had given the impression that it had always belonged to Adam Warfield. Clearly, Abernathy hadn't given Longarm the full story.

"I reckon that means your pa has passed on. I'm sorry. When did it happen?"

"About six months ago."

After Abernathy had begun making plans to run his spur line to Rimfire, Longarm thought.

"He died suddenly of a heart ailment. It was quite a shock. But Adam and I knew that we would have to take over the line and keep it operating. It's what Father would have wanted. It meant so much to him to help out the people of Rimfire."

The railroad would help them even more, but Longarm didn't mention that. "Were you already working for him when he passed on?"

"That's right. Adam was the superintendent of the line, and I ran the office and kept the books. I still do, and Adam's job hasn't changed all that much, either. At least, it hadn't until recently, when business got bad and we had to let some of our drivers and guards go."

"And take over those jobs yourselves."

Rose nodded. "Yes." She sighed. "Of course, until today Adam wouldn't allow me to drive . . . and after what happened, he probably never will again!"

"You own equal shares in the line?"

"Yes."

"Then he can't very well stop you, can he?"

Rose gave a hollow laugh. "You don't know my brother, Mr. Parker . . . I mean Custis. Adam's very stubborn, and he can be a little hotheaded when he doesn't get his way."

Hotheaded enough to bushwhack a scout who worked for the railroad? Longarm couldn't help but wonder about that.

He thought about asking Rose if her brother had been driving one of the coaches a couple of days earlier when Phil Jefferson had been killed. That seemed to be prying a little too blatantly, though, so he didn't bring it up.

Besides, if he carried out the plan that had begun to form in his mind, he ought to have a chance to find out everything he needed to know. All that was required was a little patience, and maybe a little more luck.

They continued on their slow way toward Rimfire. When they reached Fielder's Cut, where the stage road ran between two steep hills, Rose pointed it out as the place where she had been ambushed before. Longarm drew his rifle and scanned the hills as the stage passed through the cut, but it appeared that the bushwhackers were long gone. No one took any shots at them.

The sun dropped close to the horizon, then touched it and began to dip beneath it. By the time the orange ball was gone, the western sky was lit up beautifully with all kinds of colors.

"How far are we from the settlement?"

"Maybe a mile and a half."

Longarm nodded. "We ought to keep going. There'll be enough light to see for a little while, and we ought to be spotting the lights of town pretty soon."

That was how it turned out. As dusk settled down over the Wyoming landscape, Longarm's keen eyes picked up a scattering of yellow lights up ahead. He knew that the glow came from the windows of buildings in Rimfire.

The ruts made the road easy to follow, especially with the lights to steer by. Another half hour went by. The sky was almost completely dark. Millions of stars had winked into existence in the sable blanket overhead. But now they were close enough to town that Longarm could not only see the lights, he could also hear the tinny strains of music, probably coming from one of Rimfire's saloons.

The stage road turned into the main street at the southern end of town. Longarm saw it stretching out for five or six blocks in front of him, lined with businesses on both sides. The residences were on the cross streets and side streets.

Rimfire seemed prosperous. A couple of general stores were still open and brightly lit, as were several restaurants and cafés. Those businesses were all in the southern half of the settlement. Half a dozen or more saloons and gambling dens and dance halls clustered in the northern half. A big public well in the middle of the street, complete with a windmill and elevated water tank, formed an unofficial dividing line.

Longarm had seen scores of cow towns like this scattered across the West, from the Rio Grande to the Canadian border. Rimfire had the added advantage of having mines located nearby, too. The settlement faced a very promising future as it served as the supply center for the surrounding ranches and coal mines.

Rose pointed the team toward a building on the right side of the road. Lamplight glowed in the front window and in an open doorway. Behind the building were a barn and a corral. As Longarm rode closer, he could make out a sign attached to the awning over the boardwalk in front of the building. It read "RIMFIRE STAGECOACH COMPANY."

A man's figure suddenly appeared in the doorway. He must have heard the creaking of the coach's wheels through the open door. At the sight of the approaching vehicle, he came quickly across the boardwalk and jumped down into the street, hurrying forward to meet the coach.

"Rose! What's wrong? Why aren't you on the way to Laramie?"

Rose hauled back on the reins and brought the stagecoach to a stop. "I'm sorry, Adam. I had to turn back. The front axle cracked."

"Blast it! What else could possibly go wrong?"

"That's not all. The axle cracked because the team stampeded and took the road too fast."

Adam Warfield threw his hands in the air. "I knew I shouldn't have let you make that run by yourself! I knew it was a mistake, that you couldn't handle the team—"

"Adam." Rose's voice cut into her brother's frustrated, angry ranting. "The team didn't just get away from me. The horses stampeded because someone started shooting at me in Fielder's Cut."

That silenced Warfield, all right. He stared up at his sister for a long moment, and that gave Longarm a chance to study him in the light that spilled through the doorway.

Adam Warfield was a big, heavy-shouldered man with a shock of dark hair and a strong jaw that looked like it was often thrust out pugnaciously. He was probably ten years older than Rose. At the moment he wore town clothes, the dark trousers and vest from a suit, but the collar of his white shirt was undone and the sleeves were rolled up on brawny forearms. He didn't have a tie.

He didn't appear to be armed, either, Longarm noted. At the same time, Warfield took notice of him.

"Who's this?"

"Mr. Parker saw the team running away and stopped them. Then he repaired the axle as best he could, so that I could get the stage back here to town."

Longarm dismounted as Warfield came over to him. Warfield was still obviously upset, but he at least tried to be gracious as he stuck out his hand.

"Thank you for helping my sister, Mr. Parker. If there's anything I can do to repay you—"

"Actually, there is." Longarm gripped Warfield's hand. "You can give me a job."

Chapter 9

Warfield gave Longarm a confused frown instead, while Rose spoke from the driver's seat of the stagecoach. "Custis, I told you that we've had to let most of our drivers and guards go. We can't afford to give you a job, no matter how grateful I am to you for your help today. There's no money for wages."

"I'll work for room and board. That'll sure beat what I've been makin', which is not a blasted thing."

Warfield shook his head. "I'm sorry, it's impossible. I appreciate what you did for Rose, but—"

"Your sister told me a little about the trouble you've been havin' with the railroad, Mr. Warfield. If you're so shorthanded that you can't put guards on your coaches, then I reckon you'll probably continue to have trouble."

"No offense, Parker, but that's none of your business."

Longarm thumbed his hat back on his head. "The Chinese have a sayin' about how when you save somebody's life, you're responsible for them from then on. I reckon I saved Miss Warfield's life today, and I'd hate to see anything happen to her when she takes that coach out again."

Warfield's jaw stuck out, just like Longarm figured it would when the man got mad. "Are you threatening my sister, Parker?"

"Nope, not at all. You've got me wrong. I'm just saying that whoever took those shots at her is liable to try to ambush her again next time. She'll stand a lot better chance of gettin' through safely if she's got a guard with her."

"A guard like you."

Longarm shrugged. "I can handle a gun when I have to."

Warfield slashed the air with his hand. "Forget it. I don't need some saddle tramp telling me how to run my business . . . or how to take care of my sister."

He started to turn away. Longarm put a hand on his arm to stop him. That brought an angry roar from Warfield.

"Let go of me, damn you!"

He whirled around and swung a big fist at Longarm's head.

Rose had warned him that her brother was hotheaded, Longarm recalled. But even so, he hadn't expected Warfield to take a swing at the man who'd saved his sister's life.

That was what was happening, though. Instinctively, Longarm took a quick step to the side, so that Warfield's fist passed harmlessly by his ear, missing by a good six inches. That threw Warfield off balance and made him stumble forward a step.

Longarm grabbed his shoulder to keep him from falling. "Take it easy—"

With another yell, Warfield drove forward, turning his stumble into a fresh attack. He crashed into Longarm, wrapped his arms around the big lawman's body, and bore him backward off his feet. Both men fell heavily in the dusty street.

"Adam, no!"

Warfield ignored his sister's shout. He started slugging at Longarm, throwing short, frenzied punches that thudded against Longarm's ribs. None of them landed with any real power, but Longarm wasn't going to just lie there and take it, regardless of whether or not Warfield was hurting him. He brought up a knee and sank it in Warfield's stomach, then grabbed his shoulders and heaved him aside.

Without Warfield's weight pinning him down, Longarm rolled away and came up on one knee. Warfield was a few feet away, doubled over from the pain of the knee to his guts. Panting, he lifted his head and glowered at Longarm.

"Take it easy, old son. There's no need for us to fight—"

Longarm didn't get to finish. Warfield scrambled up and charged him again.

Longarm made it to his feet in time to meet that attack head-on. He blocked the wild, looping punch that Warfield swung at him. This wasn't the way Longarm had planned for his first meeting with Adam Warfield to go, but the other man had called the tune. Longarm stepped in and smashed a hard right into Warfield's face.

The blow landed solidly and knocked Warfield back a step. Longarm followed it with a left that caught Warfield on the jaw and jerked his head to the side. Warfield staggered and went to a knee. From there he tackled Longarm again, catching the lawman around the thighs and bringing him down.

Longarm kicked free, rolled again, and came up with his fists cocked. Warfield was up again, too, his size allowing him to throw off the damage Longarm had done to him so far. Both men were close to the same height, but Warfield was probably thirty pounds heavier.

Not only that, but the punches Longarm had landed

seemed to have knocked some of the wildness out of Warfield, too. He wasn't roaring incoherently and charging like a maddened bull anymore.

"I don't care who you are, I'm gonna pound you into the dirt, mister. Nobody lays hands on me."

Longarm made one more try to talk some sense into the man. "Listen, Warfield, if you'd just settle down, you'd see there's no reason for us to fight."

"Shut up! I'm tired of people coming in here, thinking they can run roughshod over me. I'll show you! I'll show you all!"

He came at Longarm again, and the way his fists snapped out in short, controlled punches, Longarm knew that Warfield had some regular boxing experience. With his size, he might have even fought in the prize ring at one time.

Longarm had experience, too . . . at staying alive. He had learned in a rough-and-tumble school that showed no mercy to those who couldn't master its lessons. He blocked most of Warfield's punches, absorbed the punishment inflicted by those he couldn't, and threw his own punches that thudded home again and again on his opponent's body and face. Blood began to smear Warfield's features, looking black instead of red in the faint light that came from the building.

Longarm wasn't even thinking about Rose anymore as he and Warfield stood toe to toe and slugged away at each other. He was vaguely aware that she wasn't shouting at them anymore, but that was all.

The sudden thunderous boom of a shotgun made both men step away from each other, their hands falling. Longarm looked toward the stage line office and saw Rose standing on the boardwalk, holding a shotgun she must have brought from inside.

"That was only one barrel! Stop it or I'll use the other one on you two idiots!"

"Rose!" Warfield held a hand out toward her as she pointed the Greener at him and Longarm. "Put that gun down. You don't know what you're doing."

"The hell I don't! I'm stopping you fools from beating each other to death for no good reason!"

Longarm thought that her voice held a note of hysteria. He backed away from Warfield, putting some distance between them so that Rose couldn't threaten both of them with the scattergun at the same time.

"Your brother's right, ma'am. You need to point that thing somewhere else. I don't think you want to hurt anybody."

Warfield snarled at him. "Damn it, Parker, stay out of this! This is between my sister and me."

"Not when I'm in the line of fire of a load of buckshot, it ain't. It's my business, too."

Voices came from up the street. The shotgun blast had drawn some attention from the townspeople, and now they were on their way to see what the commotion was all about.

"See what you've done, Rose? Now there'll just be more trouble."

She stared at her brother, struggling for a second before she could speak. "You . . . you sanctimonious hypocrite! You attack a man for no good reason, and then you accuse me of causing trouble?" She threw the shotgun on the boardwalk at her feet, causing both Longarm and Warfield to wince, but the weapon's other barrel didn't go off. "Go ahead! Beat each other to death! See if I care!"

She turned and stormed into the office, slamming the door behind her.

A middle-aged, barrel-chested hombre with a tin star

pinned to his vest came up, holding a revolver. "What's goin' on here? Adam, was that a shotgun I heard?"

Warfield sighed. "Yes, Sheriff Holcomb, it was. But it was just an accident. Rose didn't mean to fire it."

Longarm didn't dispute that, even though it wasn't true. He didn't see any point in complicating matters more than they already were.

Holcomb leaned forward and squinted at Warfield. "You look like you tangled with a wildcat, son." He glanced over at Longarm. "You havin' trouble with this stranger?"

Warfield shook his head. "Just a friendly tussle, I guess you'd say."

The sheriff grunted. "Well, if that's the case, I'd hate to see an *un*friendly tussle between you two!" Without holstering his gun, he stepped over to Longarm. "Who're you, mister, and what're you doin' in Rimfire?"

Longarm knew he could put an end to the local lawman's suspicions just by telling Holcomb that he was a deputy U.S. marshal. He wasn't ready to do that, though. Despite the unexpected trouble with Adam Warfield, he hadn't given up on the plan he had formed on the way into town.

"Name's Parker, Sheriff, and I'm not lookin' for trouble, if that's what you're askin'. I came into town with Miss Warfield after she had a problem with the stagecoach."

Holcomb looked quickly at Warfield. "Problem? What sort of problem, Adam?"

"A cracked axle." Warfield's heavy shoulders lifted and fell. "I guess this fellow did give Rose a hand. He and I just had a misunderstanding about it."

The sheriff nodded slowly. "All right. I reckon that makes sense. You don't need any help, then?"

"No, we're fine here. Aren't we, Parker?"

Longarm nodded. "Yep. No hard feelin's as far as I'm concerned, Sheriff. I'm a peaceable man."

Holcomb finally pouched his iron and then pointed a finger at Longarm. "See that you stay that way." He turned to the small crowd of curious onlookers that had gathered. "All right, folks, go on about your business. No reason to stand around gawkin'."

As the crowd began to disperse, Longarm turned to Warfield. "I meant what I said, Warfield. I'm not lookin' for trouble, and there are no hard feelings on my part. Fact of the matter is, if you want to walk up the street with me to one of those saloons, I'll buy you a drink to prove it."

Warfield shook his head. "No." Then his stubborn stance seemed to ease a little. "But if you'll come in the office, I've got a bottle of whiskey in the desk."

Longarm grinned. "I reckon we can both use a shot."

Warfield took hold of his jaw, moved it back and forth a little, and grimaced. "I'm probably going to need it to help dull the pain of those wallops you gave me."

"You landed a few punches of your own."

The two men went inside the building. Longarm didn't see Rose anywhere, but he noticed that a rear door was standing open.

So did Warfield. He nodded toward the open door. "If you're wondering, I guess Rose went out the back. Our house is directly behind here on the side street, and she can get to it by going past the barn and the corral. She's probably still upset. You don't know my sister, Parker, but . . . she holds a grudge."

"Runs in the family, does it?"

Warfield laughed hollowly. "I don't hold grudges. Oh, I admit that I fly off the handle too easily. I've got a bad temper, no denying it. But once I've blown up, it's over."

Longarm had his doubts about that. From everything he'd heard, Warfield was holding a grudge against Clayton Abernathy. But that was different, he supposed. Abernathy was threatening Warfield's business. You might even call it his life's work.

Longarm glanced around the office. It was furnished in a strictly functional manner with a desk, several chairs, a file cabinet, and a small table. A map of Wyoming hung on the wall with the stagecoach route from Rimfire to Laramie marked on it.

Warfield went behind the desk and leaned over to open a drawer. He took out a bottle half-full of amber liquid and a couple of glasses. He pulled the cork from the bottle, splashed whiskey in the glasses, and pushed one across the desk toward Longarm.

"Help yourself."

"Don't mind if I do." Longarm picked up the glass. They didn't bother with making any sort of toast. They just threw back the whiskey.

Longarm licked his lips appreciatively. "Much obliged."

Warfield toyed with his empty glass. "About that job you wanted . . ."

The words took Longarm by surprise, but he was glad to hear them. It meant his plan still had a chance of working. He figured that the easiest way to find out the truth of what Adam Warfield was doing was to gain the man's confidence.

"You'd hire me, after the two of us whaled the tar out of each other like that?"

Warfield waved that away. "I wouldn't want a man working for me who wouldn't stand up for himself. I figure a man like that wouldn't stand up for me and my company, either."

"Well, you're probably right about that."

"And if you go to work for the Rimfire Stagecoach Company, you'll run into trouble, Parker. I can practically guarantee that. You'll be risking your life . . . and that's a lot to risk for room and board."

Longarm shrugged. "I've always been a gamblin' man, now and again. Your sister said something about how the fella putting in that railroad spur line is the one behind your troubles?"

Warfield lifted the bottle and cocked an eyebrow. Longarm held out his glass for a refill.

"Pull up a chair. It's a long story."

Chapter 10

"Our father, Donald Warfield, was a stagecoach man. He started out as a driver for John Butterfield and Ben Holladay. He worked his way up to being a superintendent for one of the sections of the Butterfield line, until he decided to go out on his own. I was a driver for Holladay by that time, following in my father's footsteps, I guess you could say, but I was glad to quit and go with him. He started a couple of small lines in New Mexico Territory, with my help, but once they were successful, he sold them. He always said that he liked the challenge of starting a business more than he did the work of running one. Until he came here to Rimfire, that is. He fell in love with the place and said this was where he was going to stay."

Adam Warfield sipped the whiskey in his glass and then sighed.

"He was right. He's buried in the churchyard up the street."

"I'm sorry he passed away. But I reckon he was happy here, doin' what he wanted to do."

Warfield nodded. "Until that bastard Clayton Abernathy showed up in town and started talking about how he was going to build a railroad line up here. He got everybody excited. They figured that a railroad would be a lot better than a stage line."

For the most part, they were right about that, thought Longarm. Passengers could travel faster and in more comfort on a train, mail and freight could be shipped more securely, and having a railroad here would be a real boon for the ranchers in the area. They could drive their herds to Rimfire when they were ready to ship the cows to market, rather than having to drive farther south to the main railroad route.

Like it or not, the expansion of the railroads across the West was the death knell for stagecoach transportation, except in a few isolated areas where it wouldn't be worthwhile for anybody to build a spur line. Longarm knew that, and he suspected that Adam Warfield did, too. Warfield was stubborn, though, and wanted to hang on as long as he could.

Did that mean he would resort to sabotage and murder in order to delay the inevitable? Longarm didn't know yet, but he couldn't see any other motive for what had been happening.

Warfield took another drink and went on. "Abernathy got what he wanted. He cut my father's legs right out from under him. You should have seen that ruthless buzzard gloating, Parker. He was about to destroy his old enemy, and he enjoyed every minute of it."

Longarm frowned. "Wait a minute. Old enemy? You mean your pa and Abernathy knew each other before Abernathy decided to build a spur line up here?"

"That's right. They'd known each other for years. You said something earlier about somebody holding a grudge. Well, that's Clayton Abernathy for you. He never forgave my father for marrying my mother."

Longarm's fingers tightened on the glass in his hand. It seemed that there were some things Abernathy hadn't bothered to mention to him.

"Fought over a woman when they were younger, did they?" He made the question sound like a casual one.

"It wasn't really much of a fight. My mother was already engaged to my father. Then Abernathy came along, fancying himself a dashing young railroader, and decided that he was going to take her away from him. Of course, it didn't work. She told him in no uncertain terms that she had no interest in him and would never leave my father for him, and that was the end of that . . . at least it was in the minds of everyone except Abernathy. He stayed mad about it. I'm convinced that he still is. He never accepted the fact that he couldn't get everything he wanted, just because he wanted it."

Of course, he was hearing all this from Warfield's side, Longarm reminded himself. But he had to admit, Abernathy had struck him as pretty arrogant, and he had no trouble believing that the railroad baron would react as Warfield had just described.

Abernathy must have been happy when the opportunity came along to build a railroad line to Rimfire. It would be a lucrative business deal, and he could get revenge on his old enemy as well, as Adam Warfield had just pointed out.

"So you think because of all this, Abernathy hired gunmen to take those potshots at your sister?"

"He's the only one who would do such a thing. And that's not the only trouble we've had, either. We've had horses run off and coaches damaged. Somebody started a rockslide that closed down one of the passes between here and Laramie for a while. Because of all that, we've had trouble getting the mail through in a timely manner. That gives the government the option of breaking its contract with us and giving it to Abernathy instead, once the railroad gets here. I'm sure that's exactly what Abernathy has in mind." Warfield sighed. "So you see, Parker, if you go to work for us, you'll be walking right into a bad situation that's only going to get worse."

Longarm shrugged. "Wouldn't be the first time."

"I just want you to go into this with your eyes open, that's all."

"I understand. But it looks to me like you and your sister need help, and I don't know where else you're gonna get it."

"Neither do I. Lord help me, neither do I." Warfield tossed back the rest of his drink. "So, you still want the job?"

"I do."

Warfield leaned forward and extended his hand across the desk. "Then Lord help *you*, because you're going to need all the help you can get."

Warfield told Longarm there was a cot in the tack room in the barn where the line's former hostler had slept. The hostler was one of the employees who'd been let go, so now Warfield did most of the work with the horses himself. Longarm would pitch in on those chores, too, so he could sleep in the tack room and put his saddle horse in the corral with the other animals. He would take his meals at the house with Warfield and Rose.

"We'll get that axle changed first thing in the morning, so be ready to get up and get to work."

Longarm nodded as he stood in the door of the tack room with his saddle in one hand, his rifle in the other, and his saddlebags slung over his shoulder. Warfield told him good night and left the barn.

Longarm found places for his gear, then settled down on the cot and smoked a cheroot as he thought about everything that had happened.

So far he hadn't seen anything that ruled out Warfield as a suspect in the attacks on the railroad, but neither had he come across any evidence indicating that Warfield was guilty. The man had a motive, that was all. Longarm didn't know if Warfield was a good enough shot with a rifle to have killed Phil Jefferson or if he'd even had the opportunity. Nor could Longarm figure out how Warfield could have afforded to hire a dozen gunmen to attack the railroad construction camp. Clearly, the Rimfire Stagecoach Company was just scraping by without even an extra nickel to spare.

Then there was the matter of the ambush attempt on Rose Warfield and the other problems the stage line had been experiencing. Adam Warfield was convinced that Abernathy was behind them. Financially, that was certainly possible. Abernathy had plenty of money to recruit hired gunmen.

But as far as Longarm could tell, Abernathy didn't have a really strong reason for doing so. Adam Warfield claimed it was so that the government would have an excuse for breaking the mail contract, but the government would probably do that anyway once the railroad reached Rimfire. The politicians who ran things in Washington didn't need any excuses for what they did. They just went ahead and did it, especially when it meant some bribes or kickback money for their own pockets.

That left sheer spite as the only motivation for what Warfield claimed Abernathy was doing. Abernathy might well be capable of such a thing, but again, Longarm would need proof.

Anyway, he hadn't been assigned to investigate what was happening to the stagecoach company. Like it or not, his responsibility was to Abernathy.

But if the railroad baron *was* up to no good, and Longarm happened to uncover that in the course of his investigation . . . well, there was no telling where these things might lead.

Longarm dozed off with that thought in mind, after putting out his cheroot. The past thirty-six hours had been hectic and occasionally dangerous, and he had the veteran frontiersman's knack of falling asleep quickly when he wanted to, then sleeping lightly but restfully, ready to wake up and deal with trouble on a second's notice.

No such trouble disturbed him this night. He woke before dawn the next morning, got up and tended to his horse and the other horses, then walked over to the house where Adam and Rose Warfield lived. When he knocked on the back door, Rose called out for him to come in.

The twin tantalizing smells of coffee brewing and bacon frying greeted him. Rose stood at the stove. She looked back over her shoulder at him and smiled.

"Good morning, Mr. Parker."

"Mornin', ma'am."

"I trust you slept well?"

"I sure did. How about you?"

"Fine, once I calmed down." She turned her attention back to the stove. "But I was a little surprised this morning when I heard that Adam had hired you after all."

Longarm pulled out a chair at the kitchen table without waiting to be invited. "Like your brother explained it to me, he gets mad easy, but then he gets over it. As soon as he stopped and thought about it, he could see that hirin' me was a good idea."

"For us, maybe. Not for you. You've bitten off more than you can chew."

"I reckon we'll have to wait and see about that. There's an old saying about eatin' an apple one bite at a time."

She carried a plate piled high with flapjacks and bacon

over to the table and set it in front of him, along with a cup
of the steaming hot coffee. "I think you'll find this more
filling than an apple."

Longarm dug in. The food tasted as good as it smelled,
maybe even better. As he ate, he couldn't help but cast a
glance or two at Rose, who returned to the stove to continue preparing breakfast for herself and her brother.

She wore denim trousers again today, and the way they
hugged her hips was mighty appealing. Instead of the frilly
white blouse she'd had on underneath the buckskin jacket
the day before, this morning she wore a faded blue man's
work shirt. From the way it fit her, Longarm knew it
wasn't a hand-me-down from her brother. She had bought
it for herself, like the trousers. She was determined to help
her brother and do a man's work around here, and she was
dressing the part.

Adam Warfield came into the kitchen. "I'll go give the
horses some grain and fill up the water trough."

"Already done, Boss."

Warfield stopped and frowned at Longarm. "How did
you know what to do?"

"I've taken care of horses plenty of times before. Fact
of the matter is, I've worked around stagecoaches quite a
bit. I can switch out a team, handle the reins, ride shotgun,
whatever you need."

Warfield pulled back a chair to sit down on the other
side of the table. "Well, then, it looks like I made a good
decision by hiring you." He winced slightly as he sat down.
"Except for these bruises and stiff muscles I've got from
that ruckus we had."

"You'd have those either way. I'm a mite stiff and sore
this morning, too."

"Not too sore to help me replace that axle, I hope."

Longarm smiled. "Soon as I finish up this fine meal
Miss Warfield's fixed for us, I'll be rarin' to go."

After they had eaten, the two men went back to the barn. It was an hour's hard work to block up the front end of the big Concord coach, remove the front wheels and the cracked axle, replace the axle, and put the wheels back on.

Longarm and Warfield were both sweaty and greasy when they finished with the job. They were at the pump cleaning up when Rose came out to the barn, wearing her buckskin jacket and carrying a shotgun tucked under her arm.

"I'll hitch up the team and get started to Laramie."

Her brother stared at her in surprise for a second. "After what happened yesterday? I don't think so."

"The mail's already a day late. We can't afford any more delays."

Warfield threw down the rag he'd been using to dry his hands. "Then I'll take the coach. Or Parker can."

"You have work to do here, Adam."

"So do you."

Rose shook her head. "All the books are up-to-date, and all the bills are paid . . . somehow. The best way I can contribute right now is by taking this coach to Laramie and back." She glanced at Longarm. "But I was thinking that perhaps Mr. Parker would be willing to go along as shotgun guard."

Warfield looked at Longarm, eyes narrowing. "I'm not sure that's a good idea. It wouldn't exactly be proper for the two of you to travel together, now would it?"

"Oh, good grief, Adam! We rode into town together yesterday. Anyway, I don't have anything scandalous in mind."

Warfield grunted. "Maybe *you* don't. But you'll have to spend a couple of nights on the trail, coming and going."

"At way stations where there'll be a hostler to serve as chaperone. Anyway, I'm sure Mr. Parker is a perfect gentleman. Tell my brother, Mr. Parker."

Longarm scratched at his jaw. "Well . . . one thing nobody's ever accused me of is bein' perfect . . . but my ma back in West-by-God Virginia raised me to treat ladies right."

Warfield shook his head. "I don't like it."

"It'll be fine, Adam, I promise you."

"What about those bushwhackers? They could be keeping an eye on the town, just waiting for you to leave so they can try again to kill you."

Rose nodded toward Longarm. "That's why I'm taking Mr. Parker along. He can fight them off if they try anything."

"Ma'am, if I could make one suggestion . . ."

"Of course, Mr. Parker, what is it?"

"We'll take that Greener of yours, but I'll want my Winchester, too. A scattergun's mighty good for close work, but if any varmints come after us, I'd just as soon deal with 'em at a distance. The farther the better, in fact."

Rose nodded again. "That makes sense. Of course you can take your rifle." She faced her brother. "Well, Adam, are you going to be reasonable about this, or would you rather be your usual stubborn self?"

Warfield didn't look happy about it, but after a moment he shrugged in agreement. "You're right about the mail needing to get through. And if I don't get that other coach repaired, it's not going to be fit to use much longer. All right, Rose, you can take this run. But be careful." He looked sternly at Longarm. "And you be on your best behavior, Parker."

"Sure thing, Boss."

Longarm kept any sign that he had an ulterior motive off his face. That motive didn't involve romping with Rose Warfield—although he suspected that any such activities would be prime romping, indeed—but rather he thought that by the time he had spent several days in close company with her, she would have learned to trust him. If she knew anything about her brother waging war against Clayton Abernathy's railroad, Longarm was confident that he'd be able to get it out of her.

He didn't like using her like that, but the job had to be done. If Adam Warfield was guilty, Longarm would bring him to justice.

It didn't matter that he instinctively liked both of the Warfield siblings considerably more than he liked Abernathy. Even Adam Warfield, with his hot temper, struck Longarm as a better hombre than the railroad baron.

"Is the new axle on there?"

Warfield nodded in response to his sister's question. "The coach is ready to go."

Rose smiled at Longarm. "Then get your rifle and your other gear, Mr. Parker. We'll be rolling as soon as we can get a team hitched up. Then it'll be next stop Laramie, so to speak. Not counting the way stations between here and there."

"Yes, ma'am," Longarm said. "Next stop Laramie."

Chapter 11

As Longarm had told Rose and Adam, he had worked around stagecoaches before. Shotgun guard wasn't a bad job. You got to be out in the open air and sunshine, riding on the driver's seat was at least as comfortable as riding inside the coach, and you were up high enough that you had a good view of the countryside all around.

The only drawback was that from time to time, owl-hoots tried to shoot you. Longarm dealt with that nearly every day in his job, anyway, so it was nothing unusual.

In this particular instance, the job was even more pleasant because of the company involved. He sat on the high seat with Rose Warfield beside him to his right, handling the reins. The shotgun lay on the floorboards at Longarm's feet, and he held the Winchester with the stock propped against his left thigh.

Rose had donned the buckskin jacket and that battered old hat with the turned-up brim. As they rolled south, away from Rimfire, she glanced over at Longarm and caught him grinning at her.

"What's so amusing, Mr. Parker?"

"Thought you was gonna call me Custis."

"All right, Custis, what are you grinning at?"

"You just remind me of an old compadre of mine named Salty Stevens. He's got a hat like that, too, and he's been known to drive a stagecoach, among other things. Of course, you're a mite taller than he is, and you don't have a bushy white beard, either."

"Thank goodness."

"Yeah, a set of whiskers wouldn't do much for your looks."

She gave him a stern frown. "You don't need to be discussing my looks. You promised my brother that everything between us would be proper."

"Yes, Boss."

Rose laughed. It was a good sound. "Don't start that, Custis. As far as I'm concerned, we're working together."

"Well, yeah, but you own half this stagecoach. There's no gettin' around the fact that you're the boss, at least while your brother's not around."

"Adam doesn't run *everything*, you know. When we need to decide something, we discuss the situation and make the decision together."

Having seen Adam Warfield in action, Longarm doubted that Rose would be able to change his mind once he'd made it up, but he kept that thought to himself. Since this conversation with Rose was headed in the direction he wanted it to go, he kept it moving along.

"What are the two of you going to do about that railroad?"

Rose heaved a sigh. "What *can* we do? There's no law against building a railroad. Clayton Abernathy has a whole flock of lawyers working for him, so I'm sure that he acquired all the right-of-way legitimately and is doing everything by the book. Legally, we can't stop him from building that spur line to Rimfire."

"Seems like there ought to be *something* a fella could do . . ."

Rose shook her head. "There's not." A tone of bleak resignation entered her voice. "All we can do is hang on for as long as possible, I suppose, even though all it really means is waiting for the railroad to arrive and put us out of business no matter what we do."

"Well, that's just not fair. Your brother thinks that Abernathy's to blame for those bushwhackers shooting at you yesterday, as well as all the other problems you've been havin'. It seems to me that if a fella's gonna do things like that, he ought to expect folks to fight back."

"Fight fire with fire, you mean?"

"Well . . . yeah."

"If we tried to do something like that, Abernathy would have the law on us. Don't you think things are bad enough as they are, Custis, without adding to our troubles?"

Longarm shrugged. "I suppose they are. I tell you, though, if somebody busts me in the mouth, I'm gonna bust him right back."

"That doesn't solve anything, though, does it?"

"Depends on how hard I hit him, I reckon."

That brought another chuckle from Rose. "Yes, I suppose so."

They rode along in silence for a while after that, which gave Longarm a chance to think about what Rose had said. Either Adam was behind the attacks on the railroad and was keeping his sister in the dark about it, or he actually wasn't to blame for Phil Jefferson's murder and the other incidents.

Or else Rose knew all about it and was lying to him now. That was a third possibility, Longarm realized. She had sounded completely sincere, but over the years he had run into plenty of women who were excellent liars.

If Adam was to blame and Rose knew about it, Longarm had planted a seed that might grow into something. He had let her know that he might not be opposed to striking back at Clayton Abernathy in any way they could, legal or otherwise. Longarm would give it a few days after he and Rose got back to Rimfire and see if she said anything about that to her brother. If she did, chances were that Adam would sound him out about helping in the next attack against Abernathy.

That would be all the proof Longarm needed to make an arrest.

Somehow, he didn't look forward to that prospect at all.

When they approached Fielder's Cut from the north, Longarm narrowed his eyes and searched the steep slopes on both sides of the trail with his gaze. He was looking for anything out of place, especially the glint of sunlight on metal. That would be an almost certain indication that ambushers were lurking up there.

He didn't see anything unusual, but he thought it would be a good idea to err on the side of caution anyway. "Whip up the team. Let's not waste any time gettin' through there."

Rose reached for the whip that rode in a holder next to the brake lever. "That's just what I was thinking." With a flick of her wrist, she sent the whip snaking out over the backs of the horses, then snapped it back with a sharp crack. The team responded by surging forward against their harness.

The stagecoach rolled quickly through Fielder's Cut. Longarm had the Winchester in both hands now, ready to bring it to his shoulder and fire if he needed to.

Nothing happened. The coach cleared the cut without incident and left it behind. That was one obstacle they didn't have to worry about, Longarm thought.

But chances were, there would be plenty more before they got to Laramie.

They reached the first way station late in the morning, close enough to midday that they would stop there for lunch. The old man who worked there came out of the low, stone-and-log station building and was waiting for the coach when Rose brought it to a stop.

"Howdy, Miss Rose. I was expectin' you yesterday."

"Sorry, Bert. There was some trouble."

"Nothin' too bad, I hope."

"A cracked axle. I had to turn around and go back to Rimfire."

The old man, who was tall and lanky and had a thatch of graying rusty hair under a battered derby, cast an interested eye at Longarm as he and Rose climbed down from the driver's seat. "Who's this gent?"

"This is Custis Parker. Custis, meet Bert Moss."

Longarm nodded to the old-timer. "Pleased to meet you, Bert."

"Likewise." Bert looked at Rose. "Thought you weren't hirin' anybody else."

"Custis has agreed to help us in return for room and board. He gave me a hand yesterday and then came along to ride shotgun today because something else happened. Somebody started shooting at me while I was coming through Fielder's Cut."

Bert's bushy eyebrows rose in surprise. "Shootin' at you? Dadgum it, Miss Rose, maybe it ain't a good idea for you to be drivin' these here stagecoaches! Find yourself another jehu."

"I'll be fine. And nothing happened today when we came through the cut."

Bert gave her an ominous frown. "Them sidewinders who work for Abernathy are likely just bidin' their time 'fore they get up to some other mischief."

Longarm cocked an eye at the old man. "You think Abernathy's to blame for what's been happening, Bert?"

Bert snorted. "Who the hell else? Pardon my French, Miss Rose."

She smiled at him. "That's all right. Who the hell else, indeed."

"Well, I got a pot o' stew on the stove. You folks go in and help yourselves while I get the team changed out."

"You want me to give you a hand?"

Bert shook his head in response to Longarm's question. "Naw, I been handlin' this chore by myself for so long, it ain't no problem. All the hosses know me, and they don't give me no trouble."

Since he seemed sure about it, Longarm nodded and went on into the station with Rose. The barn and corral were next to the building, and Longarm could see through the open door as Bert unhitched the horses one by one and led them over to the corral. The old man began bringing back fresh horses and hitching them up while Longarm and Rose sat down at a rough-hewn table and began eating bowls of the stew Bert had prepared. It was good, although the chunks of meat in it were a little tough and stringy. Longarm had eaten a lot worse in his time.

Bert had a pot of coffee on the stove, too, and Longarm and Rose helped themselves to cups of Arbuckles. The black brew was strong enough to get up and run around on its own two legs, just the way Longarm liked it. He hadn't brought his flask with him, or else he might have tried to sweeten the coffee with a dollop of Maryland rye. Rose probably would have disapproved, though.

Bert came inside. "Teams are switched out and ready to go. No passengers on this run, eh?"

"No, I think everyone in Rimfire who wants to travel is waiting for the train." Rose was smiling as she said it, but Longarm heard the strain in her voice.

"I don't understand it. Them trains are loud and they

stink and you can't ride 'em without breathin' smoke and cinders. Give me a good stagecoach any day."

"If everyone felt like you, Bert, we wouldn't have a worry in the world."

Bert took his hat off and scratched his head through his thinning hair. "Well, ever'body in the world ain't as smart as me, Miss Rose."

"No, and that's a shame."

Bert squinted at Longarm. "You look a mite familiar to me, Parker. That is your name, ain't it?"

Longarm nodded. "Yep."

"Ever been to Yankton, over Dakota way?"

"Passed through there a few times."

"For some reason when I look at you, I think of Yankton. Know a saloon there called Clancy's?"

Longarm shook his head. "Can't say as I've ever heard of it."

That was a bald-faced lie. A couple of years earlier, he'd had a dustup in Clancy's with some owlhoots he'd been chasing. Gunplay had ensued, and Longarm had been forced to kill all three of the varmints. It caused quite a sensation in Yankton for a few days, until the next shoot-out came along and made folks forget about it. Longarm wondered if Bert had been in Clancy's that night and had dived for cover along with all the other patrons when hell broke loose.

"Well, could be I'm thinkin' of somebody else, I reckon. Don't really matter, as long as you take good care o' Miss Rose here. All of us who work for her and her brother are mighty fond of her."

"Honestly, Bert, Mr. Parker's job isn't to take care of me, as you put it. We're working together. You might as well say that my job is to take care of him."

Bert just grunted and went to get a bowl of stew.

After they had eaten, Rose went around back to the

privy to tend to her needs, leaving Longarm to stand beside the coach and talk with Bert.

The old-timer didn't waste any time. "You best not try anything funny with that gal, Parker. Her brother won't take kindly to it if you do, and neither will I. She ain't gonna 'take care of you,' if you know what I mean."

"I never said she was. I'm just along for the ride, in case whoever bushwhacked her yesterday tries again." Longarm fired up a cheroot. "You know, if some damned railroad baron was tryin' to run me out of business, I wouldn't take kindly to *that*. Reckon I'd try to do something about it."

"What could you do? That bastard Abernathy's got all sorts o' money and powerful friends."

"Neither of those things would stop a bullet in the right time and place."

Bert drew in a sharp breath and stared at Longarm for a few seconds. "You hush up about such things! Adam and Miss Rose ain't the sort who'd have anything to do with that. Don't you go suggestin' it to 'em, neither. They got enough trouble without havin' the law come down on their heads."

Longarm shrugged. "I'm not suggesting anything to anybody. Just saying, that's all. If Abernathy's hirin' bushwhackers, maybe the Warfields ought to do the same."

"No, sir." Bert shook his head emphatically. "That ain't a good idea at all."

Rose's voice came from behind them as she walked around the corner of the building. "What's not a good idea?"

Longarm and Bert turned to face her. Bert didn't miss a beat in answering her.

"Goin' through Suggins' Pass. Parker here thought it might be a shortcut, but I done set him straight, Miss Rose."

Longarm nodded. "Yeah, I don't know the country around here all that well, so I'll go along with what Bert

says. I reckon by now you know the best route all the way
to Laramie."

"That's right. Are you ready to go, Custis?"

"Yes, ma'am."

Longarm would have helped her climb onto the driver's
seat, but Rose stepped forward and moved so quickly that
he didn't have a chance to. He pulled himself up and settled
down beside her, cradling the Winchester across his lap.

"We'll see you in three days on the way back, Bert."

The old-timer lifted a hand and waved in farewell.
"Good luck, Miss Rose!"

She cracked the whip and got the horses moving. The
stagecoach rolled away from the station.

Longarm didn't look back. He was already scanning the
trail ahead, on the lookout for trouble.

Chapter 12

They stopped at the next way station and changed teams at mid-afternoon, then pushed on. The stage road had already veered well away from the graded right-of-way where Clayton Abernathy's railroad would run. It was no longer in sight as the coach rocked along on the rutted trail.

"What's the schedule for these coaches, anyway? Reckon I'd better get familiar with it, if I'm gonna be ridin' shotgun." Longarm made the question sound like simple curiosity.

"When the line was doing its best business, we had two coaches on the road all the time, one southbound from Rimfire to Laramie and one running the other direction. But since the passenger traffic has dropped off to almost nothing, we've had to cut back to one stage. The round trip takes four days, so we have a stage departing from Rimfire every fifth morning, and the same is true of Laramie, with the departures staggered two days apart."

Longarm followed all that and nodded. "Your brother

said something about another stage. Why do you need more than one with that schedule?"

"Because sometimes we have to make a special run. If several passengers showed up at the office in Rimfire tomorrow morning and needed to go to Laramie in a hurry, Adam would sell them tickets and drive the second stage himself. We can't afford to turn away any business, and it doesn't really cost anything extra. The horses at the way stations have to eat whether they're being used or not, and the station managers keep on drawing their wages." Rose paused. "Anyway, we'll probably wind up having to sell that second coach sooner or later. We used to have four coaches, but two of them are already gone."

"Sorry. That's a shame."

Rose popped the whip above the backs of the team. "It is what it is. Business is a harsh mistress, Custis. She won't be dictated to."

"I reckon not. That's probably why I never went into business for myself. Too many risks."

Rose laughed. "You don't strike me as the sort of man who worries much about risks."

"Maybe not . . . but I never had to try to meet a payroll, either."

Rose drove on toward the way station where they would spend the night, and as she did, Longarm studied the landscape around them. It was a mixture of rolling hills, ranges of small, weathered mountains, and arid flats broken up by arroyos that were like gashes in the earth. The trail wasn't really that rough, but it twisted around a lot to avoid the most rugged stretches of ground.

Longarm frowned as the road ran close to one of those arroyos. It was deep enough to hide almost anything, and he didn't like the looks of it.

He raised his voice a little so Rose could hear him clearly over the rumble of the coach and the pounding of hooves. "I've got a bad feelin' about that gully over there. Maybe you better swing wider around it."

"You mean get off the road?"

"The ground's flat enough, off to the left. The coach won't have any trouble with it. And I'd feel better if we had a little more room between us and that arroyo."

Rose began working the reins to swing the team to the left. "All right, Custis, if you say so. Do you think—"

She didn't get a chance to finish her question. Men on horseback suddenly came boiling up out of the arroyo. Guns blasted. As Longarm twisted around and lifted the Winchester to return the fire, one of the slugs richocheted off the brass rail around the top of the coach.

"Go! Get all the speed out of those horses you can!"

Rose acted instantly on Longarm's shouted command. She leaned forward, started snapping the whip, and yelled, "Hyyyaaahhh!" The team surged ahead into a gallop.

That unexpected burst of speed put them ahead of the riders. Longarm faced to the rear, planted his left foot on the floorboard, braced his right knee on the seat, and rested his elbows on the coach roof. He started spraying lead at the pursuers, who raced after them less than fifty yards behind the coach.

The dust being kicked up by the wheels made it difficult to get a good look at the men, but when the billowing cloud cleared up for a second, Longarm saw them well enough to tell that over their heads they wore hoods that completely covered their faces. He had halfway expected to see them wearing bandannas and dusters, like the men who had attacked and burned the railroad construction camp. More than once in his career, he had seen a gang of owlhoots play two sides in a dispute against each other. From the looks of it, that wasn't what was happening here.

Which just lent more credence to the idea that Clayton Abernathy and Adam Warfield weren't content to compete in business. Their rivalry extended to hiring gunmen to go after each other's operation.

Those thoughts flashed through Longarm's head, but he didn't really have time to speculate about such things right now. He had his plate full enough with the half dozen hooded riders chasing the stage and blasting away at it.

The saddle of a galloping horse wasn't a very good platform for accurate gunfire, but unfortunately, neither was a swaying, bouncing stagecoach. Longarm cranked off several rounds from the Winchester, but none of the pursuers fell. They didn't even slow down. They were mounted on fast horses, and they were drawing closer.

"Keep your head down!" He glanced over his shoulder and saw that Rose was already following the shouted command, even before he had given it. She was hunched forward, clinging desperately to the reins. So far the horses were still under her control, rather than stampeding the way they had the day before, but Longarm didn't know how long that would last.

A fresh volley of shots from the pursuers made him duck, too, and as he did, he saw one of the men pulling even with the rear of the coach. Just as Longarm had done the day before, the man reached over, grabbed the canvas cover of the baggage boot, and leaped out of his saddle. Longarm swung the rifle toward the man as he clambered up to the top of the stage, but before he could fire, something smashed into the Winchester and tore it out of his hands. One of the pursuers had gotten off a lucky shot that struck the rifle's breech.

That allowed the man to reach the top of the stage and grab for his gun. Longarm's hand flashed across his body to the Colt in the crossdraw rig. Both guns came out and blasted at almost the same instant, but the shot from Longarm's .44 was just a shaved heartbeat of time faster. The hooded man's aim was deflected just enough that his bullet missed Longarm. At the same time, he surged to his feet atop the coach, clutching at his belly where Longarm's slug had punched deep into his guts. With a scream he went backward off the coach, disappearing into the dust.

Longarm glanced over at Rose and felt his heart thump violently in his chest as he saw the blood on the left shoulder of her buckskin jacket. Her left arm hung uselessly at her side, but she still gripped the reins in her right hand. Her face was contorted in pain.

"Rose!"

"I'm all right . . . Custis!" The words came out through gritted teeth. "I can . . . handle the team!"

Longarm wasn't so sure about that, but he had to trust that she could because the other pursuers were still closing in, and now he had lost his Winchester. He reached down and lifted the shotgun to the seat where it would be handy. Then he squeezed off four rounds from his Colt, emptying it. One of the remaining pursuers jerked under the impact of a bullet and slewed around in his saddle. He stayed mounted but fell back quickly.

The other four had almost caught up. Longarm crouched low on the seat and reached for the loops on his shell belt. He started fumbling fresh cartridges from them so that the hooded men would know his Colt was empty. They urged their horses to greater speed, and he could almost see through those hoods to the savage grins of triumph on their faces.

Then he shoved the bullets in his pocket, jammed the Colt back in its holster, and grabbed the shotgun. His fumbling had drawn the riders in range, just as he had hoped it would, and before they could peel off and try to get out of the line of fire, he leveled the twin barrels of the Greener at them and pulled both triggers.

The thunderous roar of the shotgun pounded his ears. He saw two of the men go backward out of their saddles, shredded by buckshot. One of the horses fell, sending its rider sailing through the air. Only one of the hooded men was still mounted, and he seemed to decide suddenly that the stagecoach wasn't worth chasing after all. He hauled his horse to a stop.

"Rose, you all right to keep going?"

"Yes, I . . . I'm fine."

Longarm doubted that. The bloodstain was spreading on her shoulder. She needed medical attention, but he didn't want to risk stopping yet. Some of those hooded hombres were out of the fight, probably for good, but the others might still represent a threat.

"Don't slow down, then. Let's put some distance between us and those bastards."

She nodded. He reloaded his Colt and shoved fresh shells into the shotgun. After scanning the landscape behind them and seeing no sign of the pursuers anymore, he slid down onto the seat again and took the reins from her.

"I can handle this now." He looked around. "You know where we are?"

Rose sagged against him. "No, I . . . I've never been this far off the road before."

The chase had led across country. They had reached the edge of the flat they had been crossing. Hills dotted with scrubby pines lay in front of them. Longarm thought it might be a good idea to find a place where they could fort up while he took a look at Rose's wounded shoulder, so he headed the coach up the slope, taking it easier now because the ground was rougher. Even so, Rose was jolted around, and he heard the sharp hiss of her breath several times as pain must have stabbed through her.

The coach reached the top of the rise and started down the other side. Longarm saw a cluster of boulders at the top of the next hill and knew the rocks would provide some decent cover if he and Rose needed it. He headed for them and was halfway up the second slope when the coach gave a sudden lurch and tilted sharply forward and to the left as it came to a grinding stop. Rose was thrown against Longarm and cried out in pain. He caught her and kept her from falling.

"Custis, what happened?"

Longarm braced his booted feet against the floorboards and leaned over to look down at the left front wheel, which had come off the axle. "Looks like we lost a hub nut."

"Is the wheel . . . damaged?"

"Doesn't appear to be."

"Good. We can . . . fix it . . . then . . ."

Rose's head fell forward as her voice trailed off. Longarm turned and lifted her so that he could see her face. Her features were as pale as ivory under the turned-up brim of the old hat, which today was held snugly on her head by its chin strap. She was still breathing, so Longarm figured she had passed out from the shock of being shot and loss of blood.

Awkwardly, but as carefully as he could, he climbed down from the stagecoach and brought her with him. Then he gathered her in his arms and started walking up the hill toward the boulders. When he got there, he found a place where the ground was relatively smooth and flat and lowered her onto the sparse grass. Her head lolled to the side.

He worked the buckskin jacket off of her, then tore the shirtsleeve away from her shoulder. Relief went through him as he saw that the bullet had just creased her, plowing a shallow furrow across her upper arm just below the point where it joined the shoulder itself. From the looks of the wound, the slug had missed the bones, so there proba-

bly wouldn't be any lasting damage. It was a messy, painful injury, but Longarm felt like there was a good chance
Rose would be all right.

He wished he had some whiskey to clean the wound,
but water would have to do. He got the canteen from the
coach, pulled her shirt out of the waistband of the denim
trousers, and tore a piece from it. After soaking the cloth,
he used it to gently swab away the blood around the wound,
then poured more water directly over the bullet gash. The
bleeding hadn't stopped completely, but it had slowed to a
lazy ebb.

Longarm tore more strips off Rose's shirt and bound
them around her shoulder as bandages. He couldn't help
but notice how the damage to her shirt revealed an expanse of smooth, creamy skin at her midsection. At the
moment, though, he was a lot more concerned with her
health. He checked the pulse in her neck, found it rapid
but fairly strong. Her breathing hadn't faltered.

He had done all he could for the moment. He went
back down the hill to the coach and started unhitching the
team. The horses were important if he and Rose were
going to get out of here, so he didn't want anything happening to them. He led them back up the hill and picketed
them on a grassy stretch behind the rocks.

Then he started looking for the hub nut that had come
off the wheel. There might be a spare one in the gear box
under the coach, but if he could find the original one, so
much the better. Luckily, once the nut fell off, the vehicle
hadn't been able to go very far before the wheel came
loose. About ten yards from where the coach had come to
an unexpected halt, he found the nut and put it in his
pocket.

When he returned to the cluster of boulders, he saw
Rose's eyelids fluttering. She was trying to come to. He
knelt beside her, slipped a hand behind her head, and used

the other to trickle a little water from the canteen into her mouth.

She sputtered a little but swallowed the water. Her eyes opened. For a few seconds, she peered fuzzily up at him, apparently not recognizing him at first. Then her lips moved and she was able to form a whisper.

"C-Custis . . .?"

"That's right. You just lay still and rest, Rose. You're gonna be fine."

"I was . . . shot . . ."

"You just got nicked on the arm. You lost some blood and passed out."

She closed her eyes and sighed. "My . . . God. You're going to . . . think that I faint . . . at the drop of a hat. This is . . . twice in two days."

"Gettin' shot and havin' a team stampede on you ain't what I'd call the drop of a hat. Don't worry. You still seem tough as nails to me."

Rose laughed softly. "I don't know what I'd do . . . without you around . . . to save my life, Custis."

"You won't have to find out anytime soon. I ain't goin' anywhere."

And if he couldn't get that stagecoach fixed, he thought as he glanced down the hill toward the stalled vehicle, neither of them would be.

Chapter 13

When Rose felt strong enough to sit up, he left her sitting
there with her back braced against a boulder and his Colt
in her lap in case of trouble. With her wounded arm, she
couldn't handle the shotgun. He walked back down to the
stagecoach to study on the problem. He had to lift the coach
somehow so he could put the wheel back on and tighten the
nut on the hub, but since it was sitting on a hillside, he
couldn't just jack it up as he would if it were on flat ground.

He looked around for enough smaller rocks to wedge
around the opposite rear wheel so that it couldn't go anywhere. That took a while, and by the time he was ready to
open the gear box under the baggage boot and dig out the
jack, the sun was almost down.

He walked back up the hill to explain things to Rose.
"I'm gonna go ahead and try to get the wheel back on before we lose the light, but even if I do, it's too late to push
on today. Especially since we don't know exactly where we
are."

She nodded. "I agree." Most of the color was back in her
face now, and Longarm thought that by the looks of the

bandages on her arm, the wound had finally stopped bleed-ing. "Tomorrow morning we should be able to find our way back to the road."

"Yeah, we left it headin' east, so we'll just go back west and we ought to hit it sooner or later."

"Custis . . . we don't have any supplies."

Longarm nodded. "I know. We'll be pretty hungry by the time we get to that next way station. But we won't starve to death."

"No, I suppose not. At least we have plenty of water."

Since they had been planning on taking their meals at the way stations or in Laramie, they hadn't brought along any food. If Longarm made any more of these runs as shotgun guard, he would be better prepared. He'd bring some jerky, anyway.

He went back to the coach and started jacking it up. It was backbreaking work for one man to lift that much weight, even with the help of the jack. He had to be care-ful, too, not to overbalance that stage so that it toppled over backward and rolled down the hill. That really would be disastrous. At the same time, he had to raise the coach high enough so that the wheel could be slipped back onto the axle.

When he thought he had reached that point, he locked the jack in place and quickly grabbed the wheel. He had already checked it to make sure none of the spokes were cracked, and it wasn't damaged in any other way. The wheel was heavy and hard to wrestle into place, but after a few minutes, he managed. Holding it on with one hand, he reached into his pocket with the other, took out the hub nut, and twisted it onto the hub.

Then it was just a matter of tightening the nut with the wrench he had taken from the gear box. While he had the wrench in his hand, he checked the nuts on the other wheels and tightened them, too. Most of the light had faded from the sky and stars were beginning to appear in the velvety blue expanse overhead by the time he was finished.

He let the coach down carefully. The wheel he'd replaced seemed to be holding just fine. He gave the nut a last couple of twists. After stowing everything away, he went back up the hill to join Rose.

He hunkered on his heels beside her. "I think we'll be ready to roll first thing in the morning. We were lucky the wreck didn't do any more damage than it did."

"I know. But we're still stuck out here for the night."

"We'll be all right." Longarm tried to sound reassuring. "It'll get a mite cold before morning, but there are lap blankets inside the coach we can use to wrap up in."

"I wish we had some coffee and something to eat."

"So do I, but it's probably best if we try not to think about that. Just be glad that we're alive. With all the lead that was flyin' around, we could've got ventilated without much trouble."

"Yes." Her voice held a bitter edge. "All because Clayton Abernathy can't be satisfied to just wait and put us out of business by conventional means."

Longarm settled down beside her on the ground and leaned back against the rock. He thumbed his hat to the back of his head.

"It seems to me like Abernathy don't have much to gain by causing all this trouble for you and your brother. Like you said, all he has to do is wait for his railroad to reach Rimfire, and he'll get what he wants."

"It's revenge because of what happened with my mother. He wants to destroy us to . . . even the score with her for choosing my father, I guess you'd say. That's the only thing that makes any sense."

But did it, really? Longarm asked himself. Abernathy had struck him as a pretty hardheaded businessman, and not the sort of hombre who'd waste money. Hired gunmen didn't come cheap. Abernathy was rich, sure, but he hadn't gotten that way by throwing dinero around needlessly.

Nothing else made any sense, though, as Rose and her brother Adam had both pointed out. Longarm was convinced that the attack hadn't been a random robbery attempt. Not after the shots fired at Rose the day before.

Longarm would have liked to lay his hands on one of those men who had been lurking in the arroyo, waiting to ambush them. He was willing to bet he could have gotten some answers out of the hombre. Unfortunately, the survivors of the fight were probably miles away by now.

Just in case they weren't, Longarm knew that he was going to have to stay awake most of the night and stand guard. It was possible that killers were out there somewhere in the gathering gloom right now, searching for him and Rose.

He got to his feet. "I'll fetch those blankets. You need to get some rest."

"Thank you, Custis, I'm pretty tired. Getting shot and losing a lot of blood will do that to you, I suppose."

He chuckled. "Take it from me, it sure will."

When he got back from the coach, he spread one of the blankets on the ground, then draped another one over Rose after she lay down carefully on her right side.

"Custis . . . have you been shot a lot of times? What you said before made it sound like you had."

"I've been nicked more often than I like to think about."

"Are you . . . an outlaw?" She rushed on, as if trying to explain herself. "I mean, I know you said you were just drifting and looking for a job, but . . . before that . . . were you on the dodge, as they say?"

Longarm couldn't stop himself from laughing. He hoped that his reaction didn't offend her.

"No, ma'am. I don't reckon I can prove it right here and now, but I can honestly say that I ain't wanted by the law in any of the states or territories of this great nation of ours. I've never been in prison, either."

Except for a few times when he'd been working undercover, and that didn't really count, he told himself.

"Well . . . good. I feel bad about even asking, but you seem so competent with a gun, and able to handle any sort of trouble that comes up . . . so I just wondered. I hope I didn't hurt your feelings."

"Not hardly. Stuck off out here in the middle of nowhere with a fella you barely know like you are, I don't blame you for wantin' to find out as much as you can about me."

"You said you were born in West Virginia?"

Clearly, she wanted to talk, so he slid a cheroot from his shirt pocket and put it in his mouth without lighting it. He didn't want the flare of a lucifer to give away their position to any searching eyes.

"Yeah, that's right. Born and raised and figured I'd stay there my whole life, until that little ruckus between the North and South came along. Once I'd seen more of the world, my feet were too restless to stay home."

"You fought in the war?"

"Yep, but don't ask me for which side. I disremember. When it was over, though, I came west. Figured I'd had enough to do with both North and South and wanted to see some place new. I cowboyed for a while and ate at least a ton of dust following herds of cattle up the trails from Texas to Kansas. It didn't take me long to decide I'd had enough of that. I've been sort of on the drift ever since, working at this, that, and the other."

That was a slightly edited version of his adult life, but it was close enough for government work, he decided. It seemed to satisfy Rose, too. She sounded sleepy when she spoke again.

"At least you've had adventures. I've been stuck in a kitchen and an office all my life."

"Until now."

Rose laughed softly. "Yes, until now. And now I've been chased by badmen and shot."

"Yep." Longarm's voice was solemn. "A life of adventure's a mite overrated sometimes."

Rose didn't say anything else, and after a minute Longarm heard her deep, regular breathing and knew that she had dozed off. That was good. The rest would help her heal.

He sat there in the quiet darkness with the shotgun beside him, waiting for trouble that he hoped wouldn't come.

The night passed quietly, for which Longarm was thankful. Along toward dawn, he got to feeling so groggy that he woke up Rose to see if she could stand guard for a little while and let him get some rest. She was willing and claimed that she felt much better after sleeping for quite a few hours.

Longarm gave her his gun again. "If you hear anything that don't sound right, wake me up. Don't go to shootin' at things in the dark unless you just have to."

"I won't, Custis. How long do you want me to let you sleep?"

"Wake me when you can see the sun just startin' to edge up over the horizon, if I'm not already awake."

She sat up, and he stretched out and pulled one of the blankets over him to ward off some of the chill that had crept into the night air. Here in Wyoming it got cool every night, even in the middle of summer. Sleep overtook him almost as soon as he closed his eyes.

Something warm pressing against him woke him later. It took a second for him to realize that Rose was lying snuggled up in the crook of his arm with her head pillowed on his shoulder. She must have gotten sleepy and been unable to withstand the temptation to lie down again.

Longarm lay there unmoving and relied on his senses to tell him what was going on around them, if anything. He didn't hear anybody moving around, and the horses seemed calm, too, which they wouldn't be if anyone was messing with them. Longarm sniffed the early morning air. No hint of tobacco smoke, so no one had fired up a quirley anywhere nearby. All he smelled was the fresh, clean, womanly scent of Rose's hair and body. He gazed up at the sky and saw an arc of orange over the eastern horizon. Dawn wasn't far off, but it wasn't quite here yet.

And Rose wasn't asleep, as he had first thought, either. She moved her head and pressed her lips against the bare skin of his neck. At the same time, her hand slid over his hip and moved to his crotch. She rubbed his shaft through his trousers. It began to harden immediately as her touch made blood rush to it.

"Now, I know you ain't doin' that in your sleep."

Rose laughed softly. "You probably think I'm terribly bold and wanton, Custis."

"It ain't that so much as it is that I promised your brother I'd treat you proper-like."

She snuggled closer to him and lifted her head so that she could whisper into his ear. "That's all well and good, but the proper way to treat a woman who wants a man as much as I want you, Custis, is to give her a good and proper fucking." She must have felt him stiffen in surprise, because she laughed again. "Yes, I know that word. I grew up around stagecoach drivers, remember?"

"You seem like a gal who knows what she wants, too."

Her hand tightened on him. "I am. I was attracted to you as soon as I saw you, and now you've saved my life twice. Don't think it's just gratitude, though. I want you . . . because I want you."

"You've got that wounded arm."

"Yes, and it hurts. So making love with you will help take my mind off of it."

Longarm couldn't help but chuckle. Rose was bound and determined to have him, and as a man who knew a thing or two about women, he knew what a waste of time it was to try to change their minds once those minds were made up.

"All right, but we'll have to be careful. We don't want to start that wound bleedin' again . . . and we don't want anybody sneakin' up on us, either."

"We'll just have to stay alert and not get *too* carried away."

Longarm wasn't sure how likely that was, but he was willing to give it a try.

He eased his shoulder out from under Rose and helped her stretch out on her back. "You just lay there for now."

"That's not fair. I'm supposed to be repaying you."

"You said it wasn't about gratitude."

"Well, not completely . . ."

Longarm grinned at her as he unfastened her trousers and started to slide them down over her hips. "Oh, I'll be gettin' repaid, no doubt about that."

Quickly, he bared her from the waist down. The sun still wasn't up, but there was enough light in the sky so that it cast a rich, reddish-gold mantle over her. He put a hand on the inside of each thigh and parted her legs as he knelt between them. Rose was already breathing harder.

"Custis, what are you—"

She found out what he was going to do as he lowered his mouth to the opening between her legs. He spread the folds apart with his thumbs and delved into her with his tongue. Rose gasped and arched her hips. She was already wet and quickly grew even wetter as he licked and sucked from one end of her sex to the other. He lingered around the delicate little nubbin of flesh and circled it with his tongue, which made her cry out and clutch at his head with her good hand.

From the way she reacted, no one had ever done that to her before, but she got the hang of it almost right away. She ground herself against him and squeezed his head with her thighs as spasms of ecstasy rippled through her. With practiced ease, Longarm took her higher and higher, until he felt something shatter inside her.

"Oh . . . my . . . *God*!"

Her muscles went limp and her legs fell away from his head. He kissed her soft stomach as it heaved from the power of the sensations that he had sent coursing through her. Slowly, he worked his way up her body, unbuttoning and opening her shirt so that his lips and tongue could trace a path over her skin.

"How's that arm feel now?"

"It doesn't . . . hurt . . . a bit!"

"Good. Maybe you can sit up and straddle me—"

He didn't have to make the suggestion twice. She was so eager that she almost didn't give him time to get his own trousers and long underwear down. As soon as he was ready, with his hard cock jutting up from his groin like a shaft of iron, she grabbed hold of it with her good hand, swung a leg over his hips, and lowered her hips so that she could bring the head to her drenched opening. She slid down onto it, groaning as she engulfed him inch by inch.

She took in as much of the long, thick shaft as she could, then began bobbing up and down gently on it. Longarm groaned, too, as she rode him. The slick, heated core of her femininity clutched him in a maddeningly pleasurable grip. His excitement swelled along with his manhood.

In a matter of moments, he felt his climax approaching. Rose was working herself up to a second one as she rode him. Her eyes were closed, and she panted softly as she thrust her hips at him. Longarm knew that neither of them could withstand much more of this exquisite torture, but he was determined to hold out as long as he could. He reached up past the tattered remains of her shirt and filled his hands with her breasts, kneading and caressing the warm globes of flesh as he stroked her hard nipples with his thumbs. Rose tipped her back and cried out again. She galloped even harder.

Sensing that the dam was about to break, Longarm dropped his hands to her hips and braced her as he slammed up into her again and again. Then he drove as deep as he could and let go, flooding her inside with white-hot juices. Rose shuddered as her own culmination washed over her.

It took a minute or so for Longarm to catch his breath. When he had, he sat up and held her on his lap with his cock still partially buried inside her. Rose nuzzled his neck and then kissed him.

"That was so wonderful, Custis. It was just what I needed."

"Me, too." He glanced at the horizon and saw that the sun was halfway up. It had risen while he was rising, too. "And I hate like blazes to say it, but we'd better get moving."

Rose sighed. "I know. Let me just . . . sit here like this for a minute longer, all right?"

Longarm tightened his arms around her as she rested her head on his shoulder again.

"Take your time, darlin'. Take your time."

Eventually, they both stood up and Longarm helped

Rose get dressed. He pulled on his trousers and boots and got busy hitching the team to the stagecoach. When he checked the hub nut, it was still secure. He didn't think they would have any trouble making it to Laramie . . . assuming, of course, that no more bushwhackers started chasing them and shooting at them.

Their lovemaking had taken Longarm's mind off the fact that both of them were hungry this morning, but his stomach was rumbling by the time he had the coach ready to roll. He would just have to ignore it. He and Rose both drank from the canteen, then he helped her to the driver's seat and climbed up beside her. He had suggested that she might be more comfortable riding inside the coach, but she had vetoed that idea.

"I'd rather be up here with you, so that I can see what's going on."

Longarm didn't blame her for that. Putting the rising sun behind them, he got the team moving and headed the stagecoach west.

As they came down out of the hills, they could see for several miles across the flat in front of them. Longarm spotted a couple of riders far off to the north, but they were moving away instead of coming toward the coach, so he didn't worry about them. Probably just a couple of cowpokes on their way somewhere.

Smoke rose in the distance ahead of the coach, at least three miles away, and Longarm wondered if it came from the railroad camp. He pointed it out to Rose.

She nodded. "That's about where it would be, all right. I hate to say it, but I hope that means something else has happened to slow down those blasted rails."

"Looks more like the smoke from a locomotive. Chances are, they're movin' the work train up."

Longarm didn't add that the work train had had time to

get back to the camp from Laramie since the attack on the camp a couple of nights earlier. Rose didn't mention it, either, so she either didn't know about the incident or was keeping that knowledge to herself.

"I can't bring myself to hate the men who are working for Abernathy. They're just honest laborers, I suppose. They don't know anything about the bad blood between my father and Abernathy, and it's not their responsibility to keep this stagecoach line from collapsing. So I feel bad about it when I catch myself hoping that something has happened . . . but I do it anyway."

"I don't reckon you got anything to be ashamed of, Rose. Nobody could blame you or your brother for wantin' to keep the line operating."

"No, I suppose not. That's why I didn't argue with Adam when he decided that we needed to ask for help."

Longarm glanced over at her, his eyes narrowing slightly as he frowned. "What do you mean, 'ask for help'? You said yourselves that Abernathy ain't doin' anything illegal, so you can't have sent for the law."

Rose shook her head. "No, Adam wrote a letter to an old friend of our father who's a very successful business-man. He thought maybe this man could advise us on what we should do, if anything." She smiled slightly. "I think Adam had in mind that if we had to, we could offer to sell this man an interest in the line in hopes that would give him an incentive to keep it going. He's very rich, you know, and has a big ranch down in Texas and all sorts of other businesses scattered across the West. Adam said he could help us if anyone could."

An uneasy feeling stirred around inside Longarm. He knew of someone who fit that description, but . . .

"How long had it been since your pa heard anything from this fella?"

"Oh, a long time, I think. Years. Maybe ten years or more. But Adam found an old letter from him among Father's papers, after Father passed away."

"And this hombre down in Texas, does he, uh, have a name?"

"Well, of course he does." Rose gave Longarm a puzzled look. "His name is Alex Starbuck."

Chapter 14

If Longarm had been closer to the two riders heading north toward Rimfire, he would have recognized them instantly.

One was a tall, lean, well-muscled man whose golden skin, raven-black hair, and slightly slanted eyes testified to the fact that his mother had been a beautiful Japanese woman, his father a brawny American sailor. His clothing was a mixture as well, mostly the sort of duds a cowboy might wear: black trousers, a white, collarless shirt, a black leather vest, and a black Stetson with a tightly curled brim. Instead of boots, though, he wore rope-soled sandals on his feet. Also, there was no gunbelt around his waist; in fact, he carried no visible weapons except for a Winchester in a saddle sheath.

But tucked into pockets on the vest were a number of *shuriken*, the deadly, razor-sharp, five-pointed throwing stars favored by Japanese martial artists. Sheathed on each forearm under his shirt sleeves were *tanto*, throwing knives. The heavy buckle on the belt around his waist could become a weapon in his hands, as well.

That wasn't the extent of it. The man's hands and feet could move with blinding speed and bone-crunching power. He was a superb martial artist, having been trained for it since childhood. But he might have become a *ronin*, a masterless warrior, if Captain Alex Starbuck had not brought him to America to serve as bodyguard and companion to the captain's young daughter.

The man's name was Ki.

The person riding beside him was a woman, probably in her mid-twenties, although it was difficult to be certain because while her beauty was a mature one, it was also an ageless one. She had thick waves of reddish-gold hair under a flat-crowned brown hat. The hair fell to her shoulders, framing a lovely face dominated by keenly intelligent green eyes and then spilling on down her back. She wore a gray shirt with the sleeves rolled up a couple of turns on her forearms. The top couple of buttons on the shirt were undone, revealing a tanned throat and the beginning of the valley between firm, full breasts. A pair of denim trousers hugged her hips snugly and were tucked into high-topped brown boots.

A gunbelt was strapped around her hips, with a .38-caliber Colt Lightning double-action revolver riding in the holster. The gun had been specially made, with ivory grips replacing the usual hard rubber ones. It was the only thing flashy or fancy about the woman, other than her sheer beauty.

When she was out on the trail like this, Jessica Starbuck didn't look like one of the richest individuals in the entire country, a woman who controlled a vast business empire inherited from her father.

Jessie had done more than just sit back and enjoy being wealthy. She had battled the enemies responsible for the deaths of her mother and father until they were defeated, and she had helped to destroy that evil cartel when it tried to rise again. She had served as an unofficial troubleshooter for the companies in which she held an interest, traveling all over the West with Ki to take on all sorts of villains and defeat a number of evil schemes. She had expanded her holdings, although the centerpiece of the empire was still the vast Circle Star Ranch in South Texas. Her accomplishments were legion, especially considering her relatively young age.

Yet she had retained the core values of honesty, loyalty, and courage that her father had instilled in her. When the letter from Adam Warfield arrived, addressed to her father and asking for help, it hadn't taken Jessie long to decide what to do about it.

This man Warfield obviously didn't know that Alex Starbuck was dead, and from the sound of his letter, he was in desperate straits. Jessie and Ki had been on the first train north, leaving the railroad in Laramie and striking out on the fine horses they had brought with them. They could have taken the stagecoach to Rimfire, but Jessie and Ki preferred the freedom and flexibility of having their own mounts.

Jessie studied the mostly flat and sparsely grassed terrain ahead of them. "I wonder how far we are from Rimfire."

"Having studied numerous maps of the territory, I'd estimate it's another ten miles or so." Ki was well spoken. Anybody who expected singsong pidgin English from him because of his Oriental ancestry would have been very surprised. "We should be there by the middle of the day."

"We ought to be coming to another way station on the stagecoach line, too. Maybe we can get some breakfast there."

Knowing that there should be a way station fairly close by, they hadn't taken the time this morning to prepare breakfast at the camp where they had spent the night.

Jessie wanted to get on to Rimfire as quickly as possible so she could talk to Adam Warfield and get all the details of the situation. She wasn't very optimistic about being able to help him.

Jessie knew Clayton Abernathy and didn't like him. The Starbuck holdings included interests in several railroads, so it was inevitable that Jessie would have met Abernathy and had dealings with him. In fact, she had been there at Blanco Verde when Abernathy and some of the other railroad barons had gotten together to form their so-called Railroad Ring. Jessie had been asked to join, but she didn't want any part of it. The whole thing reminded her too much of the Cartel, which had cost scores of innocent lives and ruined many others.

Maybe she was just being a little contrary, she had thought when she read Adam Warfield's letter, but if she could do something to frustrate Clayton Abernathy's plans and help someone else at the same time, she wanted to.

Keen eyes could see a long way out here in this level landscape. Jessie and Ki both spotted the way station when it was still a couple of miles ahead of them, although they couldn't make out any details until they were closer. Then they could see that the station consisted of a squat, stone-and-timber building, a barn, and a corral.

As they came even closer, Jessie noticed a faint popping sound in the distance. She looked at Ki.

"Is that . . .?"

He nodded. "Gunshots. And they sound like they're coming from the vicinity of the station."

"We'd better go see what it's about."

Without waiting to see whether Ki agreed with her, Jessie heeled her horse into a run. The buckskin gelding responded instantly, stretching its legs in a hard gallop. Ki followed close behind on his pinto.

The horses covered the ground in a hurry. Jessie saw

dust begin to billow up in the air near the station. As she and Ki came closer still, she was able to tell that the dust came from a small herd of horses being driven away from the station. Several men were pushing the horses along, while several more fired back toward the building.

Jessie and Ki didn't have to talk to anybody at the station to figure out what was going on. Those horses were being rustled. They had probably been kept in the corral and used to switch out teams, which meant they belonged to the Rimfire Stagecoach Company.

And since Jessie and Ki had come up here to Wyoming to lend a hand to Adam Warfield, the owner of the stagecoach company, their course of action was clear.

They would try to stop those varmints from getting away with the horses.

Jessie kept her mount moving at top speed while she drew her Winchester from the saddle sheath. When she was young, her father and Ki had seen to it that she learned to ride and shoot as well as any man and better than most. Since then, a life of danger and excitement had honed her skills even more. As she and Ki closed in on the stolen horse herd, she brought the rifle to her shoulder and guided her mount with her knees as she opened fire on the rustlers.

Ki joined in the fight as well, throwing lead toward the men trying to drive the horses away from the station. Muzzles flashed in a couple of the building's windows, showing that the defenders inside there were still in the fight, too. In fact, as Jessie and Ki circled to their right, they wound up with the rustlers in a cross fire.

The men were able to use the dust and the spooked horses for cover as they fought back. Guns banged and chaos ruled. Jessie saw a rider loom up out of the dust about twenty yards away, driving several of the stolen horses in front of him. He sent them lunging straight toward Jessie and her buckskin.

Jessie reined her mount out of the way at the last moment, barely avoiding what could have been a disastrous collision. She wasn't out of danger yet. The rustler was right behind the stampeding horses. The revolver in his fist roared and spouted flame as he fired at Jessie.

She heard the wind-rip of the bullet's passage perilously close to her ear. The Winchester was a little awkward for close work like this, so she held the rifle in her left hand while her right palmed the Lightning from its holster with almost magical speed. The gun bucked against her palm as she squeezed the trigger.

She fired two shots in less than the blink of an eye. Both slugs punched into the chest of the man who had just tried to kill her. The impact of the bullets rocked him back in the saddle, but he didn't fall off his horse. He clutched at the horn and kept himself in the saddle. Jessie was close enough to see that his eyes were wide with shock and pain.

She especially noticed his eyes because they were the only part of the man's face she could see. The rest of it was covered with a hood that looked like it had been made from a flour sack. The man's hat was crammed down tightly over the hood.

He struggled to bring up his gun for another shot at Jessie, and she was about to put another round in him when a thick streamer of dust blew between them, cutting them off from sight of each other. When it began to disperse, the rustler was gone. Jessie bit back a curse as she thought that the man must have taken advantage of the opportunity to turn his horse around and flee.

He wouldn't get far, she was confident of that. Not with two bullets in his chest. He probably had only moments to live.

She twisted in the saddle and craned her neck, looking for Ki. Guns still went off, but there was less shooting than there had been a few moments earlier.

Jessie didn't see Ki, but she knew he could take care of himself. She wheeled her mount around and went after the horses. The quicker she could start rounding them up, the less they would scatter all over hell and gone.

She started by turning the ones that the rustler had used to try to trample her. The speedy buckskin cut them off and headed them back toward the way station. Jessie had used the buckskin as a cutting horse on the Circle Star, so it knew what to do. Once the runaway horses were trotting back in the right direction, Jessie went after some more.

She had slid the Winchester back in the saddle boot and holstered the Colt Lightning, but she kept her eyes open for more rustlers. They must have scattered when she and Ki lit into them, she decided, because the dust was settling now and she didn't see any more riders with hoods over their heads. The gunfire had finally stopped, too.

"Jessie!"

She looked around and saw Ki trotting toward her on his pinto. He was driving several of the horses in front of him. She waved to let him know she was all right, then prodded more of the milling horses to join the animals Ki had gathered.

Ki brought his mount alongside Jessie's as the two of them started the horses toward the station. "Were you hit?" His voice was calm, but she heard an undercurrent of worry in it.

"No, I'm fine. How about you?"

Ki shook his head. "None of their bullets found me. One of them carried away a *shuriken* in his throat, though."

"I know what you mean. One of the varmints was packing two of my bullets in him when he lit a shuck away from here."

The sudden pounding of hoofbeats made both of them stiffen in the saddle. Jessie instinctively reached for her gun as she saw a man riding toward them, but she stopped with her hand on the Lightning and didn't draw it. The man approaching them wasn't wearing a hood or a hat. He was bare-headed and carried a rifle. His face was dark with anger.

When he saw Jessie and Ki, he reined in sharply and pointed the rifle at them. "Don't move!"

Jessie kept her hands in plain sight so the man wouldn't get spooked any more than he already was. "Take it easy, mister. You might not have been able to tell it with so much dust flying around, but we're the ones who stopped those rustlers from getting away with the horses."

The man was big and dark-haired, with a muscular chest and heavy shoulders. He didn't lower the rifle.

"Who are you?"

The sharply voiced question irritated Jessie. She didn't like having guns pointed at her, especially by someone she had just helped, and she didn't appreciate being interrogated, either.

But she was smart enough to know that the fastest and easiest way to settle this confusion might be to put her cards on the table.

"My name is Jessica Starbuck."

The name had quite an effect on the man. His eyes widened. The barrel of the rifle drooped, but whether it was because the man understood they weren't enemies or simply because he recognized the name and was surprised, Jessie didn't know.

Evidently it was the latter. "Starbuck! Are you related to Alex Starbuck?"

"He was my father."

The man frowned. "Was?"

"That's right. He passed away several years ago." Jessie made a guess. "And you're Adam Warfield, who wrote a letter to my father asking for help."

The man must have thought that he couldn't be more surprised than he already was, but now he saw he was wrong. He lowered the rifle the rest of the way and stared at Jessie.

"That's right. What are you doing here, Miss Starbuck?"

"You asked my father for his help and mentioned that he and your father were friends years ago." Jessie shrugged. "I know my father would have wanted to do whatever he could for you, and since he's not here . . ."

"You're taking his place."

"That's right."

"A woman?"

That drew a laugh from Ki. "I don't know if you noticed or not, Warfield, but Jessie ventilated one of those rustlers, and together we kept them from stealing your horses." Ki waved a hand toward the horses, which had stopped and were grazing peacefully now on the grass. "This *is* your herd, isn't it?"

Warfield lowered his rifle the rest of the way and nodded. "That's right. I'd brought some fresh horses out here to the way station yesterday and planned to drive the ones we've been using for a while back to Rimfire. All of them were still in the corral when those men attacked. The station keeper and I had to fort up inside the building, and while they had us pinned down, they opened the corral and drove all the stock out." Warfield frowned at Ki. "And who are *you*?"

"My name is Ki."

"Ki what?"

"Just Ki."

"You work for Miss Starbuck?"

A faint smile curved Ki's lips under the thin mustache he wore. "In a manner of speaking." Though he had started out as an employee, Ki was more like a member of the family now and had been for many years. He regarded Jessie as his sister—an occasionally reckless little sister—and she thought of him as a protective older brother.

Something had occurred to Jessie. "No offense, Mr. Warfield, but why would anyone want to steal these particular horses? They're just draft animals. They're worth some money, of course, but not nearly as much as they would be if they were fine saddle mounts."

"You can't run a stage line without horses for your teams." Warfield's voice was full of anger and bitterness. "This herd represents almost half of the horses I own. If I'd lost them, it would have made keeping the stage-coaches running a lot more difficult, if not impossible. That's all Clayton Abernathy cares about."

Jessie nodded. "You said in your letter that you believe Abernathy is to blame for your troubles. It so happens that I know Clayton Abernathy."

"And you don't believe he would do such a thing?"

"On the contrary. I believe Clayton Abernathy is capable of almost anything."

Warfield looked surprised again, but he recovered pretty quickly. "I can see we have a lot to talk about, Miss Starbuck. If you and your friend will help me get these horses rounded up and back in the corral, then we can go inside and have some coffee."

"And some breakfast?"

That finally got a smile out of Warfield. "Sure. Although once you taste Horace's cooking, you may want to turn around and go back where you came from."

Chapter 15

Adam Warfield wasn't exaggerating about the food dished up by the short, stocky old-timer who took care of the station and the horses. His name was Horace Dunn, and he was bald except for a fringe of white hair around his ears and the back of his head. He had a high-pitched voice and a fussy manner. The bacon on the plates he set in front of Jessie and Ki was half-raw, and the flapjacks were just a little shy of being charcoal.

But Horace's coffee was actually pretty good, and that made the rest of the meal tolerable.

Jessie looked across the table at Warfield, who had already had breakfast but sipped on a cup of coffee while she and Ki ate. "I didn't expect to meet you until we got to Rimfire," she said, "but since fate has brought us together sooner, why don't you go ahead and tell me about Abernathy."

Warfield's broad shoulders rose and fell in a shrug. "There's not much to tell. He's building a railroad spur line to Rimfire, and he's going to put me and my sister out of business."

"Your sister?"

"Rose. She owns half of the stage line. We inherited it from our father, Donald Warfield."

"Who was friends with my father?"

Adam nodded. "That's right. About twenty years ago, Alex Starbuck was partners for a while in a stage line that my father started down in New Mexico Territory. It was always meant to be a temporary thing—an infusion of cash, I guess you'd say—and it worked out well for both of them. They had met even before that, when my father was driving a Butterfield coach that your father was taking to El Paso. Together they fought off some outlaws who tried to hold up the stage."

Jessie smiled. "Yes, that sounds like something he would do. Both the fighting off the outlaws and then helping your father out later on. He never forgot a friend."

"That's what my father told me and Rose about him. Later, after Dad passed on, I found some letters he'd gotten from Alex Starbuck, and that gave me the idea of writing to him and asking for help." Adam gave Jessie a solemn look. "I'm sorry to hear that he's dead."

"Thank you. Like I said, it was a while back . . . and the men responsible for what happened to him paid for their crimes."

The harsh finality that crept into Jessie's voice when she said that made Adam raise his eyebrows a little. He didn't say anything, though, despite the obvious curiosity on his face.

"So you and your sister have been running the stage line ever since your father passed away, right?"

Adam nodded. "We were doing most of the work before that. Dad's health had gotten bad. I'm convinced that when Abernathy showed up in Rimfire and started talking about how he was bringing in the railroad, that was what pushed my father over the edge. His heart failed not long after that. They were old enemies, you see, my father and Clayton Abernathy. I don't think Dad could stand to think that Abernathy was going to win."

"Business enemies?"

Adam smiled and shook his head. "Not until this business with the railroad. Once upon a time, they were rivals for my mother's hand. It wasn't much of a rivalry, though. She was already engaged to my father, and she wasn't just about to leave him for a buzzard like Abernathy."

"Buzzard" was a pretty good description of the railroad baron, Jessie thought, both his appearance and his rapacious appetite for money and power. Maybe thirty-five or forty years earlier, he hadn't looked as much like one of the carrion birds as he did now, but Jessie would have been willing to bet that his personality was about the same.

Ki spoke up. "You believe that Abernathy is to blame for the attacks on your stagecoach line that you described in your letter?"

"I do."

"Why would he do such things? In all likelihood, your stagecoach company won't be able to survive the competition from the railroad once it's complete."

"I know." Adam's voice was heavy with resignation. "And while that would be a bitter pill to swallow, I suppose I could stand it. That's not good enough for Abernathy, though. Just putting us out of business won't satisfy his lust for revenge. He has to destroy us."

"In that case, why doesn't he just hire gunmen to kill you?"

"Some of those bullets came mighty close today."

Jessie thought Adam had a point there. But she wasn't sure she was ready to accept his explanation for what had been happening around here. Clayton Abernathy was a lot of things, none of them good, but Jessie couldn't recall ever hearing about him letting his business dealings turn personal.

Maybe this was a special case. Competition over a woman could make some men go utterly mad . . .

She pushed her plate of half-eaten food away and took another sip of coffee. "I'm curious about something, Mr. Warfield."

"Please, call me Adam."

Jessie smiled. "All right, Adam, tell me . . . when you wrote that letter to my father, what exactly did you expect him to do to help you?"

Adam didn't answer for a moment. Then he heaved a sigh. "I don't really know. I knew that Alex Starbuck was a big, successful businessman. I thought maybe he'd know how to handle something like this. I hoped he would advise us on what we could do to fight back against Abernathy. Rose and I even discussed offering to sell him part of the company at a very good price, so he'd have a personal stake in the situation. I don't know what good that would have done, but . . ." He shrugged again. "When you're desperate, you grasp at any straw you can find."

"Of course you do." Jessie turned the matter over in her mind. She still wasn't sure that Adam was right about Abernathy being behind the rustling and all the other attacks, but she had an idea that might help smoke him out into the open if he was. "I have one suggestion, if you're interested."

"Of course I'm interested! After the help you and Ki have given me today, I'll listen to anything you have to say, Miss Starbuck."

She smiled. "Make it Jessie. And sell a third of your stagecoach line to me."

Adam and Ki both stared at her. Ki regained his voice first. "You're sure you want to buy an interest in a stagecoach line that's almost certainly doomed to failure, Jessie?" He glanced at Adam. "No offense."

Adam shook his head. "None taken. You're just stating the facts." He looked at Jessie. "But Ki's right. Buying into the Rimfire Stagecoach Company is a losing proposition."

"You were willing to sell part of the company to my father."

"Well, yes."

"So, I'd like to have a personal stake in this fight, too, if I'm going to help you. With the money I can put into the deal, you can buy more horses, hire more men, do anything that needs doing that you've been putting off because you didn't have the cash."

"That's just postponing the inevitable, isn't it?"

"Maybe. Maybe not. I don't like to give up on a business once I'm involved in it. And when Abernathy sees that he's not going to be able to roll right over you, maybe it'll frustrate him enough that he'll do something to prove he's the one who's been trying to destroy you. You might not be able to stop the railroad in the long run, Adam . . . but if you can send Clayton Abernathy to prison for hiring killers and sending them after you, at least that would be something."

Adam smacked his palm down on the table with a sharp crack. "It sure would!" Then despair visibly gripped him again. "But a man like Abernathy would never go to prison. Not with all the lawyers he can hire."

"He can't hire any more than I can . . . and mine will be better." Jessie's voice was as coolly confident as her smile.

Adam thought about it for a few seconds more, then jerked his head in a nod. "All right. It's a deal."

"Won't you need to talk to your sister about it? She owns part of the company, too, doesn't she?"

"Rose will go along with whatever I decide. At least I think she will. But she'll be back from Laramie in a couple of days. We can talk to her then. I suppose things can wait that long."

"What's she doing in Laramie?"

Adam grunted and shook his head as if in amazement. "She drove the stagecoach down there. We've had to let all our drivers go, so she talked me into letting her take one of the runs."

Ki frowned. "You let a woman drive a stagecoach all the way to Laramie?"

"I didn't like it. Rose can be persuasive, though, and mighty stubborn. Anyway, she's not alone. Parker, our new shotgun guard, went with her. He seems to be a good man. He helped her out the other day when the team ran away from her. Probably saved her life."

Fleetingly, Jessie thought that she knew a man who sometimes called himself Parker. But it was a very common name, so she put that idea out of her head.

"We're agreed, then. Pending discussion with your sister, I'm going to buy a third interest in the Rimfire Stagecoach Company."

"We haven't talked about the price."

Jessie shook her head. "Doesn't matter. I'll meet whatever price you ask, and when this is all over, if you want, I'll sell that third of the company back to you for the same price."

"That's mighty generous of you."

Jessie thought about what a pure-dee son of a bitch Clayton Abernathy was and how he was part of the bunch that had tried to rope her in on their shady shenanigans, and she smiled.

"Take my word for it. I intend to get full value received." Earlier, they had driven all the horses back into the corral.

When they were finished with breakfast and ready to start toward Rimfire, Jessie, Ki, and Adam mounted up and cut out the ones that Adam intended to take back to the settlement with him, leaving the fresher animals here to use as stagecoach teams for the next few weeks.

"They hold up better that way over the long run, when they get an occasional period of extended rest."

Jessie accepted Adam's explanation. She didn't know much about running a stagecoach company, so she was more than willing to take his word on such things.

The three of them were able to handle the small horse herd easily. They pushed the animals northward at a steady pace, not getting in any hurry. By midday, they'd reached another way station, where a lanky old-timer named Bert Moss had lunch ready for them. Bert was a better cook than Horace—although it was hard to mess up beans—but his coffee wasn't as good.

After they had eaten, they resumed the trip to Rimfire. Adam kept looking around as if he expected bushwhackers to jump them at any second. Jessie and Ki were in the habit of staying alert at all times, so such caution was nothing new to them.

As they approached a gap between two steep bluffs, Adam pointed it out to Jessie. "That's Fielder's Cut. Day before yesterday, my sister Rose was driving the stagecoach through there when somebody opened fire on her from the bluffs. She said it sounded like there were several gunmen. That's when the team stampeded and got away from her."

"But this man Parker helped her, you said?"

Adam nodded. "That's right. He was able to stop the team, but not before the front axle cracked from all the bouncing around the coach was doing. He repaired it well enough for Rose to turn around and go back to Rimfire. We replaced the axle there. It's been a problem, keeping the coaches in good enough shape to use them. I did some work on the other one yesterday morning, before I brought those fresh horses out."

"You only have two stagecoaches?"

"We had four, but we've had to sell a couple of them to keep enough money in the bank for operating expenses. Anyway, our business has fallen off so much that two coaches are enough to meet the demand."

"We'll have to see what we can do about that."

Adam gave her a doubtful look. "You can't just manufacture demand out of thin air."

Jessie smiled. "You'd be surprised. If you cut fares enough, people who have been postponing traveling might decide to go ahead and make their trips."

"But if you don't charge enough, you'll lose money."

"It's better to lose a little money in hopes of making more later."

Adam shook his head. "You're the tycoon, not me."

Ki laughed. "Tycoon. It's hard to think of you that way, Jessie, especially when you're dressed like a cowboy and packing iron."

She grinned back at him with the comfortable ease of long familiarity.

Adam spoke up. "I, uh, think you look just fine, Miss Starbuck . . . Jessie."

"Thank you." They were in Fielder's Cut now, and Jessie's eyes scanned the slopes above them. She was about to decide that there wasn't going to be any trouble . . .

When she spotted a flash of sunlight reflecting off metal on the bluff to their right, and a split second later, a rifle cracked and a bullet whined through the air just over their heads.

Chapter 16

"Go!"

The shout burst from Jessie's lips as she jammed her boot heels into the sides of the buckskin and sent the horse leaping into a gallop. As the same time, she leaned forward in the saddle to make herself a smaller target and drew her Colt. The actions were all instinctive. She had been in so many fights she didn't have to think about what she was doing anymore.

More shots blasted from both sides of the cut. Bullets whistled around the three riders. One of the horses from the stagecoach teams screamed and threw its head up as blood gushed from a wound in its throat. The horse's legs went out from under it, creating an obstacle in the trail as it fell. The other horses shied away from it, adding to the confusion. Jessie, Ki, and Adam had to rein in as the herd milled around in front of them.

Ki whipped his Winchester from its scabbard and started spraying lead along the bluff to the left. Adam did the same, aiming at the right-hand slope. Jessie twisted from side to side in the saddle as she triggered the Lightning at every puff of powdersmoke she spotted above them. The gunmen were hidden behind rocks and trees, though, so there wasn't much to shoot at.

The hammer of Jessie's gun clicked on an empty cylinder after five rounds. Instead of taking the time to reload, she pouched the iron and jerked her hat off her head instead. She had to get that horse herd moving again so she and her companions wouldn't be trapped here. She drove her mount into the rearmost horses and slashed at their rumps with the hat as she shouted at them.

Those horses leaped ahead to get away from her and banged into other animals that started running, too. In a matter of seconds, the herd stampeded. They might scatter when they cleared the cut, but if they stayed here, the bushwhackers would kill them all, humans and horses alike. Another horse was already down, kicking and flailing as it bled to death.

Ki and Adam kept shooting, giving Jessie some covering fire as she drove the frantic horses ahead of her. Dust clogged the air in the cut. Suddenly Jessie broke out of it and saw that they were clear. Just as she'd expected, the herd broke apart, but at least as the horses spread out, they continued running in the general direction of Rimfire. That would make rounding them up later easier.

Behind her, Ki and Adam hipped around in their saddles and threw more lead at the bluffs. When their rifles ran out of bullets, the two men galloped hard after Jessie and the stampeding stagecoach horses. Ki saw a few spurts of dust around them where slugs fired from the bluffs struck the ground, but none of the shots came close, and in a matter of moments, he and Adam had raced out of effective range.

"You hit?"

Ki shook his head in response to the question Adam

called to him over the pounding hoofbeats. "What about you?"

"I'm all right! Do you know if Jessie was wounded?"

"I didn't see her get hit!" Despite that, Ki would feel a lot better when they caught up to her and he could make certain that she wasn't wounded.

He looked back at the bluffs to make sure that the gunmen hadn't mounted up and set off in pursuit of them. He didn't see anyone.

Up ahead, Jessie started trying to gather the herd. Some of the horses hadn't scattered very far, so she was able to prod them back into a group without much trouble. As far as she had seen, only two of the horses had been killed by the crashing volleys of rifle fire. When she looked back, she saw that Ki and Adam were both following her and appeared to be all right. The results of that ambush could have been a lot worse.

In fact, that thought brought a faint frown to her lovely face. Down in the cut as they had been, and caught in a cross fire to boot, the hidden gunmen should have been able to do more damage to them. It was surprising that none of them had been wounded and only two horses killed.

Jessie didn't know what that meant, if anything, but she was going to ponder on it. Later, though, because right now she needed to concentrate on getting what was left of the herd back together.

A minute later, Ki and Adam caught up and pitched in to help her. When they had the herd gathered, Adam did a quick count and confirmed what Jessie had thought earlier.

"We only lost two horses." Adam sleeved sweat off his forehead. "Mighty lucky."

Jessie nodded. "Yes, mighty lucky. Are there any more natural traps like that between here and Rimfire?"

"No, I don't think there are any other good places for an ambush. We should have a pretty good view of where we're going."

"How much do you think those two horses were worth?"

"Around two hundred apiece, I'd say."

"Four hundred dollars, then." Jessie's voice was decisive.

"Why do you want to know?"

She looked over at Adam. "Because if I'm going to be a part-owner of this company, and it turns out that Clayton Abernathy was responsible for what happened back there, I intend to see to it that he settles his debt. Every damn penny." As Adam had predicted, they made it to Rimfire without being ambushed again. The place was a nice-looking frontier settlement, Jessie saw as they drove the horses into the corral next to the barn owned by the stagecoach company. Maybe still a little rough around the edges in places, as befitted its origins as a wild-and-woolly cow town. Civilization was all well and good, but to be truly interesting, a place needed a few of those rough edges, too.

When they had the horses in the corral, Ki swung the gate closed. Jessie rested her hands on her saddle horn and leaned forward to ease tired muscles as she looked over at Adam.

"Is there a good hotel in town?"

He nodded. "The Gaston House is probably the best. Maybe not real fancy, but clean and comfortable, and they'll treat you right."

"I don't care about fancy. I just want a nice, long, hot bath. Do you think they can accommodate me?"

"I'm sure they can."

Jessie saw a faint flush tinging Adam's ears pink, and

she knew what he was thinking. He'd just had a mental image of her sitting nude in a tub of hot, soapy water . . . and he liked what he saw in his mind's eye.

It wasn't beyond the realm of possibility that he might get to see the real thing before everything was said and done. He was a big man, and handsome in a rough-hewn way. Jessie liked that. She had never found men who were pretty all that appealing. To her way of thinking, a man ought to look like a man.

But she was getting way ahead of herself there, and she knew it. She barely knew Adam Warfield. There would be time for other things later, if they were meant to be.

"Ki and I will head on down to the hotel, then."

Adam spoke quickly. "You'll have dinner with me, though?"

Jessie smiled and shrugged. "If you'd like. That's probably a good idea. We can discuss our business plans."

"Yes, uh, that's just what I was thinking. Our business plans."

He still had that bathtub picture stuck in his head, Jessie thought.

"Just give me a chance to get . . . cleaned up first." That was really too mischievous of her, she told herself. She shouldn't torture the poor man by making him think of her bathing again.

On the other hand, it had been a long, hard day, and it was a little entertaining to watch him gulp like that.

"The hotel dining room in, say, two hours?"

Adam nodded. "I'll be there."

Jessie smiled and reined her horse into motion. Ki fell in alongside her. When he spoke, it was quietly enough so that only she could hear.

"It doesn't happen very often, but every now and then you're a bit of a tease, Jessie Starbuck."

She laughed. "I know. I'm awful, aren't I?"

Ki didn't answer that question. Instead, he asked one of his own.

"Do you really think there's any way we can help Warfield and his sister? Clayton Abernathy has a right to build a railroad, as long as he's doing it legally, and from what Warfield told us, there's nothing illegal about the railroad itself."

"I intend to send a letter to my lawyers on the next stagecoach telling them to look into that very thing. We might as well make sure that every possibility is covered. If there's anything shady or corrupt about the way Abernathy acquired the right-of-way, we might be able to use that to stop him."

Ki made a little circling gesture with his hand. Jessie knew he meant it to encompass the entire settlement around them.

"If you do that, you'll be stopping the citizens of Rimfire from getting the benefits of railroad service, won't you?"

"Well . . . I suppose that's true. Blast it, Ki, do you always have to be right?"

He smiled. "Just doing my job."

"I don't recall my father ever telling you that you had to be my conscience, just my friend."

"If I didn't help you follow your conscience, I wouldn't *be* your friend, Jessie."

They reached the hotel, a sturdy-looking, two-story building of whitewashed timber. A sign reading "GASTON HOUSE" hung on the awning over the boardwalk in front of the building. Jessie and Ki reined to a stop and swung down from their saddles. They tied their mounts to the hitch rail. Jessie took her saddlebags and slung them over her shoulder, then drew her Winchester from the saddle boot.

"I'm too tired to argue philosophy right now. Let's just go inside and get rooms."

Ki nodded. "Once we've done that, I'll take the horses back down to Warfield's barn. If you're going to invest in the company, I think it ought to be all right for us to put our horses up there."

The hotel lobby was furnished with a certain shabby elegance. It wasn't busy. A clerk sat on a stool behind the desk, and a couple of men in flashy suits and bowler hats lounged in armchairs reading week-old editions of the local newspaper. Their outfits marked them as traveling salesmen. Jessie made a mental note of that. The drummers probably would need to be moving on in the reasonably near future. That meant a couple of potential passengers for the stagecoach line.

The young clerk got up off his stool to watch Jessie and Ki as they crossed the lobby toward the desk. It wasn't every day that a beautiful young woman who was well armed and dressed like a cowboy came in here. In fact, it might not have ever happened before. And certainly the clerk had never seen anyone like Ki, because— to be honest—there wasn't anyone else like Ki.

The young man put his hands on the desk and cleared his throat as Jessie and Ki came up to the desk. "May I, ah, help you?"

Jessie set the Winchester on the desk. "We need a couple of rooms. The best ones you have available, in fact. And whatever room you put me in, I want a tub and plenty of hot water brought up there, pronto."

"I . . . I'm not sure—"

Jessie took a handful of double eagles from her pocket and stacked the five coins on the desk in front of the clerk. His eyes widened even more at the sight of that much money.

"A hundred dollars ought to hold us for a good long while. Let me know when it gets close to running out."

"Yes, ma'am!" The clerk grabbed the register and set it in front of her, along with a pen and inkwell. "If you'll just sign in . . ."

Jessie signed *Jessica Starbuck, Circle Star Ranch, Texas.* She wasn't trying to keep her presence here in Rimfire a secret. In fact, the more people who knew she was in town, the better. She intended to stir things up in hopes of spooking Clayton Abernathy into making a wrong move, and it was entirely possible he had spies in the settlement.

The clerk took keys from the rack. "I'm putting you and your, ah, friend in Rooms Five and Nine, Miss Starbuck. They're both first floor front, with fine views of the street, but I'm afraid they're not adjoining."

"That's all right. No need for them to be."

"Yes, of course. I'll see about getting that tub brought up right away."

Jessie nodded as she picked up her rifle. "The sooner the better. You do have a dining room here in the hotel, don't you?"

"Yes, ma'am. The best food you'll find in Rimfire."

"Good. I have a dinner engagement in a little less than two hours."

"If you need some help with your bags . . ."

Jessie patted the saddlebags draped over her shoulder. "These are all I have. I reckon I can handle them."

She started for the stairs leading up to the first floor while Ki headed for the front door. "I'll tend to the horses."

She nodded. "Thanks. See you at dinner."

She climbed the stairs, found Room Five, and let herself in, leaving the door open. The sight of the big bed with its thick mattress and soft comforter made her yearn to stretch out on it, but not yet, she told herself. Not while she was covered with trail dust.

She put the saddlebags on a chair and leaned the Winchester in a corner. Hearing footsteps, she looked out and saw two men carrying a big galvanized metal tub down the hall toward her room. She stepped back to let them bring it in.

One of the men was the young clerk. "The water's heating. Our maids will bring it up."

Jessie nodded. "Thank you."

The young man lingered, clearly summoning up his courage. Finally he was able to voice what he was thinking.

"No offense, ma'am, but are you *really* the famous Jessica Starbuck?"

Jessie gave him a big smile. "No, dang it, you're too smart for me. I'm really Calamity Jane."

"No, ma'am! I've seen Calamity Jane, and you don't look anything like her!"

Laughing, Jessie ushered him out of the room. A few minutes later, a couple of maids arrived carrying buckets of steaming water. They poured the water into the tub and went back downstairs to fetch more.

That process took a while, but when it was done, the tub had a couple of feet of hot water in it. Jessie locked the door, pulled a chair over next to the tub, and set her coiled gunbelt and holstered Colt on it so that the weapon would be in easy reach if she needed it. Then she stripped off her dusty clothes and dropped them in a corner.

One of the maids had brought a chunk of soap, too, and left it on the table next to the bed. Jessie picked it up and stepped naked into the tub, sighing in satisfaction as she felt the hot water on her skin. It wasn't steaming anymore, but it was still plenty hot as she lowered herself into it.

The tub was big enough for her to stretch back some, rest her head on the edge, and close her eyes as she let the heat unkink stiff muscles. It soaked into her, and as she lay there, she found herself thinking about Adam Warfield. A different sort of heat kindled inside her. She wondered how deeply he would blush if he could see her like this. She wondered if the real thing would match his mental image of her.

Maybe they would both find out. Yes, sir, maybe they would.

Chapter 17

When Jessie came downstairs about an hour and a half later, she wore a simple but elegant blue gown and soft white slippers. A string of pearls was around her neck. Anyone who had seen her arrive earlier wouldn't have thought that she could carry such an outfit in a pair of saddlebags, but she was an expert at packing the things that she would need. And sometimes a lady needed to look elegant.

The clerk gawked at her from behind the desk. After a moment, he found his tongue.

"M-Miss Starbuck, you look . . . well, you look beautiful!"

"Thank you. What's your name?"

"Spencer, ma'am."

"Then thank you, Spencer."

"Uh, Mr. Warfield is here. He asked me to tell you that he's in the dining room with the, ah, Chinese gentleman."

Jessie shook her head. "Ki isn't Chinese. He's half-Japanese. But actually, he's an adopted Texan, I suppose you could say." She flashed a smile at the young man.

"Yes, ma'am. Anyway, they're in the dining room."

Jessie nodded and crossed the lobby to the arched en-•
trance into the dining room. Like the rest of the Gaston
House, it wasn't fancy, but the white linen tablecloths were
snowy and the crystal and china sparkled in the lamplight
that filled the room.

About half the tables were occupied. As Jessie came
into the room, she was aware that both men and women
were looking at her. She was used to that and didn't let it
bother her. She moved smoothly toward the table where
Ki and Adam Warfield waited for her. Both men came to
their feet.

They had cleaned up, too, although Jessie doubted if
they had soaked in a hot tub for an hour like she had. Ki
had donned a short, black leather jacket that matched his
vest, and Adam wore a gray tweed suit. He had shaved,
and a couple of tiny nicks were still visible on his strong
jaw.

"Miss Starbuck. Jessie. You look lovely."

"Thank you."

Adam moved to hold her chair for her. Ki didn't try to
beat him to it. He was content to sit back and let Adam
play the gentleman this evening.

When they were all seated again, Jessie asked what was
good here. Adam smiled.

"Well, this is cattle country, so I'd recommend the
steak. Unless that's a little too unrefined for your tastes."

"I grew up on a ranch, remember? Steak will be fine.
With all the trimmings, of course."

Ki nodded. "For me, as well."

"I thought maybe you ate some sort of special diet . . ."

That brought a chuckle from Ki. "Like rice and vegeta-
bles? As if American food would somehow corrupt and
defile my Oriental purity? No, Mr. Warfield, I'll take a nice,

thick, juicy steak. I suppose I've already been corrupted by your country."

"I didn't mean any offense."

Ki made a slight motion with his hand to show that he wasn't offended.

Jessie reached over and put a hand on Adam's arm. "Don't pay any attention to him. He has an odd sense of humor at times."

Ki shook his head. "No, I'm just inscrutable."

"Well, I'm ordering the steaks." Adam motioned for the black-suited waiter.

A bottle of wine sat on the table. Adam and Ki already had some in their glasses. Adam poured the wine for Jessie.

"I hope this is to your liking. I'm sure it's not like what you could get in San Francisco or some place like that. Rimfire, Wyoming, is a long way from fancy."

Jessie sipped the wine and nodded. "I like Rimfire, Wyoming. It looks like a fine town." She didn't want this dinner to get too serious, but some things couldn't be avoided. "It would grow even more with a railroad."

Adam leaned forward, resting his hands on the table and hunching his shoulders a little. "You're saying that I ought to let Abernathy win for the sake of the town? I thought you wanted to fight him, Jessie."

"I do . . . because he's Clayton Abernathy, and I don't like him or trust him to be honest. But in the long run, Adam, it's hard to defeat progress."

Adam grunted. "And hard to defend trying to do so. I know, Jessie. To be honest, I like the people here. I'd like to do what's best for them. But my father started that stagecoach line. It meant an awful lot to him. I can't just let it go under without putting up a fight. You can understand that, can't you?"

Having carried on with her own father's enterprises,

Jessie certainly could. She smiled across the table at Adam.

"We're going to put up a fight. At the very least, we're going to find out who's responsible for those attacks, and we'll see to it that they pay for what they've done. After that . . . well, we'll have to wait and see."

"I can go along with that." Adam lifted his glass of wine. "Here's to the Rimfire Stagecoach Company . . . and its new partner." Jessie and Ki clinked their glasses against his. And if anyone here in the dining room was secretly working for Clayton Abernathy, Jessie thought, the spy was probably getting an eyeful right about now. The food in the hotel dining room was good, and Jessie enjoyed the meal. The conversation centered around the stagecoach company and the other stage lines Donald Warfield had started. Jessie could tell how much Adam thought of his late father. They really were a lot alike, she and Adam, and once again she felt that the things they had in common could grow into a friendship, and that friendship into something more.

Jessie resolved to take that slow, however. In the end, she might not be able to help him save his company, and a romantic relationship between them would only complicate matters. Still, she had never been one to deny her feelings forever. She might postpone acting on them, but sooner or later, if the urge was there . . .

Jessie put that out of her mind as Adam walked her back to her room after dinner. She resolutely kept her thoughts on business instead.

"Tomorrow, we'll go over the books. I want to take a look at the stock, too, as well as that second coach, the barn, and everything else the company owns."

"You're a canny businesswoman, aren't you, Jessie?"

Her answer was straightforward. "I try to be. When I'm

going into some new enterprise, I don't like to run into any surprises."

"I can't blame you for that. I'll show you anything you want to see and answer any questions you have. Then Rose will be back the day after tomorrow, if everything has gone all right, and we can finalize the deal."

Jessie smiled. "That sounds fine to me. Good night, Adam."

"Good night." He looked like he wanted to put his hands on her shoulders and kiss her, and if he had, Jessie wouldn't have stopped him. But instead, he just smiled, nodded, and turned to walk away along the hotel corridor.

Jessie lingered outside her door, waiting until Adam reached the landing. He looked back at her when he did, smiled and nodded again, then started down the stairs.

Jessie turned the key in the lock and opened the door.

Flame lanced from the darkness inside the room.

Jessie was already moving, having heard a floorboard creak just as she swung the door back. Whoever was lurking in the room had shifted slightly as Jessie started to come in, and that had given him away. As Jessie threw herself forward and to the side, she heard the flat *whap!* of a bullet tearing through the air near her head.

By the time she hit the floor just inside the room, her fingers had deftly plucked a derringer from a hidden pocket in her gown. It was a single-shot Bulldog, but since it fired a .44-caliber round, that single shot packed a punch. Jessie couldn't afford to waste it, though, so she rolled across the floor, hoping to draw another shot from the would-be killer.

She did. Another muzzle flash lit the room for a split second with its garish light. Jessie was ready. She thrust the Bulldog at the spot where the gun had just gone off and pulled the trigger. The derringer's report was loud for such a little gun, especially in the close confines of the hotel room.

Jessie's ears rang from the shots, but she was able to hear a grunt of pain and knew that her bullet had found its target. She leaped to her feet, still clutching the derringer in her right hand, and swung blindly in the direction of the ambusher. Gun and fist thudded hard against something she hoped was the varmint's head. She lowered her own head and rushed forward, bulling into the man and shoving him toward the curtain-covered window.

The gunman must not have expected his quarry to put up such a fierce fight. He let out a startled yell as Jessie drove her shoulder into his chest and forced him backward. He fell through the curtains and hit the window, which gave with a splintering crash under the impact. The man continued yelling as he toppled over the sill and plunged out of sight.

Jessie dropped the derringer and slapped her hands against the wall on both sides of the window to keep her momentum from carrying her on through the shattered pane. She looked down and saw that the man hadn't fallen very far, only a few feet to the top of the roof over the hotel's front porch. That roof was probably how he had gotten into her room to start with. He'd have been better off if he'd left the window open behind him, rather than closing it.

Jessie thought about climbing through the window and going after him, but as she looked down at him, he rolled over and brought his gun up. She was a little surprised he had managed to hang on to it. She jerked backward as he fired. The bullet hit the window frame and chewed splinters from it. Two more wild shots rang out, the slugs going through the broken window to thud into the wall, high on the other side of the room.

As Jessie leaned forward again, she caught a glimpse of the man rolling off the edge of the roof so that he dropped toward the street below. She rushed to the open door and nearly ran into Adam Warfield in the hall as she was leaving the room.

"Jessie! I heard shooting. What happened?"

"Bushwhacker!" That one word was explanation enough. "Come on!"

She brushed past Adam and sprinted for the stairs. She had left the derringer in the room, so she was unarmed now, but she didn't let that slow her down. She was confident that she had wounded the man lurking in her room, and she wanted to put her hands on him so she could question him and find out who had sent him.

Clayton Abernathy came to mind instantly as the most logical suspect.

Ki had lingered over coffee in the dining room, but he'd heard the shooting upstairs, too, of course. He was in the entrance to the dining room as Jessie and Adam reached the bottom of the stairs.

"Jessie?"

"I'm fine. Bushwhacker!"

She didn't have to explain to Ki, either. He joined them in their rush to the front doors. Behind the desk, the young clerk Spencer just stared at them in amazement.

Jessie didn't slow down as she crossed the boardwalk. She didn't use the three steps down to the street, either, but bounded right over them instead, landing with an agile grace as she twisted to her left. That was where the man would have landed when he rolled off the roof.

He wasn't there. Jessie didn't see any sign of him.

"Damn it!" The oath burst from her lips. "I know I hit him. I guess he wasn't hurt enough to slow him down."

Ki paused and knelt beside a dark splotch on the ground. He touched it, then rubbed his fingertips together.

"You hit him well enough that he's losing some blood."

Spencer's voice came from the front door of the hotel. "Miss Starbuck, is . . . is everything all right?"

Jessie turned toward him. "A lantern, Spencer. Quick!"

The young man jerked his head in a nod. "Yes, ma'am!" He disappeared from the door.

"Should I get the sheriff?"

Jessie shook her head in response to Adam's question. "I expect he'll be along anytime now. He must have heard those shots."

Ki straightened from the splash of blood. "The whole town probably heard those shots."

Spencer came running out of the hotel with a lit lantern in his hand. "Here you go, Miss Starbuck."

Jessie took the lantern from him and held it over the blood in the street. As the light spread, she and the others could see the trail of dark red drops leading down the street. She started following them. Ki, Adam, and Spencer were right behind her.

"Shouldn't somebody get a gun?" Adam didn't sound nervous, just cautious.

Jessie shook her head again. "Ki's armed."

"He is?"

Ki moved his arms, and the handles to the *tanto* knives slid into his palms. He pulled them from his sleeves and held them up to show Adam.

The blood trail turned toward an alley. Jessie motioned for Adam and Spencer to stay back.

"He could still be in there. Let Ki take a look."

"But isn't that dangerous?"

Ki had disappeared into the shadows before Spencer finished asking the question.

No one saw Ki unless he wanted to be seen. His dark clothing allowed him to blend into the night, and he moved with such stealth that no one could hear him, either. He explored the alley in utter silence, using all of his senses to do so, then emerged from it a few moments later to make his report.

"The man had a horse tied up back there. Even though he was wounded, he was able to get away."

Jessie nodded, trying not to feel too disappointed. "I thought that might be the case."

Adam pushed his coat back and stood with his fists on his hips. "Maybe he'll bleed to death, the son of a . . . gun."

"Maybe. I'm not sure he was losing that much blood, though." Hurrying footsteps and an irritated voice made Jessie glance around. "This is probably the sheriff coming now."

Adam came a step closer to her. "Before the law gets here . . . do you think Abernathy was behind this ambush, Jessie?"

"You mean, do I think he'd want to get rid of me if he already found out that I'm going to get in the way of his plans?" Jessie nodded, because the possibility had already occurred to her. "I don't doubt it for a second."

Adam's voice was heavy with anger. "Then that's one more mark against him, one more debt he owes us. By the time this is over, he's going to have a lot to answer for."

Jessie meant to see to it that those debts were paid, too.

Chapter 18

Longarm and Rose hadn't run into any more ambushes on the way to Laramie, and so far the trip back to Rimfire had gone smoothly, too.

That was good, because Longarm had plenty of other things to think about, most notably the revelation that Adam Warfield had written a letter to Alex Starbuck appealing for help.

Starbuck wouldn't get that letter, of course. The man had been dead for a number of years. But if the letter was addressed to the Circle Star Ranch in Texas, then the chances were good that it would have wound up in the hands of Alex Starbuck's daughter Jessica.

Longarm had known Jessie Starbuck for a long time. Early on in her crusade against the Cartel, the gang of international criminals responsible for murdering her father, Longarm had been drawn into the fight. They had teamed up from time to time to battle elements of the Cartel, until that bunch of no-good snakes had been stomped for good.

Or so they had thought. Recently, the Cartel had risen from the ashes, led by the daughter of its founder, and Longarm and Jessie had been forced to defeat it again.

It had been good to see her again, despite the often dangerous circumstances. Years had passed without them seeing each other, and Longarm had missed her. Longarm sometimes thought that if there was one woman in the world he might have loved and settled down with, it was Jessie Starbuck.

But that was unlikely to happen. Longarm had packed a badge for Uncle Sam for too many years to give up his career as a lawman, and a gal like Jessie, who was rich as Croesus and owned a ranch bigger than some eastern states, wouldn't want to be married to some two-bit star packer. They were just too different—and too set in their ways—to ever make a marriage work. Longarm knew that and accepted it.

So he did his best to enjoy to the utmost any time he did get to spend with Jessie, even if folks were usually trying to kill them when that happened. As Rose Warfield drove the stage northward toward Rimfire, Longarm couldn't help but wonder if Jessie and Ki would be there when they got back. According to Rose, it had been more than a month since Adam had written that letter, so it had had time to get to Texas, and Jessie and Ki had had time respond to the plea for help.

Rose pulled back on the reins to slow the horses. "I was thinking about resting the team for a little while."

Longarm frowned. "It ain't that far to Rimfire. We'll be back there in another hour or so."

"I know. That's why I want to stop now." Rose turned to look at him. "I haven't had my fill of you, Custis."

They had spent one night in Laramie, in a small hotel not far from the stage station. There were sleeping quarters

at the station itself, but Longarm and Rose had wanted
more privacy than that.

They had taken advantage of that privacy to make love
for hours, in every possible way Longarm could think of,
and a couple that Rose had insisted *weren't* possible until
he demonstrated otherwise. It had been a wonderful night,
even though they'd had to take some precautions because
of Rose's wounded arm, but since they had spent the next
night at one of the way stations, they hadn't had a chance
to repeat the experience.

They had no passengers, and obviously Rose wanted to
stop the stage for one last hurrah before they got back to
Rimfire. Longarm had to admit that the idea was an intriguing one.

"What did you have in mind? There ain't exactly a bed
anywhere around here."

He waved a hand at their surroundings as the stagecoach rocked along slowly. There was nothing in sight but
rolling prairie, broken here and there by small buttes.

"We don't need a bed. I thought we'd get inside the
coach and . . . you know." She blushed, despite the inti-
macies they had already enjoyed.

"Well, I suppose we could give it a try. Those benches
are pretty hard, but I'm game if you are."

Rose laughed. "As long as *you're* hard, Custis, I think
we can manage."

She was right. She stopped the team, set the brake, and
the two of them climbed into the coach. Longarm sat on
the rear seat, and Rose sat on him. They set the coach to
rocking on its leather thoroughbraces. Everything worked
just fine, and they were flushed and a little breathless but
thoroughly satisfied as Rose got the team moving and
started the coach rolling once more toward Rimfire a half
hour later.

As they went through Fielder's Cut, Longarm scanned the slopes closely, alert for more bushwhackers, but once again their luck held and nothing happened. Now it was just a fairly short run on to Rimfire.

"Maybe Abernathy has given up. Maybe he's decided to leave us alone."

Longarm heard hope in Rose's voice as she voiced that thought, but it was faint. She didn't really believe it, and neither did he. Clayton Abernathy wasn't the sort to give up once he had started something.

They came in sight of the town a few minutes later. Rimfire hadn't changed any in the time they'd been gone . . . not that Longarm had expected it to. Rose steered the coach toward the station and brought it to a stop in front of the building.

Adam Warfield stepped out onto the porch, followed by a woman. Even though Longarm had been halfway expecting to see her, he still felt a jolt of mingled pleasure and surprise as he recognized Jessie Starbuck.

He wasn't nearly as surprised to see her, though, as she was to see him. He could see the shocked reaction in her eyes. Somebody who didn't know her as well as he did probably wouldn't have noticed it, because Jessie controlled her emotions in an instant and looked at him impassively, as if she had never seen him before.

"Rose!" Adam stepped forward to reach up and help his sister climb down from the driver's seat. "How are you? Was there any trouble along the way?"

Rose winced as Adam caught hold of her under the arms.

Adam saw that. "You're hurt!"

"I'm fine." She smiled. "I just got a little scratch on my left arm."

"What kind of scratch?"

"Well . . . a bullet scratch."

"A bullet—good Lord! I knew I shouldn't have let you drive that coach! You were ambushed again, weren't you?"

Rose started to shrug, then caught herself. "That's right, but Custis fought them off and we got away from them. We didn't lose the mail pouch or anything like that, Adam."

"Did they jump you at Fielder's Cut again?"

Rose shook her head. "No, they were hidden in one of the arroyos between Bert's station and the one Horace runs."

"Blast that Abernathy!"

Rose had taken notice of Jessie, who stood with her hands on the porch railing, a faint smile on her face. "Adam? Who's this?" Rose nodded toward Jessie.

Adam took a deep breath. "We have a lot to talk about, Rose. Remember that letter I wrote to Alex Starbuck down in Texas?"

"Of course I do."

Adam took her right arm and led her toward the porch. "Well, this is Jessica Starbuck, Mr. Starbuck's daughter. Unfortunately, he's passed away, but Jessie and a friend of hers have come up here to give us a hand."

"They have?"

"That's right. If you're agreeable, Rose, Jessie is going to be a new partner in the Rimfire Stagecoach Company."

Rose looked like she was having a hard time grasping everything that was coming at her, Longarm thought. He climbed down from the seat, grateful that so far Jessie was playing her cards close to her vest. She hadn't made any mention of knowing him or who he really was. In fact, after that first startled glance, she hadn't paid much attention to him at all.

Adam made the introductions. "Jessie, this is my sister, Rose Warfield. Rose, this is Jessica Starbuck."

Jessie held out a hand and smiled warmly. "Hello, Rose. I'm glad to meet you. Adam has told me a great deal about you."

Rose had a certain tentative air about her as she took Jessie's hand. Longarm figured that might have something to do with her realization that Adam and Jessie were already on a first-name basis.

But that wasn't unusual for Jessie. Despite her power and wealth, she wasn't the sort of gal to put on airs. She never minded getting out and working side by side with the Circle Star Ranch hands during a roundup or a trail drive, getting every bit as dirty and worn out as they did. That attitude was one of the things Longarm had always really liked about her.

"You'll have to excuse me, Miss Starbuck. You evidently know a lot more about me than I do about you."

Adam stepped in quickly to prevent any ruffled feathers. "We'll all sit down and have a long talk together once the horses are put away and Rose has had a chance to rest a little." He glanced over at Longarm. "By the way, Jessie, this is our new shotgun guard. Our *only* shotgun guard, I should say—"

Longarm reached up and tugged on the brim of his hat as he finished the introduction. "Custis Parker, ma'am. It's an honor and a privilege to meet you."

That way she would know that Adam and Rose weren't aware of who he really was. He was confident that Jessie would keep his secret . . . for the time being, anyway.

He wanted to have a talk with her as soon as he could, though, without causing any suspicion.

She returned his nod. "Hello, Mr. Parker. I suppose there's a chance that you'll be working for me as well as for Mr. and Miss Warfield. Will that be all right with you?"

Longarm spotted the flash of amusement in her eyes. He kept his own expression solemn as he answered.

"Yes, ma'am, that'll be fine."

Adam steered the two women toward the door. "Rose, why don't you and Jessie go on inside? I'm sure you're tired after making that long trip to Laramie and back. Custis and I will tend to the horses."

Rose looked a little leery at the idea of being in the station alone with Jessie, but she didn't argue. "All right, but don't take too long, Adam. We have a lot to talk about."

Once the two women had gone inside, Adam climbed to the driver's box and took the stagecoach into the barn. Longarm followed and set aside the Winchester he had bought in Laramie to replace the one he'd lost during the running fight with the bushwhackers. Rose had offered to pay for the rifle, but Longarm had told her that he still had some money and wanted to pay for it himself.

He started unhitching the horses, and Adam joined him in the chore. "Did anything else happen on the trip that Rose didn't tell me about?"

Quite a bit, Longarm thought, but none of it that Adam would want to hear about, since it involved his sister being plowed like a field at planting time. Instead of saying anything about that, Longarm shook his head.

"Nope. Gettin' jumped by those varmints slowed us down a mite, but Rose is a good driver. She made up the time we lost, and we delivered the mail pouch in Laramie on schedule and picked up the one we brought back."

"There were no passengers waiting in Laramie, were there?"

Longarm shook his head. "Afraid not."

"Well, a couple of drummers have bought tickets on the run leaving in the morning, so the line has a little extra income, at least."

"That's good to know." Longarm figured it would look strange if he didn't act curious about Jessie, so he asked a question. "Alex Starbuck's daughter, eh? Rose told me about you writin' a letter to him asking for help and advice. I didn't really expect to come back to Rimfire and find a third boss, though."

"Is that going to be a problem?"

Longarm shook his head. "No, like I told Miss Starbuck, it don't matter to me." He grinned. "I don't reckon I've ever had a boss quite that pretty, though."

"Don't get any ideas."

The sharpness of Adam's response told Longarm that he was already interested in Jessie. Well, that came as no surprise. Any man who was single and had a pulse couldn't help but be interested in Jessie. And probably quite a few who weren't single, as well.

"Don't worry, Mr. Warfield. I'll keep my distance."

That wasn't going to be easy. There had always been a powerful attraction between Longarm and Jessie, right from the first moment they laid eyes on each other.

Longarm's answer seemed to satisfy Adam. They finished unhitching the team, then Adam took the mail pouch from inside the coach and handed it to Longarm.

"You mind taking this down to the post office?"

"Nope."

"Then come on back to the house for supper."

Longarm smiled. "Sounds good."

They left the barn, Adam heading into the office while Longarm started down the street with the Winchester in one hand and the mail pouch in the other. He didn't think anybody would try to jump him right here in the middle of town, but after bringing the pouch all the way to Rimfire, he wanted to make sure it landed safely in the postmaster's hands.

The sun was almost down. Soon shadows would begin to form. Longarm went up the steps to the porch and loading dock of the general store that also housed the post office. He was reaching for the door when a voice spoke behind him.

"Marshal."

Chapter 19

The word was spoken softly, but it was enough to make Longarm stiffen for a second and close his hand tighter on the Winchester. He had been a lawman for a long time, and he had made a lot of enemies. The way Patch and Little Ike McCurdy had tried to kill him back in Denver, just before he'd headed up here to Wyoming, was just the latest attempt in a long line of such efforts to put him in the ground.

So it was entirely possible that somebody here in Rimfire had recognized him and wanted him dead. For a split second, he was ready to whirl around, wallop whoever it was with the mail pouch, and then ventilate the son of a bitch before he got ventilated himself.

But almost as soon as that reaction flashed through his mind, he recognized the voice, so when he turned there was a smile on his face.

"Shouldn't ought to sneak up on a fella like that, Ki. I'm gettin' older, but I ain't too slow and feeble just yet."

The tall, lean half Japanese returned the smile. "Of course not, Mar—"

"Parker. The name's Custis Parker."

"Of course." Ki's voice was a soft murmur now. "When Adam Warfield told Jessie and me that he had just hired a new shotgun guard named Parker, I think a certain possibility occurred to both of us. We didn't actually expect it to turn out to be true, though."

"There are more things in heaven and earth, Horatio, than are dreamt of in your philosophy."

The quote brought a laugh from Ki. "You're an endless source of surprises, Mr. Parker. Have you talked to Jessie yet?"

"Just howdied, that's all."

"I'm sure she'll want to have a talk with you."

"She ain't the only one. I reckon we've both got some fillin' in to do." Longarm hefted the mail pouch. "Right now, though, I got to deliver this."

"I'll come with you."

The two men went into the store. When the proprietor saw Longarm coming, he took off his apron and went into the room that he used for the post office. A window was cut into the dividing partition, with a sliding door on it. The storekeeper/postmaster opened the door and took the mail pouch from Longarm.

"Thanks, Parker. Any trouble between here and Laramie?"

"Not enough to worry about. Nobody laid hands on that mail pouch."

The man nodded. "Good. Uncle Sam wouldn't like it if that happened."

Longarm didn't say anything about being intimately acquainted with what Uncle Sam liked and didn't like. He just nodded.

"I'll have the outgoing pouch ready for you to pick up in the morning."

"That'll be fine." Longarm lifted a hand in farewell as he and Ki turned back toward the door.

Ki frowned in thought as they left the store. "Adam Warfield doesn't have any other shotgun guards. That means you'll have to turn right around and start back to Laramie in the morning."

"Yeah, that's kind of a problem. Doesn't give me much time to poke around here."

"Why don't you let me go in your place?"

Longarm looked over at his companion. "You ever ridden shotgun before?"

"As a matter of fact, I have."

"Well, it's a thought. We'll see what Jessie has to say about it."

Ki kept his voice low, so that only Longarm could hear him. "I must admit, I'll be very curious to hear what it is that's brought you here. I suspect it's something very similar to what brought Jessie and me to Wyoming."

Except that the two of them had answered a plea for help from Adam Warfield, thought Longarm, and technically, he was still working on the case involving attacks against Clayton Abernathy's railroad. If you looked at it like that, then he and Jessie were really on opposite sides for a change.

Longarm and Ki bypassed the office and the barn and walked across the back lot to the house that Adam and Rose shared on the side street. They went to the back porch and knocked on the door, and when Jessie opened it, a mixture of delicious aromas drifted out.

"I fixed supper tonight." She smiled at them. "Come on in. I see that the two of you have met."

That last was for Adam's benefit. He sat at the kitchen table, and judging by the smile on his face and the admiring look in his eyes, he had been watching Jessie move around the kitchen as she prepared the meal.

Ki played along with Jessie's comment. "Yes, I saw Mr. Parker delivering the mail pouch to the post office and introduced myself."

Adam gestured to one of the chairs at the table. "Sit down, Parker. I imagine you're tired, too, after traveling to Laramie and back over the past four days."

"Yeah, but if it's all the same to you, Mr. Warfield, I reckon I'd just as soon stand for a while. The driver's seat on that coach ain't what you'd call soft and comfortable."

Adam laughed. "I know. And I hate to ask you to ride that far again, starting first thing tomorrow morning, but I don't have much choice. I don't have another guard, so you'll have to come with me to Laramie."

Jessie stirred something simmering in a pot on the stove, then turned toward the table. "Actually, you do have a choice, Adam. Why not let Ki ride shotgun on the next run?"

"Ki?" Adam frowned in surprise. He asked the same question Longarm had a short time earlier. "Have you ever ridden shotgun on a stagecoach, Ki?"

"Yes, I have. I might add that I'm an excellent shot with a rifle, and I can handle a shotgun as well."

"Oh, I don't doubt that you can take care of yourself. I thought you were Miss Starbuck's bodyguard, though. If you come with me, you'll have to leave her here in Rimfire."

"Where I'll be perfectly safe," Jessie said.

Adam was still frowning. "I don't know . . ."

"Ki is more my friend than my bodyguard, and he knows I'm perfectly capable of taking care of myself. Alternating guards is a good idea, just like alternating drivers. The trip is too long and hard for someone to be on the trail constantly, without any breaks."

"You're probably right about that." Adam shrugged. "All right, Ki, if you want to come along, I'd be happy to have you. Parker can keep an eye on things here in Rim-fire."

Longarm nodded. "I'd be happy to. And if there's any chores around the station you want tended to, I can do that, too."

"I'll think about it. All right, it's settled, I suppose. We'll leave early tomorrow morning, Ki."

"I'll be ready."

Longarm leaned the Winchester in a corner. "Where's Miss Rose?"

"Freshening up."

"Reckon I ought to do the same thing." Longarm ran his hand over his jaw, the fingertips rasping on beard stubble. "I could use a shave."

Jessie laughed. "Later. Supper's almost ready."

Adam got to his feet. "I'll go upstairs and tell Rose."

He left the room. Longarm, Jessie, and Ki waited in silence until they heard Adam's heavy footsteps on the stairs.

Then Jessie darted across the room to Longarm and threw her arms around him. "Custis. My God, it's good to see you." She kept her voice low, little more than a whisper. "When Adam said he had a shotgun guard named Parker, I thought about you, but I never really dreamed it was you!"

Ki grinned. "I told the marshal the same thing."

"Not marshal." Longarm shook his head. "Around here, I'm just a shotgun guard, and that's the way it needs to stay for now."

Jessie looked up at him. "I don't understand. Did Billy Vail send you to investigate what's been happening to the stagecoach line?"

Footsteps sounded on the stairs again. Longarm gave a quick shake of his head.

"We'll talk about it later."

Jessie nodded. By the time Adam came back into the

kitchen, followed by Rose, Jessie was back at the stove, putting the finishing touches on the meal, and Longarm and Ki were sitting at the table.

"Everyone go into the dining room." Jessie waved a hand in command. "I'll bring the food in there."

The others went to the dining room. Rose wore a blue dress with little yellow flowers on it, and Longarm thought she looked lovely. She didn't have the same sort of breathtaking beauty as Jessie, but Longarm felt a powerful attraction to her anyway. It was probably made even stronger by his knowledge that beneath Rose's sweet, almost wholesome exterior lay the wildly beating heart of a wanton woman.

This evening, though, she just looked tired, and he supposed that the long trip had caught up with her. He felt some of that himself, and he was glad for more than one reason that he didn't have to start back to Laramie first thing the next morning.

Jessie brought in fried chicken, potatoes, greens, and some of the best biscuits Longarm had ever eaten, especially when they were dipped in gravy. The five of them sat at in the dining room, at a large round table that was covered with a lace cloth. It had belonged to her mother, Rose told Longarm, and her father had taken it with him all over the West, a reminder of the beloved wife he had lost when Adam was an adolescent boy and Rose little more than an infant.

The meal was a pleasant one. Good food, good company . . . Longarm had eaten too many meals on the trail, in smoky saloons, in squalid hash houses. That was his life. Sometimes it was good to stop and get a reminder that there were normal people in the world. People who sat down in their homes at tables with lace tablecloths. People who weren't whores, gamblers, horse thieves, bank robbers, or bloodthirsty killers.

It would be nice to live like this for a while.

But he knew he would grow tired of it. He wasn't cut out for a normal life. And even if he had been at one time, it was too late now.

Still, when he looked at Adam and Rose Warfield, he wished that they weren't facing so much trouble. No matter how things worked out with Clayton Abernathy and his railroad, the life that the brother and sister had built for themselves here in Rimfire was facing an inevitable end.

Eventually, inevitably, the talk turned to that. Adam explained to Longarm and Rose how he had met Jessie and Ki when they prevented rustlers from making off with half the stagecoach company's livestock at the way station run by Horace Dunn.

"That would have been a crippling blow if those horse thieves had succeeded. It might have been enough to put us under." Adam made a face. "Then Clayton Abernathy would have won."

Jessie pushed her empty plate away. "That wasn't all. They jumped us again at Fielder's Cut and killed two of the horses."

"Same bunch?" The question came from Longarm.

"We didn't actually get a good look at them either time. But I'm confident that it was the same men."

Adam grunted. "Abernathy's men."

"We don't actually *know* that."

Adam glanced sharply at his sister. "Who else would have any reason to try to ruin us?"

That was the same question that had been circling around in Longarm's head for days now.

In the four days he had spent on the road with Rose, she hadn't said one thing, hadn't given a single sign, that she and her brother had had anything to do with the attacks on the railroad.

Nor could Longarm see any legitimate reason for Clayton Abernathy to send hired gunmen after the stagecoach company, unless it was out of sheer spite directed at the children of his old enemy. That was possible, but it didn't ring true to Longarm.

There was something here he wasn't seeing.

His puzzlement deepened when Adam mentioned the attempt on Jessie's life the first night she had been in Rimfire.

He looked across the table at her. "Somebody hid in your hotel room and took a shot at you?"

"That's right, Mr. Parker."

"Maybe it was somebody who busted in there to rob you."

"I suppose that's possible . . . but nothing was disturbed."

"You got there before the varmint could steal anything."

"Nonsense." Adam slapped a hand down on the table. "The man was an assassin working for Abernathy."

"Why would Abernathy send a killer after Miss Starbuck?"

"To keep her from joining forces with me, of course. He's afraid that with her help, I'll be able to stop him from running us out of business."

Again, Longarm couldn't rule out that possibility, but he didn't completely buy it, either. Why would Abernathy bring the law into the mix if he'd hired assassins? It was true, though, that Jessie's unexpected arrival in Rimfire had upset what seemed to be a balance between Abernathy on one side and the Warfields on the other. That had to have something to do with the attempt on her life.

Despite all the hashing it back and forth, nothing was settled, of course. Too many questions still remained for that. When the meal was over, Longarm took his rifle and went back to the barn. He was eager to stretch out on that cot in the tack room and get some rest. He knew he could trust Jessie and Ki to get themselves back to the hotel safely.

He might have thought that nobody would dare try anything right here in town, but after hearing about the gunman hiding in Jessie's room, he knew that obviously wasn't true.

He snapped a lucifer to life on his thumbnail and lit the lantern hanging on a nail in the tack room. Deciding to wait until morning to wash up and shave, he stripped his shirt off and then sat down on the cot to take off his boots. He had done that when he suddenly heard a small noise in the barn. Most people wouldn't have noticed it at all, but his hearing was exceptionally keen.

In his stocking feet, Longarm stood up and moved to the door of the tack room. With a whisper of steel on leather, he drew his .44 from its holster. He blew out the lantern and then stood there, listening intently.

A moment later, he heard the noise again. It was a footstep. He was sure of that now. Someone was sneaking up on the tack room, and given everything that had happened lately, chances were it was somebody who didn't have his best interests in mind.

He jerked the door open and thrust the Colt out in front of him as he stepped into the darkened barn.

He was still moving when hands closed on his arm and hauled hard on it. A hip was thrust out, ramming into his thigh. He felt his feet leave the ground as he suddenly felt himself sailing into the air.

Reacting instantly, Longarm twisted in midair, reached out with his free hand, and clamped it around his assailant's arm. He heard a surprised yelp as he pulled the shadowy figure along with him. He landed hard on his back, the impact knocking most of the air out of his lungs, but he had already brought up a foot, planted it in the midsection of his opponent, and levered the figure up and over.

The throw was calculated. Longarm knew there was a pile of straw behind him where the person who'd grabbed him would land. He rolled over and hesitated just long enough to drag a breath of air into his lungs before he leaped and landed sprawling atop the lithe figure.

"And here I thought maybe you were getting slow and soft in your old age." Jessie sounded breathless, too.

"Not hardly."

Longarm brought his mouth down on hers.

Chapter 20

By the time Longarm and Jessie were sitting up side by side on the pile of straw a few minutes later, they had both caught their breath. They hadn't made love, but they had spent a very pleasurable interval kissing and getting reacquainted. Now they leaned against each other with the ease of longtime familiarity.

"All right, Custis, it's time for you to 'fess up. What are you doing here?"

"I could ask you the same question."

"No, you couldn't. You know why I'm here. Adam wrote to my father asking for help. Ki and I figured we'd see what we can do to deliver. That's what my father would have wanted."

Longarm didn't doubt that for a second. He hadn't known Alex Starbuck except by reputation . . . but that reputation was a sterling one.

"I'm working on a case. You were right about Billy Vail sending me here."

"Did Adam write to the Justice Department, too? He didn't mention anything about that."

"It wasn't Adam who asked Uncle Sam for help." Longarm paused. "It was Clayton Abernathy."

He felt Jessie's muscles go stiff. She sat there beside him without saying anything for a long moment, and during that time, she gradually pulled away so that the two of them weren't touching anymore.

Finally, she spoke in a hushed, strained tone.

"Abernathy? You're here working for that bastard Clayton Abernathy?"

"No, I'm here working for Billy Vail and the federal government." Longarm didn't bother trying to keep the irritation out of his voice. He had known Jessie for long enough that she shouldn't jump to such conclusions about him. "But Abernathy's the one who lodged the complaint about attacks and sabotage directed at his railroad."

"What attacks and sabotage?"

Quickly, Longarm explained things to her, starting with the destruction of supplies, the bombing of the trestle, then finally the murder of Phil Jefferson and the attack by the masked riders that had destroyed half the construction camp.

Jessie listened in silence and didn't interrupt him. When he was finished, she asked a question.

"You can't honestly believe that Adam and Rose Warfield have anything to do with all those terrible things, can you?"

"It don't matter all that much what I believe. Abernathy believes that they're responsible for his troubles, and that's what I was sent to find out."

"Sent to prove, you mean."

Longarm shook his head. "I'm here to get to the truth, whether it agrees with what some railroad baron thinks or not."

"Well, that's a relief. I thought for a second that you were going to—"

"Don't say it."

Jessie finished the sentence despite the warning. "Railroad the Warfields."

Longarm groaned. At the same time, he was relieved that the tension between him and Jessie had eased to the point that she could make a bad joke.

Jessie became more serious. "I've been here for a couple of days, Custis, and I can tell you, Adam Warfield doesn't have anything to do with those attacks on the railroad. I won't deny that he hates Abernathy, but he's not a killer."

"You sound mighty sure about that."

"I am. He's just not the type to do anything like that. Anyway, there's the practical side of it, too. Adam couldn't have done all those things by himself, and he doesn't have anybody to help him. He's had to let all the stagecoach company's employees go except for the men who take care of the way stations, and they're all old. They wouldn't run around with masks over their faces, shooting up a railroad camp and burning down half of it."

Longarm nodded slowly in the gloom of the barn. "I'm inclined to agree with you about that. He might've hired some gun wolves, though."

"With what? He doesn't have any money! He can barely keep the stage line going."

"Well, now that you mention it, that matches up pretty well with what I was thinkin'. Although I reckon Adam could be hidin' the fact that he's got money and making it seem like he's a lot poorer than he really is."

"Rose could be doing the same thing."

Longarm shook his head. "No, I don't think so. I've spent a heap of time with her the past few days, and she never slipped. I think she's tellin' the truth, as far as she knows it."

"And *I* think that Adam's telling the truth."

"You know I respect your opinion, Jessie, but you've been fooled a few times in the past, especially when the fella who did the foolin' was a big, good-lookin' galoot."

She pulled even farther away from him. "And I suppose *you've* never let a pretty face sway your opinion in the past? You've been right about every woman you've ever met?"

"Blast it, you know that's not true! Hell, you've probably fooled me a time or two yourself."

Jessie crossed her arms over her chest and smiled at him. "I'd say it was a lot more times than that, Custis. I always just figured that what you didn't know wouldn't hurt you."

Longarm felt irritation well up inside him again. Most of the time he and Jessie got along just fine, but every now and then, she liked to slip a burr under his saddle. She was good at it, too.

"So you think that Adam's innocent of going after Abernathy's railroad, and I think that Rose is in the clear. You know, it could be that we're both right."

"But in that case, who's attacking the railroad? Who has anything to gain by stopping that spur line except Adam and Rose?"

All Longarm could do was shake his head. "I don't know. That's what I've been puzzlin' over for days now. But how about this . . . Let's say that the varmints who have been causing trouble for the stage line work for Abernathy."

Jessie grunted. "I think that's a reasonable assumption."

"Abernathy believes that the Warfields are coming after him, so he goes after them."

Jessie leaned toward Longarm, suddenly interested in what he was saying. "So the real reason for the attacks on the railroad isn't to stop the spur line, but rather to prod Abernathy into attacking the stage line?" she asked.

Longarm nodded. "If that's true, then the real targets are Adam and Rose."

Jessie heaved a disappointed sigh. "Who have no real enemies other than Clayton Abernathy."

"That we know of."

"True, but I can vouch for the fact that they're well liked in the community, Custis. I haven't heard a bad word about them since I've been here in Rimfire. It's an interesting theory, but it still has a hole in it."

"Yeah, it seems like every theory I come up with has that same hole. This damn case is too simple. The War-fields on one side, and Abernathy on the other. The stage-coach versus the railroad."

"We all know who's going to win that one in the long run."

"Yeah, but the long run ain't my concern. My job is to find out who's been attacking the railroad and put a stop to it. The whole business of progress and the march of civilization . . . that'll just have to sort itself out."

"Well, I'm glad we got to talk about it, anyway . . . even if you do suspect Adam."

"And even if you suspect Rose."

Jessie laughed. "This doesn't happen very often, does it, Custis? The two of us being on different sides of an argument, I mean."

"No, it don't. And I don't like it, neither."

"Well, it doesn't change the important thing."

"What's that?"

She leaned over and kissed him on the cheek. "That I'm always glad to see you again, Custis Long." Longarm and Jessie agreed to keep it secret for the time being that they knew each other and that Longarm was a deputy U.S. marshal, and Longarm knew that Ki could be counted on to maintain that confidence, too.

Jessie's visit to the barn had given Longarm a lot to think about. It kept him awake for a while after she slipped out and returned to the hotel, but despite that, he didn't have any more answers the next morning than he'd had the night before.

He helped Adam get the horses ready for the next run to Laramie. Ki tucked a Winchester under his arm and went to the post office to pick up the outgoing mail pouch. Rose and Jessie prepared breakfast . . . although Longarm sensed that the process had involved a little tension between the two women. Everyone gathered in front of the office to see the stagecoach off.

After the two drummers climbed inside the coach and Longarm stowed away their sample cases in the boot, Adam and Ki climbed to the driver's box. Adam lifted the reins and took the brake off.

"We'll be back in four days."

Rose looked up at her brother. "Be careful, Adam."

"Don't worry about us. We can take care of ourselves, can't we, Ki?"

Ki just smiled, and Longarm knew he was playing at being the inscrutable Oriental again.

Adam slapped the reins against the horses' backs and got them moving. He lifted the broad-brimmed black hat he was wearing for the trip and waved farewell with it. Ki just swayed easily on the seat and didn't acknowledge that they were leaving the settlement.

Jessie stared after the departing stagecoach with a thoughtful expression on her face. "You know, I'll bet I could take a turn at driving the coach on one of the runs."

Rose shook her head. "You might be able to ride shotgun, but I don't think you could handle one of those teams."

"Why not? I grew up on a ranch and have been around

horses my whole life. I've driven buggies and buckboards and supply wagons plenty of times."

"That's not the same as a stagecoach. It's no Sunday afternoon drive in the park."

Longarm saw anger flash in Jessie's green eyes and knew that she had taken offense at Rose's comment, and with good reason. It had been pretty condescending. Jessie had never been the type for a Sunday afternoon *anything* in the park.

He decided that it might be best if he tried to head off trouble. "Why don't we go on back inside, ladies? Nothin' else we can do out here. In fact, short of takin' care of the stock that's left here, there ain't really any chores we need to do."

"I need to go over the books and see if we can squeeze out any extra cash." Rose surprised Longarm a little by looking at Jessie and saying, "Would you like to give me a hand with that? If you're buying a third of this stagecoach line, you ought to familiarize yourself with our records."

Jessie nodded. "I couldn't agree more." She glanced at Longarm. "What are you going to do, Mr. Parker?"

"Don't worry, I got somethin' in mind." He grinned. "I was thinkin' about a nice, long siesta. That is, if that's all right with my boss."

Jessie and Rose spoke at the exact same instant and said the same words.

"That's fine."

Then they looked at each other, both sets of eyes narrowing slightly. The truce between them held, but Longarm sensed that it had just been strained again.

Longarm was glad that he wasn't going to be spending much time here in Rimfire over the next couple of days. The last thing he wanted to do was get caught in the middle of a fight between two beautiful women, although he was aware that some hombres found that sort of thing downright intriguing.

He waited until Jessie and Rose had gone into the office, then he strolled out to the barn. The gray gelding he had rented in Laramie was in one of the stalls, looking fat and sassy. Longarm reached over the partition to pat the horse on the shoulder.

"I'll bet you'd like to get out on the trail and stretch your legs a mite."

"Where are you thinking about going, Custis?"

He turned his head to look over his shoulder and saw Jessie coming into the barn. He glanced past her to make sure that Rose wasn't with her.

"Don't worry, I told her I was stepping out back for a minute. I noticed you slipping out here to the barn and figured you might be planning to go somewhere."

"It's been several days since I was down at the railroad camp. Thought I might ought to check in with Fenton and Delahunt and see if there's been any more trouble."

"Who?"

"Earl Fenton's the construction boss, and Morgan Delahunt's the engineer in charge of the project."

Jessie nodded. "That's probably a good idea. Between the two of us, we can account for the whereabouts of both Rose and Adam over the past few days. If anything has happened at the railroad, we'll know that they're in the clear."

"At least personally. Either or both of 'em still could've hired somebody to make trouble for Abernathy."

"You don't really believe that, though, do you?"

"Nope, and neither do you."

"So you need to find some new lead."

Longarm scraped his thumbnail along his jawline as he frowned. "That's what I was thinkin', all right."

Jessie came up on her toes and pressed her lips quickly to his. "Good luck, Custis."

Longarm smiled. "You reckon you and Rose can get along while I'm gone?"

"Of course we can. We're a couple of grown, intelligent women." She paused. "But you'd better hurry back, as much as you can."

Chapter 21

Jessie agreed to keep Rose occupied while Longarm was gone and, if necessary, make excuses for his absence. With that worry off his mind, Longarm saddled the gray, led the horse out of the back of the barn, and rode away by a circuitous route so that Rose wouldn't see him leaving.

The railroad right-of-way had been graded all the way to Rimfire, then terminated in a lot on the western edge of town where a depot would be built. Construction wouldn't start on the building until the rails were closer. Right now the foundation was marked off, but that was all that had been done, Longarm saw as he rode by the place and began following the graded roadbed.

There was no way he could get lost with that trail of scraped, flattened earth to guide him. A few days earlier, end-of-track had been about twenty miles south of Rimfire. Longarm expected that by now it would be a mile or two closer.

Unless, of course, there had been more trouble.

He rode at a steady pace, and the gray did indeed seem to enjoy the chance to stretch its legs. The miles fell away behind Longarm. From time to time he glanced eastward, toward the stagecoach road, which had curved away from the right-of-way and was no longer in sight. He wondered how Ki and Adam were doing and hoped that they didn't run into any more ambushes.

Although if there was anyone Longarm trusted to be able to take care of himself in a fight, other than him, it was Ki. The man was hell on wheels when he got going.

Late in the morning, Longarm spotted smoke rising from the prairie ahead of him. From the looks of it, he could tell that it came from a locomotive. He supposed they were moving the work train up or back for some reason.

As he came closer, he began to be able to see the camp itself, a dark smudge spread out across the flat, sparsely grassed terrain. He supposed Delahunt had returned from Laramie with more supplies and tents to replace those lost in the raid several nights earlier. The camp looked as big as it had been before the masked men wreaked flaming destruction on it.

The smoke had stopped rising into the clear blue sky. Longarm's eyes narrowed as he saw another train behind the work train. The smoke could have come from it as it was arriving at the camp, he thought. The second train was shorter than the work train. It consisted of a locomotive, a coal tender, a single passenger car, and a caboose.

Longarm started to get a bad feeling as he looked at that train.

He wasn't going to turn around and leave after coming all this way. He rode on, hearing now the ring of steel on steel as workers swung hammers and drove in the spikes holding the rails to the ties. The sound of that labor was music to the ears of some men, nothing but cacophonous noise to others. It was the sound of civilization's inexorable advance.

Some of the men paused and waved as Longarm rode past. He returned the wave and continued toward the pair of trains stopped several hundred yards behind end-of-track. He looked for Fenton, thinking that he might spot the construction boss and find out if his hunch was right about that second train, but he didn't see the man anywhere.

When Longarm reached the caboose of the work train, he reined in and swung down from the saddle. He tied the reins to a grab iron on the side of the car and climbed to the rear platform. His knock on the door didn't bring an answer.

"I think Earl and Mr. Delahunt are back yonder talkin' to the big boss."

Longarm looked over and saw that one of the workers walking past the caboose had paused to call up to him. The man was pointing to the second train.

"The big boss?"

The man nodded. "That's what Earl said. Said Mr. Abernathy his own self was comin' out here to check on us, so everybody had better work hard and be on his best behavior."

Longarm bit back a curse. He'd wanted to talk to Fenton and Delahunt, not Clayton Abernathy. It would have been all right with him if he hadn't had to deal with old Buzzard Face again until he'd gotten to the bottom of everything and the case was over. Abernathy must not have understood that the rich fellas were supposed to stay back in the cities and leave the middle of nowhere to the working men.

He nodded to the railroad worker. "Much obliged for the information, pard." He supposed there was no point in postponing the inevitable.

But then something occurred to him, and he paused before climbing down from the platform.

"You know who I am?"

The workman nodded. "Sure. You're that lawman who was here last week when those masked bastards attacked the camp and burned down half of it."

"That's right. Has anything else like that happened while I was gone?"

"Trouble, you mean?" The man frowned and shook his head. "No, not really. Just a lot of hard work goin' on."

"Nobody's taken any potshots at the camp, or anything like that?"

"Not that I've heard about."

Longarm nodded. "Thanks, old son."

In a way, he wasn't too happy to hear that things had been peaceful at the railroad camp. If there had been more trouble, that fact wouldn't have cleared Adam and Rose of any wrongdoing, but it would have been one more indication that they weren't involved in the campaign against the railroad.

Longarm dropped back to the ground and left his horse tied where it was while he walked back along the second train. He figured Abernathy would be meeting with Fenton and Delahunt in the passenger car. As he passed beside the car and saw all the beautiful wood and the brilliantly polished brass and silver fittings, he knew it had to be Abernathy's private car, not a regular passenger car he had commandeered for the trip out here. Longarm would have bet a hat that it was just as fancy inside as it was outside.

Someone had put down a set of portable steps next to the rear platform. Probably a private porter that Abernathy had brought along, thought Longarm. He didn't think it likely that Abernathy would travel anywhere without bringing servants along.

That guess was confirmed when Longarm knocked on the door and a sober-faced gent in a dark suit opened it. "May I help you?"

"I'm lookin' for Fenton and Delahunt."

"Marshal Long!" The exclamation came from inside the car. "Bring the marshal in here, Felix."

The servant stepped aside and ushered Longarm into the car. "May I take your hat, sir?"

Longarm took off the snuff-brown Stetson but kept the fingers of his left hand clamped to the brim. "No, thanks, I'll hang on to it."

"Marshal Long." Clayton Abernathy came toward him, hand outstretched. The skinny fingers reminded Longarm a little of talons, but that might be because Abernathy looked so much like a buzzard, he thought. Longarm took Abernathy's hand. "I hope you're here to report that you've dealt with Adam Warfield and he's no longer a threat to this railroad."

Longarm didn't hold on to Abernathy's hand any longer than he had to. As he let go of it, he shook his head.

"No, sir, I'm afraid I haven't found out yet who's behind the attacks on this spur line."

The skin of Abernathy's high forehead wrinkled in a frown. "I told you back in Denver who's responsible for everything that's happened. Warfield is, damn it!"

"I'm afraid the law has to have proof, not just your word, Mr. Abernathy."

The railroad baron's face darkened with anger. "Now see here! I received word in Denver that the camp had been attacked and partially destroyed, so I came to see for myself. And now you tell me that you haven't arrested— or killed—Adam Warfield?"

"There's no proof he had anything to do with those things."

"He threatened me! And no one else has any reason to try to stop this spur line from going through!"

They were back to that again, the big rock wall that Longarm couldn't push down.

To gain a little time, he looked past Abernathy to Earl Fenton and Morgan Delahunt, who stood next to a small bar holding drinks. Both men looked like they would have rather been somewhere else, though. They gave Longarm uneasy nods of greeting.

The place was just as fancy as Longarm expected, with thick rugs on the floors, a heavy, opulent divan on one side and matching armchairs on the other, crystal lamps, and fover the windows thick silk curtains that at the moment were pulled back and tied with golden cords to let in light. A door at the far end of the room probably opened into sleeping quarters.

Longarm couldn't help but wonder where Danielle was. He supposed that Abernathy might have left her back in Denver. She would certainly be more comfortable there than out here in the middle of nowhere.

Abernathy was getting impatient. His mouth snapped like a beak as he spoke.

"Well, Marshal? What are you going to do about this?"

"I've been investigating." Longarm didn't tell the railroad baron that he had been in Rimfire and had in fact been to Laramie and back in the past few days. Abernathy might have a stroke if he heard that Longarm was actually working for Adam Warfield. "I came down here today to talk to Fenton and Delahunt and find out if there's been any more trouble while I was gone."

Delahunt set his untouched drink aside and stepped forward. "No, things have been peaceful enough, Marshal. We're still behind schedule because of all the earlier trouble, but we're making up ground on it. Slowly."

Longarm nodded. "I reckon that's good to hear. Maybe you won't have any more trouble."

Abernathy pointed a bony finger at him. "That doesn't excuse everything that happened before. Warfield still has to answer for that."

Speaking of stone walls, Longarm thought . . . Talking
to Abernathy about Adam Warfield was like beating your
head against one. Abernathy's hatred of Donald Warfield
was so virulent and long-standing that he was incapable
of believing anything except the worst about Donald's
son.

"Whoever raided this camp, I'm going to find them
and see to it that they pay for what they did." Longarm's
voice was flat and hard. He was running out of patience
with Abernathy. "The same thing goes for whoever murdered Phil Jefferson. They'll be brought to justice. But I'll
carry out my investigation the way I see fit, and I'll find
the truth . . . not necessarily what *you* think is the truth,
Mr. Abernathy, but what really happened."

Abernathy stared furiously at him for a long moment,
then sneered. "I don't care for your tone, Marshal. I'll be
sure to mention that when I talk to my friends in Washington."

"You go right ahead and do that. But by then, I reckon
I'll have gotten to the bottom of this mess. As long as Chief
Marshal Vail is satisfied with my work, then I reckon I am,
too."

"Perhaps I should also mention Chief Marshal Vail to
my friends. Frankly, the fact that he believes you to be his
best man makes me question *his* judgment, as well."

Longarm held a tight rein on his temper. Threatening
him was one thing. Threatening Billy Vail was a different
story altogether, and Longarm knew he was about a
whisker away from reading the riot act to this old vulture.

That was when the door to the rest of the car opened,
and Longarm heard a glad cry in a female voice.

"Custis!"

Danielle Abernathy hurried toward them, looking as
beautiful as ever in a dark green gown that clung to every
curve. Her thick red hair was put up in an elaborate ar-

rangement of curls, piled high on her head with ringlets hanging down around her ears, which also sported glittering gold earrings.

Longarm saw that Earl Fenton and Morgan Delahunt both watched Danielle as she went past them. He didn't blame them. Any man who wasn't blind would notice Danielle, and even a blind man might be intoxicated by whatever delicate scent that she was wearing. Her father stepped aside to let her pass—she was probably the only person in the world for whom Clayton Abernathy would step aside—and she put her arms around Longarm to give him a hug. Fenton and Delahunt both sighed in a mixture of resignation and jealousy.

They really would have been envious if they could have heard what Danielle whispered into Longarm's ear.

"Thank God you're here, Custis. I'm in desperate need of someone to make love to me!"

Chapter 22

Longarm stiffened, but probably not in the way that Danielle intended. He glanced at Abernathy, Fenton, and Delahunt. None of them appeared to have heard the provocative words Danielle whispered in his ear.

He disengaged himself from her embrace as gently as he could. "It's, uh, good to see you again, too, Miss Abernathy."

Mischief lurked in her eyes. "You didn't come all this way to see me, did you, Marshal?"

"No, ma'am . . . not that you wouldn't be worth it." Longarm nodded to Abernathy. "I'm still tryin' to locate the varmints responsible for the trouble your father's been having gettin' this railroad built."

"Oh." She made a little face of disappointment. "Then I suppose I shouldn't be flattered after all."

"What do you want, Danielle?" Abernathy's voice was sharp with irritation as he put the question to her. "We're discussing business here."

She turned to him. "I'm sorry, Father. I just heard voices and wanted to see who was here."

Longarm suspected that she had known good and well he was the one who had just entered the private car. She had probably seen him through one of the windows as he approached.

"Well, you've said hello to Marshal Long. Why don't you go on back to your quarters now and let us continue our discussion?"

Danielle pouted. "Oh, all right." She looked at Longarm again. "Are you going to be around here for a while, Marshal?"

"I don't rightly know just yet."

"Well, I hope you are. I'd like to talk to you again. You're such an interesting man."

She still liked to blatantly flirt with men in front of her father, Longarm noted. She either enjoyed getting on his nerves, or she just truly didn't give a damn. Longarm didn't know which and didn't suppose that it really mattered.

She wiggled her fingers at him as she left the room. Abernathy harrumphed as the door closed behind her.

"Now we can get back to business. Just how do you intend to proceed, Marshal?"

"I figure I'll keep pokin' at the hornets' nest until somethin' flies out."

Abernathy shook his head. "That's not good enough. Deal with Warfield now, Marshal, or I'll bring in people of my own who can handle this situation the way it should be handled."

"Hired guns, you mean?" Longarm didn't mention that Adam Warfield was convinced Abernathy had already resorted to that tactic.

"I mean men who can do what needs to be done!"

"The way you're talkin', Abernathy, you're gonna wind up on the wrong side of the law. You do that, and it's you I'll be arrestin'."

Longarm knew he shouldn't have said it, but he was

too angry to hold the words in. Back in Denver and now here, Abernathy had acted like he was nothing more than a hired hand, a flunky to boss around and carry out whatever orders Abernathy cared to give him. That rubbed Longarm the wrong way, and he had finally run out of patience.

Abernathy's face turned so red it looked like he was about to pop. "Get out!" He flung a bony hand at the door. "You're fired!"

Longarm shook his head and smiled grimly. "It don't work that way, mister. Once I'm on a case, the only one who can take me off is Billy Vail."

"What about the attorney general of the United States?"

Longarm's voice was a mocking drawl. "Get him out here, and I'll think about it."

Earl Fenton couldn't stand it anymore. He moved forward, getting between Longarm and Abernathy.

"Take it easy, Marshal. Maybe you and me ought to go have a talk and let things cool off."

"I'll be glad to talk to you, Fenton, but that won't change anything."

Fenton put a hand on Longarm's sleeve. "Let's go anyway."

For a second, Longarm thought about shrugging off Fenton's hand. He didn't like being hustled out of the private car this way.

But he had made his point with Abernathy, he supposed, and nothing more would be gained from prodding the man right now.

Actually, losing his temper like that hadn't been totally a matter of giving in to impulse. Some of it was calculated. That poking around he had mentioned included poking Abernathy himself. It was a strategy supported by Jessie Starbuck. The madder and more impatient Abernathy was, the more likely he was to do something that would give the game away, assuming that he was behind the attacks on the stagecoach company.

On the other hand, Longarm thought as he let Fenton and Delahunt steer him out of the private car, he couldn't forget that Abernathy had just threatened to bring in hired guns. Was the railroad baron devious enough to make a threat like that in order to conceal the fact that he had already taken that step?

Longarm didn't know. But he was leaning toward assuming that Abernathy was guilty until proven innocent.

He was guilty of being an ass, that was for damned sure.

Once they were outside, Fenton shook his head. "Man, you just don't know when to quit, do you, Long? You can't talk to Mr. Abernathy like that. Nobody can."

Longarm took out a cheroot and clamped his teeth on it. "Reckon I just did." He looked back and forth between the two men. "Now that we're out here where you fellas can speak freely, tell me . . . there really hasn't been any more trouble?"

Fenton shook his head, took off his hat, and scrubbed a hand wearily over his face. "No, there hasn't, and that's the truth. Tell the marshal what you told me when you got back from Laramie, though, Morgan."

Delahunt looked like he didn't want to answer, but after a moment he shrugged as if accepting the inevitable.

"The rumors I heard say that Mr. Abernathy maybe doesn't have the sort of, well, financial backing that he once had. Some of his associates don't like the fact that this spur line has been delayed. He's under some pressure to get it finished, and if he doesn't do that soon, he may not get a chance to."

Longarm managed not to stare, but he felt like it. What the engineer had just told him was the most damning piece of evidence yet against Adam Warfield. If Delahunt was right and the deal to build the spur line was really more fragile than it appeared to be, then it was possible the whole thing might collapse if Adam could delay it long enough.

Longarm wasn't sure how Adam could have found out about that, but it was possible. He didn't know all the sources of information Adam might have.

On the other side of the scale was the fact that Longarm liked Adam and didn't want to believe that he was capable of such chicanery. More importantly, Jessie liked and trusted Adam, and despite what Longarm had told her, he placed a great deal of faith in Jessie Starbuck's ability as a judge of character.

Add to that the fact that Adam seemed nearly broke, and it still seemed far-fetched to Longarm that he could have put together a gang of gun wolves to cause trouble for the railroad.

But he had to admit to himself that it wasn't as far-fetched as it had been a minute earlier.

"Hard to believe that Abernathy couldn't afford to finance this railroad his own self if he needed to."

Delahunt shrugged. "I'm not privy to Mr. Abernathy's financial dealings. I just work for the man."

Fenton nodded. "Same here. And as long as he keeps paying me, I'll keep working for him. I'm sure every other man here feels the same way."

"But if the wages stop coming . . ." Longarm waited to see what the construction boss would say.

"Then I reckon Mr. Abernathy wouldn't have a crew anymore."

And that would be the end of the railroad, thought Longarm. Interesting. Mighty interesting.

"Are you going back to Rimfire tonight?"

Longarm shook his head in response to Delahunt's question. "No, I reckon I'll hang around here for a day or two."

Adam and Ki wouldn't be back from Laramie for four days, and Longarm hoped Jessie and Rose would be safe enough in the settlement. Jessie was good at taking care of herself, and Longarm knew she would watch out for Rose, too, even if the two of them didn't get along all that well.

He wanted to be on hand if more trouble broke out. The way things had been going for the railroad, it was overdue. Just because Adam was off on that run to Laramie didn't mean that nothing would happen. If he had some hired guns working for him, having them attack while he was gone would be a good alibi.

"I'd steer clear of the boss while you're here, if I was you." Fenton's face was solemn as he dispensed that advice. "He was so mad at you, I thought for a second that he was gonna blow a gasket."

Delahunt nodded. "So did I." He started to turn back toward the caboose of the work train, then paused. "If there's anything we can do to help you, Marshal, please let us know. I'd hate to see this project collapse after it's come this far."

"I'll do that. I wouldn't care to see it happen, either." Longarm rubbed his jaw. "Reckon I'll take a ride around this afternoon, see if I can find any signs of anybody lurkin' around here."

Fenton pointed to the mess tent. "Better get yourself some lunch first."

Longarm grinned around the cheroot he still held in his teeth. "Now that sounds like a mighty fine idea."After he'd used his fourth biscuit to mop up the last of the stew in his bowl, Longarm dropped the bowl, spoon, and coffee cup in the dishpan and strolled out of the mess tent.

"There you are. I've been looking everywhere for you."

Longarm turned around and saw that Danielle Abernathy had come up behind him. She wasn't wearing a dress like she had been earlier. Instead, brown whipcord trousers hugged her calves and thighs and hips, and her breasts pushed out against a tan shirt with the top button unfastened. She wore a dark brown hat, and her hair fell loose around her shoulders now. Actually, in that getup she reminded him a little of Jessie, although her hair had more red in it and she was a few years younger.

"I was getting something to eat before I ride out and do some scoutin' around."

Danielle nodded. "I know. Morgan told me your plans."

Longarm had a feeling that Danielle could get Delahunt or just about any other male to tell her anything she wanted to hear.

"I'm going with you."

Longarm frowned in surprise. "I don't reckon that would be a very good idea."

"I think it would be an excellent idea. Do you know how boring it gets sitting in that fancy railroad car all day? I need to get out and get some fresh air and some exercise."

Longarm asked himself what she meant by that. Of course, she didn't necessarily mean anything by it.

But he wouldn't have bet a hat on that.

"I might run into trouble. Whoever's been attacking the railroad could still be lurkin' around these parts."

"I'm sure you'd protect me, Custis."

"I don't think your pa would like it very much, either."

Danielle made a face. "Do you think I really care what my father thinks?"

"I reckon you'd care if he took all your money and your pretty things away."

Longarm knew his answer was blunt. That was the way he'd intended it. He wanted to discourage Danielle from playing whatever game she had in mind.

But as he saw anger flashing like fire in her eyes, he knew his words had just backfired on him. All he had done was make her mad . . . and more determined than ever.

"I'm coming with you, Custis, and that's all there is to it."

He shook his head. "No, you ain't."

Her eyes narrowed ominously. "I'll scream. I . . . I'll say you tried to molest me."

"Go right ahead. Seein' as we're standin' right outside the mess tent in broad daylight, I ain't sure how many folks would believe you."

She glared at him for a moment longer, then blew her breath out in exasperation. "Oh!" With that, she turned and stalked off.

Longarm was glad to see her go for two reasons. For one thing, he wouldn't have to worry about keeping her safe while he was out trying to pick up the trail of those raiders.

And for another, the view as she stomped away in those tight pants was downright spectacular.

Chapter 23

The gray gelding had gotten some grain, water, and rest while Longarm was at the railroad camp, so the horse appeared to have its second wind as Longarm set out that afternoon. He knew he couldn't push the gray too hard after the ride down from Rimfire, but hopefully he wouldn't have to.

He planned to ride a wide circle around the camp. He had a hunch that the raiders were keeping an eye on the railroad's progress and just biding their time before they struck again. If he happened to run across their tracks, he might be able to follow them back to wherever they'd been holing up.

Setting off eastward from the camp, he soon found himself in sight of the rolling hills where he knew the stagecoach road ran. Ki and Adam were over there somewhere, although by now they were probably farther south than the area where he was looking.

The terrain here was still flat. A man could see a long way. As Longarm rode across the prairie, he felt the hair on the back of his neck prickle a little. He knew that by riding out here like this, he might be putting a target on his back. He was willing to take that chance, if it drew his quarry into the open.

He saw cattle and occasional tracks left by one or two riders, but he figured those for cowhands from the ranches in the vicinity. When he had come several miles from the railroad camp and was drawing near an area that was cut up by ridges and ravines, he turned back to the north.

A brief wink of sunlight on metal was all the warning he had, but it was enough. He leaned forward in the saddle and kicked the gray into a run as a bullet whipped through the air right behind his head. He glanced toward the nearest rocky ridge and saw another reflection. A slug kicked up dust to his right, falling a few yards short.

He had turned north right at the edge of rifle range, making the move deliberately. The men who were waiting up there to bushwhack him had been forced to take their shots earlier than they wanted to, and that had revealed their position.

Now, as from the corner of his eye Longarm saw several riders start down the slope, he knew his plan was working. All he had to do now was keep those varmints from killing him and get his hands on one of them so he could make the bastard talk.

Yeah. That was all. Simple as pie.

The gray tried gallantly, but as Longarm glanced back over his shoulder, he knew the gelding couldn't outrun their pursuers. The three horsebackers gained steadily. Longarm began to look for a place where he could fort up. He passed an old buffalo wallow, from the days when vast herds of the shaggy beasts had roamed these plains at certain times of year, but he didn't think it offered enough cover. Then he spotted a narrow creek with one bank higher than the other.

The drop-off was tall enough to shelter his horse. If the gray caught a bullet, Longarm would be in more trouble than he knew what to do with.

He reined the horse toward the creek, looking for a place where the bank had caved in. He found one, and that allowed him to get down to the level of the stream. The gray slid going down the steep slope but managed to keep its legs under it. When they reached the bottom, Longarm leaped out of the saddle and dragged the Winchester from its sheath. He worked the lever and threw a round into the chamber as he scrambled back up the slope a couple of feet and threw himself to the ground.

From here he could see the men galloping toward him. He knew that with luck, he might be able to kill all three of them before they realized what was going on.

Longarm didn't want that. He needed at least one of them alive, although he wouldn't mind if the fella was wounded.

First things first. He drew a bead on one of the men and pressed the rifle's trigger. The Winchester cracked wickedly as it kicked back against his shoulder.

The way the would-be killer flew backward out of his saddle as if he had just ridden into a low-hanging branch told Longarm that his shot had found its mark. He had aimed at the man's shirt pocket, so chances were the hombre wouldn't be getting back up again. Longarm had probably drilled him through the heart.

Longarm worked the rifle's lever and swung the barrel to the left. He fired again and saw the second man topple out of the saddle. That just left the third man, the man Longarm intended to take alive.

Where the hell was the third man?

Longarm bit back a curse as he saw that the third horse was riderless. Had the man fallen off? It was possible, Longarm supposed, given how fast the riders had been going. He raised up a little higher and swung his eyes from left to right and back again, tracking the barrel of the Winchester along with his gaze.

A sudden splashing to his left alerted Longarm. He twisted in that direction and saw that the third man had left his horse on purpose to try to flank Longarm. The man had made it to the creek on foot and dropped down from the bank to the stream. Now Longarm had just a split second to swing the Winchester around and trigger a shot before the revolver in the man's fist belched fire.

He didn't make it. The handgun roared just a whisker before Longarm's rifle. The big lawman was knocked back against the sloping bank by what felt like a giant fist punching him in the left side. The bullet's impact made the Winchester slip out of his fingers, too.

He still had his Colt, and he was reaching for the .44 in the crossdraw rig when his attacker lunged closer, thrusting the gun in his hand toward Longarm's face.

"Freeze, you son of a bitch! You touch that hogleg and I'll blow your brains out!"

The man's eyes, as cold and hard as flint, told Longarm that he meant the threat. Slowly, Longarm moved his hand away from the gun at his hip.

"That's better." The man's angular face twisted in a sneer. "You don't look like much now, mister. Take that gun out with your left hand, slow and easy."

Longarm tried to move his left arm. It refused the command.

"You shot me, remember? This arm ain't workin'."

"Make it work, or I'll just go ahead and kill you and be done with it."

Longarm gritted his teeth against the pain in his side and gradually forced his left arm to move. He grasped the Colt's butt and slid it awkwardly out of the holster.

"Now toss it over here."

Longarm pretended to be weaker than he really was as he threw the gun a few feet in front of him. He didn't want it completely out of reach.

"That's the best I can do, old son."

"All right. Don't try anything funny."

"Trust me. I ain't feelin' too humorous at the moment."

In the back of his mind, Longarm wondered why the gunman hadn't just gone ahead and shot him. The three of them had been trying hard enough to kill him a few minutes earlier.

The man answered that question without even knowing that Longarm had asked it. "I think I'm gonna keep you alive so the boss can talk to you. I got a hunch there are folks who'd like to know exactly how much you've found out about what's goin' on around here, lawman."

Longarm's lips drew back from his teeth in an expression that was half-grimace, half-grin. "I know the whole thing. I know who's been doin' what, and why. And so does my boss, because I sent him a report explainin' it all."

Longarm didn't know any such thing, but the gunman didn't know that. Longarm's hope was that by saying what he had, he would trick his captor into giving away something.

Even if that wasn't what happened, Longarm intended to maintain his confident pose. He wanted the gunman to take him to whoever was in charge. That would be the quickest way to discover that person's identity.

Of course, it would also be the most dangerous, since Longarm would then have to fight his way out of the enemy camp even though he was wounded, maybe seriously for all he knew, but he would eat those bites of the apple when he came to them.

The gunman sneered at him. "You're lyin'. You don't have any earthly idea what's goin' on around here, lawman.

And you won't until it's too late for you to do anything about it. Hell, it's already too late, because you're my prisoner." He jabbed the gun barrel at Longarm. "Now back away from that Colt."

Longarm hated to give up on getting his gun back, but for now that seemed to be the best course of action. He would pretend to be cooperating until he found out what he needed to know. He took a step back, then another . . .

A shot blasted somewhere close by.

Longarm halfway expected to feel the hammer blow of another bullet, but it was the lantern-jawed gunman who took a sudden step forward, eyes widening in surprise and pain. He tried to twist around, but whoever was behind him fired again, two more shots that slammed into the gunman's back at fairly close range. He took a couple of stumbling steps and opened his mouth as if he were about to say something.

Blood was the only thing that came out, a gout of crimson that dribbled down the man's chin and dripped onto his shirt.

He dropped his gun and pitched forward, landing face-down in the creek. The water turned pink as it flowed over his bloody, bullet-riddled back.

Longarm stared in wonder at the pale face of Danielle Abernathy, who stood there using both hands to grip a pistol. Smoke curled from the barrel of the gun. She was holding it so tightly that the barrel shook a little.

Danielle's eyes were wide and staring, as if she couldn't believe what she had just done. Sometimes in a situation like that, somebody who wasn't all that familiar with guns would panic and start pulling the trigger again, and they usually didn't stop until the weapon was empty. Longarm didn't want that to happen.

"Danielle." He kept his voice firm and level despite the

pain he was in. He didn't want to spook her. "Danielle, you need to point that gun at the ground now. That fella's dead. He can't hurt either of us now."

He might have friends who could, though, Longarm reminded himself. Only three men had come after him, but the other members of the gang could be nearby, and the shots might bring them to see what had happened, especially when the three men who had given chase didn't come back.

So he had to get through to Danielle as quickly as he could, and it was important that they get out of here before someone else showed up looking for them.

"Danielle, lower the gun. You don't need it. You're safe, and so am I."

For the moment, Longarm thought.

Danielle swallowed hard. A little color began to come back into her washed-out face. She looked at the dead man lying facedown in the creek, then she looked at the bloodstain on Longarm's shirt.

"You're hurt!"

"I don't think it's too bad." He didn't know that, but he wanted to sound reassuring. "More messy than anything else. We need to find a place where I can take a look at it, though, and try to patch it up."

Danielle nodded. "Of course."

"Where's your horse?"

"It's . . ." She looked confused for a few seconds, but then her thoughts cleared. "It's back up the creek about a hundred yards. I saw those men chasing you, and then I saw you shoot two of them. But this one . . ." She nodded toward the man in the creek and shuddered slightly. "This one ran around to get behind you, so *I* hurried to get behind him. I knew he was going to try to kill you."

Longarm chuckled, even though he was far from amused. "He gave it a good try. Thanks to you, he didn't succeed." He paused. "You saved my life, Danielle."

She smiled with a trace of her old confidence. "I hope you'll remember that the next time I ask you to let me come along with you."

"I don't have to let you. You'll just follow me anyway, like you did this time."

"Well . . . probably."

"You always carry a gun when you go out riding?"

"Of course. Father's told me what a dangerous place the West is."

Under the circumstances, Longarm sure as hell couldn't argue with that. So he opted for practicality instead.

"Help me get on my horse."

Danielle tucked the revolver behind her belt and hurried forward. She was looking more like herself with each passing second. She took Longarm's right arm and helped him over to the gray. He leaned on her as he put a foot in the stirrup and then swung up into the saddle.

"Hand me my Winchester."

She retrieved the rifle, which thankfully hadn't fallen in the creek, and handed it up to him. He slid it back into the saddle boot.

"Now get your horse."

Danielle hurried off along the creek to do so, and while she was gone, Longarm looked at the dead man and felt the bitter taste of disappointment rise into his mouth. He wouldn't be asking that bastard any questions about who he worked for, the big lawman thought. Or rather, he could ask whatever he wanted to, from now until doomsday, but a man with three bullet holes in his back wasn't going to answer.

Danielle came back riding the horse she had used to follow him from the railroad camp, a leggy black. Even in Longarm's pain-addled state, she looked good to him.

He lifted the reins. "Let's go."

"Where?"

"Away from here. Back to the railroad camp, I guess."

"All right. But my father's going to be upset with me when he finds out what I've done."

"Savin' my life, you mean?"

"Well, that and riding off by myself like I did."

Longarm figured she would be all right. Likely nobody could stay mad at Danielle for long, not even her own father.

They headed west, back toward the spur line.

They had gone maybe half a mile when Longarm passed out. He didn't feel himself hit the ground when he toppled from the saddle.

Chapter 24

Losing consciousness was easy. Climbing back up out of that black pit was hard work, and it hurt like hell.

Longarm didn't mind the pain too much. It meant he was still alive. The dead didn't hurt.

The dead don't dream, either, he thought. That meant he couldn't be dead, because he was sure dreaming. Under these circumstances, what else could it be but a dream?

He would have sworn he felt a pair of warm lips around his cock, and the wet heat of a tongue gliding around the head of that fleshy shaft.

He stirred and groaned, both from the pain in his side and the exquisite sensation of having his cock sucked and licked. As the lips tightened around the head, his manhood throbbed, and gradually the pleasure began to overwhelm the pain. He was able to forget about how much he was hurting and concentrate on how good it felt to have that done to him.

Red light played against his eyelids. When he forced his eyes open, he had to squint because he was facing the setting sun. His back was propped against something so that he was halfway sitting up. He was outside, he could tell that, and after a few moments he realized that he was leaning against a rock wall of some sort, probably sandstone.

Lowering his gaze, he saw Danielle's head bobbing above his groin as she continued pleasuring him with her lips and tongue. The garish light from the setting sun made her hair appear more red than ever.

Longarm groaned again, and this time the sound caused Danielle to lift her head from what she was doing.

"Custis, you're awake. I thought this might bring you back to life. Just sit there and rest. I'll make you feel better."

Longarm had felt a twinge of disappointment when her mouth lifted from his shaft, and he would have loved for her to go back to it.

But at the moment, there were more important considerations.

"Hold on . . . a minute. Where . . . are we?"

"At the end of a little draw I found where we could hide. It's deep enough that anyone riding by can't even see the horses."

Longarm thought about that. Now that his eyes had adjusted and he could see a little better, he could make out the walls of the draw in front of him as it twisted across the prairie. The horses stood a few yards away, cropping at some stunted grass growing on the bottom of the draw. This wasn't a bad place to hole up, he supposed, but if their enemies found them, there wouldn't be any place to run. Also, these draws were prone to flash floods if a thunderstorm came up. That didn't seem very likely, since the sky was clear except for some high, thin, wispy clouds that had turned orange in the glow from the setting sun.

"How bad . . . am I hurt?"

"Not too bad. At least I don't think so. The bullet tore a

big gash on your side but didn't penetrate. I cleaned it and tore up your shirt to make some bandages."

Now that she mentioned it, he realized that his torso was naked except for the bandages tied around it. When he moved his shoulders a little, he felt the sandstone scraping against bare skin.

"You just lost a lot of blood, and I guess that's what caused you to pass out. But I think you'll be all right."

He nodded in agreement with Danielle's assessment of his wound. It hurt like the devil but probably wasn't too serious, sort of like the crease Rose Warfield had gotten on her arm during that running fight a few days earlier.

"I appreciate you . . . takin' care of me like that."

Danielle smiled up at him. "I was glad to do it. I got a little worried about you, though, because you weren't regaining consciousness." She wrapped a soft palm around his still-hard cock and stroked up and down on it. "That's when I decided that you might need a little . . . stimulation. I must say, Custis, you responded pretty strongly for a man who was out cold."

Longarm chuckled. "I guess with some things, it don't matter much whether's a man's awake or not."

"But you're awake now."

"That I am."

"Which means you can fully enjoy what I'm about to do to you."

With that, she leaned over and closed her mouth around his shaft again. Her lips spread wide as she engulfed him, taking in more than she'd had in her mouth a few minutes earlier when he'd regained consciousness. Even so, she wasn't able to swallow even a fourth of the long, thick pole.

What she had in her mouth was enough. Longarm had to close his eyes again as waves of pure pleasure washed through him. He forgot all about being wounded.

Danielle closed one hand around his cock to steady it

as she sucked, while the other stole farther into his long underwear to cup and fondle the heavy sac at the base of his shaft. Longarm groaned for a third time as she lightly squeezed it.

"If you . . . want some of that . . . you'd better go ahead and . . . climb on!" He forced the words out between panting breaths as his arousal mounted.

Danielle lifted her head again. "No, just let me pleasure you!" She sounded a little breathless, too, as if what she was doing excited her, although not as much as it excited Longarm, of course.

He was excited enough that he felt his climax building as she went back to sucking and continued playing with his balls. He told himself that in his weakened state, it might not be a good idea to try to hold it back, so he relaxed and let her work him up to a frenzy. It was a frenzy inside, anyway, even if he wasn't moving around much.

His excitement reached its peak and culminated in a series of shuddering explosions that filled her mouth with spurt after spurt of his white-hot seed. Danielle swallowed urgently, taking what he gave her except for a couple of milky pearls that escaped from the corners of her mouth and ran down her chin. Longarm arched his back slightly to thrust his cock a little deeper into her mouth, but not deep enough to make her gag. She wrapped both hands around the shaft and milked every last drop from it.

Finally, with a last lick across the head, she was done. She smiled up at Longarm, the epitome of wanton beauty.

"Rest now. You need to regain some of your strength."

His eyelids drooped closed. He felt slumber stealing over him.

So he wasn't sure if he really heard Danielle's last murmured comment or only imagined it.

* * *

"Because you're going to need it . . ." For the second time in less than a week, Longarm found himself hiding out in the middle of nowhere with a beautiful woman. Just as with Rose, he and Danielle didn't have any food, but there was a canteen of water on each horse, so they wouldn't go thirsty. They didn't have any lap blankets from a stage-coach, so they huddled together for warmth that night.

This time, Longarm was the one who was wounded, so he had to be careful not to move around too much when he and Danielle inevitably made love. She didn't seem to mind doing most of the work. In fact, from the way she squirmed and yelped and threw her head back as she rode his iron-hard cock, she seemed to be enjoying herself just fine.

By the next morning, Longarm was plenty stiff and sore, but he felt considerably stronger. He thought he could ride, as long as they took it relatively slow and easy.

Danielle pouted when he told her that they needed to get started back to the railroad camp. "My father's just going to be angry with me for disappearing like that."

"Yeah, but you got to go back sometime. Postponing it's liable to just make things worse. Anyway, we don't have any food. If we stay out here, we'll starve."

"Couldn't you shoot some game?"

"Maybe. But the sound of the shot might draw the rest of that gang down on us. I'd rather not risk it."

"Well, then . . . we could live on love."

Longarm grinned. "It's a nice idea, but I don't reckon anybody's ever been able to actually make it work."

"Oh, all right." She sighed in exasperation. "We'll go back. You probably need better medical care than what I gave you, anyway."

"I don't see how anybody could've done any better than you did, darlin'."

Danielle got the saddles back on their horses. They mounted up and rode out, heading west. Longarm wasn't exactly sure where they were, but he had seen enough of the countryside around here so that he was able to orient himself after a while. He pointed out the direction they needed to go to reach the railroad camp.

Longarm's side hurt, even when they held the horses to an easy pace, so to keep his mind off of the pain, he started thinking back over everything that had happened since his arrival at the railroad camp the first time. He mentally replayed everything he had seen and heard, there and in Rimfire, because something was bothering him, even though he couldn't put his finger on what it was. He had suspected from the first that there was more to this affair than was obvious on the surface, and he was convinced that someone had said something that confirmed that. He just couldn't remember what it was.

Of one thing he was sure: he couldn't point to anybody who was mixed up in this case and say with 100 percent certainty that they were innocent, with the exceptions of himself, Jessie, and Ki. He hadn't been able to rule out anyone else.

Danielle's voice interrupted his musing. "I think I'm glad we're going back after all."

Longarm looked over at her. "Why's that?"

"Because I'm starving! I haven't had anything to eat since . . . since I can't remember when!"

Longarm smiled. "Yeah, my belly thinks my throat's been cut, too. But we'll be there soon."

Unfortunately, his scouting expedition of the day before had carried him quite a way from the railroad camp, and then fleeing from the gunmen who'd ambushed him had taken him ever farther. At the slow pace they were forced to use today, they didn't seem to be making much progress, and Longarm knew it would take most of the day to reach the camp.

There was nothing to be done about that except to keep moving.

By late afternoon, Longarm had spotted the camp up ahead. Just seeing it was a relief, because that way they knew they weren't completely lost. They pushed the horses a little faster. Longarm gritted his teeth against the pain and looked down to check the bandages tied around his torso. He didn't see any fresh bloodstains on them, which was always a good thing.

"I'm looking forward to eating, but that's all." Danielle sounded apprehensive. "My father's going to make life miserable for me."

"Maybe not. Maybe he'll be so glad to have you back safe and sound that he won't be too upset with you for ridin' off like that."

"I hope so. Still, I'm glad I did it, no matter what he says. If I hadn't been there, you might not have made it."

Longarm nodded. "That's sure true, and I'll put in a good word for you if you want."

"We'll see." She laughed. "He may disinherit me. Then I'll need someplace to stay."

Longarm didn't expect that to happen and said so.

The words were barely out of his mouth when he suddenly reined in and leaned forward in the saddle to listen. Danielle brought her horse to a stop, too, and looked over at him with a puzzled frown.

"What is it, Custis? What's wrong?"

"Listen."

Danielle did, and after a moment, a look of alarm appeared on her face. "Are those gunshots?"

Longarm nodded grimly. "I'm afraid so, and it sounds like they're comin' from the camp."

"Father's there!" Danielle might be afraid of Clayton Abernathy, but obviously she felt some sort of affection for him.

Longarm heeled his horse into motion again. "Come on." Painful or not, they would have to move faster now.

The horses responded, carrying them quickly toward the camp. In a few minutes they were close enough to see the work train and the private train that had brought Danielle and her father to end-of-track. Work seemed to have stopped for the moment. A lot of the men were gathered near Abernathy's private car.

Longarm didn't hear guns going off anymore, but he didn't know if that was a good sign or not.

Danielle was even more worried now. "Something must have happened to Father."

"We don't know that. Let's just see what we can find out."

Some of the men must have heard the approaching hoofbeats. They turned to stare toward Longarm and Danielle. With the young woman's long red hair flowing out behind her head in the wind, Longarm figured she would be instantly recognizable. Maybe nobody would take any shots at the riders, since the boss's daughter was one of them.

The group split as Longarm and Danielle rode up to it and reined in. Morgan Delahunt and Earl Fenton stepped through the gap, which closed again behind them. Delahunt held a pistol, and Fenton's revolver was in his fist, too.

"Marshal Long! You're just in time!" Delahunt sounded excited and triumphant. Blood dripped from a cut on the back of his right hand.

"In time for what?"

"We caught the man who's responsible for all the trouble around here. He and a confederate were about to plant a bomb that would have blown up Mr. Abernathy's private train."

Danielle leaned forward anxiously. "Is my father all right?"

Delahunt smiled up at her. "Don't worry, Miss Abernathy. He's not even here. He's gone on to Rimfire. So he wouldn't have been hurt even if those two men had succeeded in blowing up the train."

Longarm wanted to know more. "Where are these two mad bombers you nabbed, old son? What have you done with them?"

"Nothing but capture them, so far." Delahunt's voice took on a grim tone. "I think we'd all like to have a trial right here and now, though."

"There won't be any of that." Longarm's firm words left no room for argument, just in case anybody was thinking about an impromptu necktie party. "Let's have a look at them."

Delahunt nodded. "Of course." He turned to motion to the railroad workers gathered around. "Step back, men."

The crowd parted again, revealing two bruised and battered men who sat on the ground with their hands tied behind their backs. Longarm felt a shock of recognition go through him.

The prisoners were Ki and Adam Warfield.

Chapter 25

When they had started out from Rimfire, Ki hadn't known what to expect from Adam Warfield. After all, he barely knew the man.

Adam proved to be a pleasant enough companion. He talked about his experiences working on various stage lines, and Ki countered by mentioning some of the adventures he and Jessie had had while they were battling the Cartel and afterward.

Adam seemed to be especially interested in Jessie. "Tell me about her."

"What do you want to know?"

"Whatever you can think of. The things she likes to do, things about her past. I don't know, Ki. I just want to know more about her."

Ki smiled thinly. "Because you're attracted to her."

Adam shot a glance over at him. "Sorry. I don't mean to trespass on another man's range."

That brought a hearty laugh from Ki. Adam glared at him.

"Jessie Starbuck is no man's range, Adam. She's my friend, that's all. A close friend, to be sure. Very much like a sister to me. But that's all."

"Then you wouldn't mind if I, uh, paid court to her?"

"*That* would be entirely up to Jessie."

Adam nodded. "That's good to know. I'm not sure I ought to pursue it, though. After all, we're business partners now. Trying to make it anything else could mess things up."

"You always run that risk, all right."

"So tell me about her."

Ki thought for a moment. "She's the most courageous woman I've ever known, and as far as bravery and daring go, I've only met one man I'd consider her equal." He was thinking about Longarm, but of course he couldn't go into that, since Adam still believed the big lawman was just a drifter and shotgun guard named Custis Parker. "She's also very smart. Men tend to underestimate just how intelligent she really is, often to their everlasting dismay. She rides like a Comanche and she's probably the best rifle shot I've ever seen, but put her in a fancy gown and she's the belle of the ball, every bit as comfortable there as she would be out on the trail. Is that what you wanted to know?"

Adam let out a low whistle. "Sounds like a mighty impressive woman."

"She is. The most impressive I've ever known. It takes a strong man to match up with her. Anyone who's thinking about pursuing her needs to look inside himself and see if he measures up."

"I think you're right."

Adam didn't say anything else about Jessie as he piloted the stagecoach along the road. They had already passed safely through Fielder's Cut with no sign of an ambush at that bottleneck, but Ki didn't intend to relax his vigiliance. He held the rifle ready across his lap, and his dark eyes never stopped searching the landscape around them.

At midday they reached the way station run by Bert Moss. If the old-timer was surprised to see Ki riding along as shotgun guard, he gave no sign of it. At his age, he had probably seen just about everything there was to see.

"Any problems since we came through here the other day?"

Bert shook his head in response to Adam's question. "Nary a one. Been nice and quiet, just the way I like it."

They changed the teams, Ki, Adam, and the two drummers ate lunch, and then the stagecoach rolled on toward Horace Dunn's station, where they would spend the night.

They made good time during the afternoon and rolled up to Horace's station while the sun was still above the horizon. The mostly bald little stationkeeper came bustling out to meet them.

"Good to see you boys. The wolves were howlin' in the hills last night. Be good to have some company."

Adam climbed down from the seat, then opened the door for the two drummers to step out the coach. "What about gun wolves?" he asked Horace.

"Seen no sign of them, thank goodness."

Horace's cooking hadn't improved, but Ki wouldn't have expected that to happen in a couple of days. His coffee was as good as ever, though.

The five men were lingering at the table over cups of Arbuckle's when Ki heard horses outside. The sounds didn't come from the animals milling around in the corral, either. What he heard was the swift rataplan of a lot of horses moving fast.

Horace got to his feet. "Who the hell is that?" He moved toward the door.

A sudden instinct warned Ki. He started to his feet.

"Horace, don't—"

Ki was too late. Horace swung the door open as the hoofbeats thundered up outside. A different kind of thunder roared out of the night. Gun thunder, accompanied by muzzle flashes instead of lightning.

Horace cried out in pain and shock as bullets slammed into him and threw him backward. Crimson flowers already dotted his shirt and overalls in a dozen places where slugs had riddled him.

Horace wasn't the only target. The night riders continued their fusillade, throwing lead through the open door and shattering the windows with more bullets. The two drummers jumped to their feet in panic, then screamed as slugs pounded into them and knocked them sprawling onto the table.

Ki leaped over the table and crashed into Adam Warfield, bearing him to the floor. At the same time, a slug struck the lamp and shattered it, spraying flaming kerosene over the table and the floor.

Ki knew the fire would spread rapidly, fueled as it was by the kerosene, but it would be certain death to try to escape from the station. Those gunmen would cut them down in seconds. The only slim hope that he and Adam had was to put up enough of a fight that the raiders fled.

Remembering that he had leaned the Winchester in a corner, Ki scrambled across the room toward it, staying low. He called a warning over his shoulder to Adam, telling the man to stay down.

"The hell with that! I've got a six-gun, and I'm going to use it. Those bastards killed Horace and my passengers!"

Ki couldn't argue with that sentiment. He had seen brains leaking from the bullet-shattered skulls of both drummers, and Horace was shot to pieces. "Take the other window, then."

He found the rifle and levered a shell into the chamber.

After crawling to the window, he waited for the gunfire to pause, even for a second. When it did, Ki raised himself up quickly, thrust the Winchester's barrel through the broken window, and began cranking off rounds as fast as he could work the lever.

On the other side of the open door, Adam's Colt blasted again and again. In a night lit only by flames and muzzle flashes, it was hard to tell if their shots were doing any good, but Ki thought he saw a couple of the raiders topple from their saddles. Then a fresh volley from outside forced him to duck.

A blazing torch sailed in through the open door, then another and another. The men had come here tonight intending to burn out the station and equipped to do so. Breaking the lamp and scattering the kerosene was just a lucky break for them, speeding up the process.

Thick, acrid smoke already clogged the room and stung Ki's eyes and nose and throat. In a matter of moments, he and Adam wouldn't be able to stand it anymore. They would be forced to go out the door and die fighting, or stay in here and die from the smoke and flames.

"Ki! Ki, get to the back of the room!"

Ki fought down a cough. "Why?"

"Just do it!"

Ki didn't know what Adam had in mind, but staying where he was wasn't going to do any good. Using his instincts to guide him in the smoky darkness, he crawled rapidly toward the rear of the station.

Adam had gotten there first. "Here! Follow my voice!"

The floor suddenly wasn't there anymore under Ki's feet. He dropped a short distance and landed on a rocky surface. Adam's hand gripped his arm.

"This tunnel leads to the barn. My pa and I dug it when we built the station several years ago. There was still Indian trouble in these parts then, and Pa thought it might come in handy someday."

Adam's voice was hoarse and strained from the smoke, but his words were welcome. Ki knew they might have a chance after all.

Flaming debris fell down through opening beneath the trapdoor Adam had thrown back on the floor. The glare from the flames lighted their way as they hurried along the tunnel, which was shored up with thick beams. Ki estimated that they had gone about a hundred yards when they came to the end of the tunnel and a crude ladder leading up to a trapdoor in the barn.

Adam went up the ladder first, followed closely by Ki. When they were standing in the darkened barn, they paused to catch their breath.

"They don't know we're here, so we can take the bastards by surprise—"

Ki interrupted him. "No. There are too many of them, Adam. You heard all those shots. They came from at least a dozen guns."

"But they killed Horace! They're burning down the station!"

"I know, but letting them kill us won't change any of those things. If we can stay alive, though, maybe we can see to it later that they answer for what they've done."

Adam hesitated, clearly not liking Ki's suggestion, and when he finally answered, he was reluctant. "All right. But what are we going to do?"

"They don't know about that tunnel, do they?"

"No reason for them to. I don't imagine anybody knows about it except me, Rose, and Horace."

"Then they think that we're still in there. When they ride away, they'll be convinced that we're dead."

"And we can follow them."

"Exactly."

The shooting had stopped. The raiders were probably just sitting there on their horses watching in satisfaction as the station burned.

Then Ki heard a commotion outside. He stole over to the side wall of the barn and put his eye to a crack. The light from the burning station washed over the scene outside, a garish illumination that was like something out of hell or a nightmare.

Several men had tied their ropes to the corral fence. As Ki watched, they pulled the fence down and then stampeded the horses. The animals, already frantic from the smell of smoke, scattered into the night.

Adam was watching from another crack. "Damn it! We needed a couple of those horses."

"They probably won't go too far. We should be able to catch two of them."

"Now what are they— Son of a bitch! They're wrecking the stagecoach."

It was true. More of the raiders had tied their ropes to the brass rail around the roof of the coach. They dallied the lassos around their saddlehorns and backed their mounts away, slow but steady. The coach began to tip up onto the wheels on its left side. Then, with splintering crashes, those wheels broke and the coach fell onto its side. A couple of men dismounted and used axes they had brought with them to chop gaping holes in the body of the coach and then chop through both axles. The stagecoach would need a lot of work before it could be used again, if it could be salvaged at all.

Adam Warfield cursed in a low, bitter whisper as he watched the wanton destruction. "I'll kill Clayton Abernathy if it's the last thing I ever do!"

Ki didn't point out that the railroad baron might not be responsible for this atrocity. They had no proof one way or the other. However, that was something to worry about some other time. Right now, what mattered was survival.

Adam looked toward the burning station. "The mail pouch was in there. It's gone. The government will take away that contract for sure now."

"Maybe not. Losing it wasn't your fault."

"You don't reckon the government will care about that, do you?"

Adam was probably right, Ki thought. But again, it was something for later.

"As long as they don't burn down the barn, we'll have a chance to settle the score with them. Don't forget that."

"I won't. I won't ever forget that score."

Ki thought there was a good chance the raiders might set fire to the barn, in which case he and Adam would have to retreat into the tunnel again and hope that the smoke didn't choke them out.

But evidently the hooded men thought that destroying the station and the stagecoach and scattering the horses was enough for one night's work. They mounted up and rode out a short time later, when nothing was left standing of the station except the part of the walls made out of stone.

Ki and Adam waited in the barn until the fire had burned down to embers, just in case the raiders had left someone behind to keep an eye on the place and make sure no one had survived. When they ventured out, they had reloaded their guns and held the weapons ready, but no shots came searching for them out of the night.

Adam strode toward the wrecked stagecoach. "There's more ammunition in the boot under the driver's box. We'd better take all we can carry."

Ki agreed with that idea. He stuffed his pockets full of .44-40 cartridges.

"They're getting away from us," Adam said. "How are

we going to trail them at night? I can't even hear their horses anymore."

"That many men will leave a trail we can pick up easily enough in the morning. We'll have to wait until then to catch a couple of horses, anyway."

"I don't like the idea of waiting. Not after what those bastards did."

Ki put a hand on Adam's shoulder. "No, but there's one more thing we need to do in the morning before we set off after them."

"What's that?"

"Give Horace and those two drummers a decent burial."

Chapter 26

That was what they did the next morning as soon as gray predawn light filled the eastern sky. They had been able to snatch a few hours of sleep in the barn, taking turns standing guard.

Nothing remained of the unfortunate victims of the raid except charred bones, but Ki wrapped them carefully in old blankets he found in one of the stalls. He and Adam took the shovel that Horace had used to muck out stalls and took turns digging graves on a small hill behind what remained of the station.

Once Ki had lowered the blanket-wrapped bundles into the ground, Adam said a brief prayer and then began refilling the graves. After a while, Ki took the shovel and finished the grim chore.

By then the sun had begun to peep over the horizon. From the top of the hill, Ki's eyes searched the surrounding countryside. He spotted several of the horses grazing about a quarter of a mile away. As he had thought, once the animals were away from the flames and the smoke, they had calmed down, and they hadn't wandered far during the night.

Adam pointed out that the horses weren't necessarily fast. "They're draft animals, not saddle horses."

"We'll have to hope that they're fast enough for our purposes."

There were saddles and tack in the barn. Ki and Adam took bridles with them and walked out to where the horses were. Ki showed that he was an expert at handling them by approaching slowly, talking in a low, calm voice the whole time. He was able to slip the bridle he carried over the head of one of the horses. The animal started to spook, then decided against it and settled down. Ki led the horse back to Adam and turned it over to him. Then he took the other bridle from Adam and went back to get a mount of his own.

They led the horses to the barn and got saddles on them. The horses were accustomed to being hitched in a team, but not to being ridden. They didn't even like having the saddles on their backs at first. Ki worked with them for several minutes, gentling them.

"I swear, it's like they can understand what you're saying to them."

Ki smiled. "Perhaps they can. Strange are the ways of the Orient."

"Bullshit. You're just making fun of me again."

That brought a laugh from Ki. "Maybe a little."

It was good to break the somber air that hung over them, caused by the death of the three men and the destruction of the station. They might have a long ride and more danger in front of them, and they needed a touch of optimism, Ki thought.

Both men knew which direction the raiders had ridden off in the night before. They mounted up and searched out the tracks left behind by the horses. That wasn't too difficult. The hooded men hadn't been trying to hide their trail.

They must have been confident that there was no one left alive at the station to follow them, and they knew that by the time anyone else came along, the wind would have erased their tracks.

That confidence, bordering on arrogance, was their mistake, that and not knowing about the escape tunnel.

Ki took the lead, his experienced eyes following the trail easily, even when it crossed rocky stretches of ground. The tracks led east toward one of the ranges of low hills that dotted this broad, mostly flat valley. Those hills would probably have plenty of hiding places in them.

"What do we do if we find their hideout?"

"We can't take them on, just the two of us. We'll have to go back and get some help."

"Help? From who?"

Ki still didn't want to reveal Longarm's true identity, so he couldn't very well explain to Adam that he knew a certain deputy United States marshal who was hell on wheels in a fight. Not only that, but Longarm could probably round up a posse in Rimfire or, if necessary, ride back down to the main line of the railroad, tap into the telegraph wires, and send for the army.

Those hooded killers would be mighty surprised to have a company of cavalry show up on their doorstep, Ki thought with a faint smile.

He and Adam had eaten supper with Horace the night before, so they weren't starving as the morning wore on and they had no food. Ki was beginning to get hungry, though. He could probably bring down a jackrabbit or a prairie chicken with one of his *shuriken*, but they would have to eat the kill raw because he didn't want to risk the smoke from a cooking fire revealing that they were on the trail of the raiders.

When Ki suggested that, Adam shook his head. "I think I can stay hungry for a while longer."

The trail took them into the hills. Ki became more cautious, riding up draws and below ridgelines. He didn't know where the gang's hideout was, and he didn't want them to stumble right into the gunsights of some sentries.

Suddenly, he reined in and sniffed the air.

"What is it?"

"Wood smoke." Ki sniffed again. "And roasting meat. We're not far from their camp." He slid out of the saddle. "I'll go ahead on foot from here."

Adam started to dismount, too. "I'm coming with you."

Ki shook his head and held up a hand to forestall any protests. "Were you trained for years to move with less sound than the whisper of snow falling on cedars? Do you know how to blend in with your surroundings so that an enemy can look right at you and not know that you're there?"

"Well . . . no, I reckon not."

"Then stay here and hold the horses. I'll be back."

Before Adam could object again, Ki glided into some trees and disappeared. That was what it looked like to Adam, anyway. One second Ki was there; the next, he was gone.

Ki moved with speed and stealth through the growth, following the cooking smells. His path led him up a long, wooded slope. He began to hear men talking and laughing and knew he was close to the enemy camp.

At least, he assumed that the men were his enemies. He supposed it was possible that he could be sneaking up on some innocent line camp with several cowboys staying there.

His instincts told him that wasn't the case, even though he couldn't rule it out. The tingle at the back of his neck convinced him that he was closing in on the men who had attacked the way station and murdered Horace Dunn and the drummers.

The slope ended at a bench that jutted out from a tall granite cliff. The bench was wide enough that several cabins and a pole corral had been built there. At one time it had probably been the headquarters of a small ranch. Now it served as the hideout for a gang of killers. Ki was convinced of that. More than a dozen horses were in the corral. He was sure they were the animals that had left the tracks he and Adam had been following.

Smoke rose from the stone chimneys of both cabins. Men strolled back and forth between the buildings. Ki watched them from his hiding place in some brush. He hadn't gotten a look at the faces of any of the men who'd attacked the station, because they all wore hoods. He could see them now, and he knew by looking at the hard-planed, beard-stubbled features that these men were hired guns, the sort of ruthless mercenaries who could be found doing all sorts of dirty work all across the frontier.

A big, barrel-chested man in a black-and-white cowhide vest swaggered out onto the porch of one cabin, holding a coffee cup. He sipped from it, then called out to the other men.

"All right, gather round, you boys. The boss'll be here soon, and he'll tell us what we're gonna do next."

"We gonna break out the hoods again, Tully?"

The big man, who was evidently the ramrod of this gun crew, cursed and shook his head. "Damn it, Reese, you ain't got the sense God gave a doodlebug. We'll be wearin' the bandannas and dusters on this next job. One outfit for when we hit the stage line, the other one for when we go after the railroad."

In the brush, Ki's breath hissed between his teeth as the implications of what Tully had just said sunk in on his brain. Longarm had gone over the situation with him and Jessie and said that there appeared to be two different gangs operating in this area, one striking the Warfield stage line, the other plaguing Clayton Abernathy's spur line project.

But now Ki knew the truth. There was only one gang, attacking both operations.

The important questions now were: who were those killers working for, and what did that man hope to gain by setting Warfield and Abernathy against each other?

One of the outlaws called out a warning. "Somebody's comin'!"

They all looked toward the far end of the bench, where a trail emerged from the trees. A lone rider came into view.

"That'll be the boss," Tully informed the others.

Ki stayed right where he was, silent and motionless, eager to learn the identity of the mastermind behind whatever was going on here.

As the man came closer, Ki was disappointed to see that he wore a hood over his head, the same sort of covering that the gunmen had worn when they raided the way station the night before. But even though Ki couldn't see the man's face, he could tell a few things about him. He wore a brown suit and Stetson and was relatively small in stature. As he reined in and dismounted, his movements were those of a relatively young man. That ruled out Clayton Abernathy, who as far as Ki could see didn't have any motive for sabotaging his own railroad, anyway.

The hooded man handed his reins to one of the gunnies and climbed to the porch where Tully waited for him. Tully nodded a greeting.

"Howdy, Boss."

"Did you destroy that stage station?" The voice was muffled by the hood, but even so, Ki was relatively certain that he'd never heard it before.

"Burned it to the ground." Tully sounded proud. "Warfield was inside, too, along with his shotgun guard and the old codger who took care of the station. Couple of passengers, too, poor bastards."

The boss nodded. "Good. We don't really need Warfield alive anymore. The men I work for are getting impatient and want this brought to an end. You're going to wipe out the railroad camp tonight."

Tully frowned. "That won't be as easy as it sounds. Them railroad workers'll put up a fight. They're tough hombres."

"You'll be able to take them by surprise. They're going to be so shocked when Abernathy's private train blows up that they won't know what's going on until it's too late."

Tully's eyebrows went up in surprise. "That private train's gonna blow up?"

The hooded man nodded. "Let me handle that part of it. Just be close to the camp tonight, and when you hear the blast, come charging in as hard as you can. Kill everyone you see."

Tully thought it over and then shrugged. "All right. You're the boss. What about Abernathy? Is he gonna get blown up along with his train?"

The hooded man shook his head. "No, we need him alive, but this is our opportunity to strike. He's gone to Rimfire."

"Sounds good."

"The only loose end is that damned lawman. Did you find him and kill him like I told you to?"

Tully grimaced and shook his head. "He got away from us somehow, and killed three of my men, to boot. From the looks of the blood, he was hit, too, but he still got away. We searched for him most of the night but didn't find him."

A curse came from under the hood. "I don't think he knows anything, but I'd still feel better about it if he were

dead. If he shows up again, I may have to kill him myself."

"If we run into him, we'll fill him full of lead, Boss.
You can count on that."

"See that you do." The man turned and reached for
the reins. "Remember, wait for the explosion. Then hit
the camp, and hit it hard."

Ki's thoughts were whirling. While he didn't have all
the answers yet, he knew a lot more than he had a few
minutes earlier, so maybe Horace Dunn's death hadn't
been entirely in vain.

He was worried about Longarm, as well. This was the
first he'd heard about the big lawman being wounded.
Even though Longarm had gotten away from the men
who'd tried to kill him, it was possible that he had holed
up somewhere and died from his injuries.

Ki wasn't going to believe that until he saw the body
with his own eyes. If anyone was capable of beating the
odds and surviving, it was Longarm.

And the hooded man knew that Longarm was a deputy
U.S. marshal, Ki reminded himself. That let out everyone
in Rimfire. To the people in the settlement, Longarm was
just a drifter named Custis Parker.

All of it was mighty intriguing, but the rest of the answers would have to wait. Adam might not like it, but now
that Ki knew another attack on the railroad was scheduled
for tonight, including some sort of bombing, they needed
to warn the men there. Otherwise it might turn out to be a
massacre.

The hooded man mounted up, turned his horse, and
rode back to the trail leading through the trees. He was
out of sight in a matter of moments.

Ki began inching his way backward through the brush.
He had to be careful. After learning everything he had
learned, he didn't want to give away his presence here.

He had only made it a few yards when a flurry of shots suddenly blasted out somewhere behind him. As Ki's head jerked toward the sounds, he knew that the shots came from the area where he had left Adam Warfield with the horses.

Chapter 27

Ki couldn't afford stealth any longer. He leaped to his feet and took off at a run through the trees. A sudden shout behind him told him that one of the hired killers had spotted him. Guns banged, and bullets whipped through the branches around him.

Shots continued to come from in front of him, too. As he bounded down the slope, he pulled two *shuriken* from the pockets of his vest.

A moment later he came out into the open and saw that Adam had taken cover behind a tree about twenty yards away. Two men crouched behind boulders and threw lead at him. They had probably been patrolling the area around the hideout, Ki thought. Chunks of bark flew from the tree Adam was using for cover as the men continued firing at it.

Ki was between the two gunmen as he skidded to a stop. One of them must have caught a glimpse of him from the corner of an eye, because he yelled in alarm and twisted toward Ki, bringing his gun up.

With a flick of his right wrist, Ki sent the *shuriken* in that hand spinning through the air. Blood spurted as the razor-sharp throwing star buried itself in the man's neck. A choking, gurgling sound came from him as he fell backward without firing.

Ki threw the other *shuriken* toward the second man, but the gunny moved, ducking down just as the star reached him. He cried out in pain as it lodged in his cheek, just below his right eye, instead of in his throat. That caused him to rear up behind the boulder he'd been using for cover, and as he did, Adam's gun blasted. The gunman's head jerked as the slug bored through his brain and burst out the other side of his skull in a shower of blood and bone fragments.

The man collapsed and was dead when he hit the ground. Ki ran to both of the men and retrieved the throwing stars. He heard both shouting and gunshots from the pursuers who were coming down the hill after him.

"Adam, bring the horses! Now!"

Adam responded, quickly holstering his gun and running deeper into the trees to grab the reins and lead the two mounts out into the open. He and Ki mounted up and wheeled the horses around.

The horses broke into a gallop just as some of the gunmen from the hideout reached the bottom of the slope. They yelled curses and blazed away with their six-guns, but Ki and Adam were already moving too fast. Slugs whistled through the air around them, but none came too close for comfort. Ki led the way over a little ridge, and the hired killers were no longer visible behind them.

Ki knew it would take the men a few minutes to return to the hideout and get their horses. He and Adam could use that time to get a lead on the pursuit. They would need every break they could get.

Adam raised his voice to be heard over the pounding hoofbeats. "What the hell happened up there? Did you find the hideout?"

"I found it! And there's only one gang of hired killers, Adam, not two!"

Adam stared over at Ki for a second, but then he had to turn his eyes back to the rugged ground over which the horses galloped. That didn't stop him from expressing his disbelief.

"That's crazy! You're saying the same bunch attacked both the railroad and the stage line?"

"That's right. They dressed differently and hit both operations so you and Abernathy would blame each other for what was going on!"

Adam gave a stubborn shake of his head. "I don't believe it! Abernathy's responsible for the attacks on us!"

"That's not the way it sounded to me! And I saw the man the killers are working for!"

Adam stared again. "Who was it?"

Ki had to shake his head. "He wore a hood. I couldn't see his face."

A bitter curse came from Adam. "Then it could have been Abernathy."

"No! This man looked and sounded younger."

They rode in silence for a few moments. Ki glanced over his shoulder but didn't see any sign of pursuit yet.

He wasn't fooled by that. The hired guns were back there. He was sure of it.

They reached the edge of the hills and rode out onto the flatland. Ki headed due west. Adam raced along beside him.

"Where are we going?"

"The railroad camp!"

"Why the hell would we want to do that?"

"Because the gang plans to blow up Abernathy's private train and wipe out the camp tonight! We have to warn them!"

"Abernathy can go to hell! I don't care if he hired those

gunmen or not! He's still trying to ruin the stage line with his railroad!"

Ki couldn't dispute that, but there was nothing illegal about Abernathy building a spur line to Rimfire. At least, if there was, Jessie hadn't uncovered it yet, and Ki knew that if there was anything shady to find in Abernathy's operation, Jessie would find it.

"What about all the workers who'll be killed? They haven't done anything to you, Adam!"

"They're putting me out of business, damn it!"

"And for that you'd stand by and let them be killed?"

Adam grimaced. Ki knew that his words were having an effect. Adam Warfield was a decent man. He wouldn't want innocent people to be blown up or gunned down.

"All right! We'll warn them at the railroad camp! But you can't expect me to like helping Abernathy!"

Ki looked over his shoulder again and saw dust rising behind them. From the looks of it, quite a few riders were back there. The hired killers were giving chase, just as he'd expected.

But he and Adam had a substantial lead. If their horses didn't give out, there was a good chance they would reach the railroad tracks before the gunmen could overtake them.

If they had been mounted on regular saddle horses, it wouldn't have even been a race. These stagecoach horses were slower than regular mounts, though.

But they had plenty of strength and stamina. Ki could feel that in the muscles of the horse under him. The animal stretched out and ran easily, as if it could keep up that pace all day.

Still, the outlaws gained steadily. The cloud of dust behind Ki and Adam moved closer. Eventually, Ki could look back and make out the horses and riders themselves at the base of that dust cloud.

He called a question over to Adam. "Do you know how far we are from the railroad?"

"Mile, mile and a half, maybe."

The hired killers were no more than half a mile behind them now. It would be close.

A few minutes later, Ki spotted some dark shapes ahead of them, low on the horizon. As he and Adam galloped on, those shapes turned into a pair of trains, one parked on the tracks behind the other. That had to be the work train in front, with Clayton Abernathy's private train behind it.

Ki checked the pursuit again and saw spurts of powdersmoke from the raiders. The range was much too great for handguns to be effective, but the outlaws were banging away anyway, in sheer frustration. It would take a man with a keen eye and a rifle, preferably a Sharps Big Fifty or something like that, to hit them at this distance.

Evidently the raiders didn't have anyone like that, because the next time Ki looked back, he saw that they had slowed down. They knew their quarry had almost reached the railroad, and they didn't want to tip their hand unnecessarily. They couldn't be sure about how much Ki had heard while he was eavesdropping on the meeting between Tully and the hooded mastermind. It was possible that he didn't know about the planned explosion and raid.

If they still tried to carry the plan out, they would find out how wrong that notion was.

Adam, too, saw that the hired killers were turning back. He let out a whoop.

"They're giving up!"

Ki nodded. "Yes. Now all we have to do is find out who's going to plant that bomb. The man behind all this has to be someone who works for the railroad."

"How do you know that?"

Ki hesitated. It would probably be all right now to tell Adam about Longarm being a deputy U.S. marshal, but he didn't want to do that without knowing for sure that the lawman was all right with it. So he settled for giving Adam an answer that was also true.

"Only someone who's supposed to be there could get away with planting a bomb to blow up Abernathy's private train. A stranger would be noticed."

"Yeah, I guess you're right. So Abernathy's got a turn-coat working for him."

"It looks like it, yes."

"Being betrayed is nothing more than what he deserves. But I reckon he doesn't have getting blown up coming to him."

Ki could have made some snide comment about how generous it was of Adam to feel that way, but he didn't waste his breath.

They were close enough to the railroad camp now that some of the men had noticed them. The workers were wary of strangers, and with good reason, considering everything that had happened. Several of them walked out away from the trains to meet Ki and Adam. They all carried rifles.

"Hold it right there!" The shouted order came from a tall, brawny man when the two riders were about twenty feet away. "Who are you, and what do you want?"

Ki realized that most, if not all, of the men who worked building the railroad had never met the man they would be putting out of business. They didn't know who Adam was. Ki glanced over at Adam and hoped that the man could read the warning in his eyes.

Ki edged his horse forward and spoke before Adam could say anything. "We're looking for work. Would you gents happen to be hiring?"

"The Chinese may have built the Central Pacific, but they're not building this line, mister."

Ki swallowed the irritation he felt at being taken for

Chinese. It happened frequently, especially around railroads, since so many coolies had been imported from
China as tracklayers.

"I'm not Chinese, and neither is my friend here. We
could sure use some jobs, though."

The broad-shouldered man seemed to be thinking about
it. Finally he shrugged.

"Can you swing hammers?"

"Of course we can."

"Might give you a try, then. We can always use a few
more able-bodied men. Put your horses in the corral. We
can feed you supper, anyway, even if you don't get hired.
I'm Earl Fenton, the boss of this crew."

Ki nodded politely. "Much obliged, Mr. Fenton."

The men in the welcoming party had relaxed a little
and lowered their guns. Ki and Adam didn't look threatening. Adam wore a six-gun, but that wasn't unusual. Ki
didn't have any visible weapons. They didn't seem to be
looking for trouble.

Ki and Adam dismounted and led their horses toward
the corral. Adam spoke in a whisper that only Ki could
hear.

"What's the idea?"

"The man who gives the orders is here somewhere. I'm
hoping we can smoke him out."

"What about that fella Fenton?"

Ki shook his head. "Too big. The man I saw at the hideout was smaller."

"I thought you were worried about that bomb going
off."

"It's not supposed to until tonight."

"What if they move up the schedule because they're
afraid you found out their plans?"

"The boss was gone before any of the others saw me

and knew I might have overheard about the bomb. He'll be the one who's going to plant it, so what we need to do is keep an eye on Abernathy's train. Maybe we can catch him in the act."

"That's a lot of *mights* and *maybes*."

"Yes, but it's also our best chance of uncovering who's behind this. And isn't that what we want?"

One of Adam's hands clenched into a fist. "Yeah. We sure do."

They put their horses up, then walked along both trains, apparently idly. It was mid-afternoon by now, and a long time since either man had eaten. Ki put aside thoughts of hunger and concentrated instead on the task that had brought them here.

He didn't see anyone lurking suspiciously around the locomotive and the three cars that made up Clayton Abernathy's private train. They seemed empty at the moment. Ki recalled the hooded man saying that Abernathy had gone into Rimfire. He had probably taken his daughter with him.

Would the mastermind wait until dark to plant the bomb? It seemed likely, but the man might be confident enough to make his move before the sun went down.

"Hey, there! You two!"

The loud voice made them stop and turn. Earl Fenton, the construction boss, stood there, hands on hips.

"You said you were willin' to work for your supper, and I've got a chore for you. Come with me."

Ki glanced at the railroad cars. He hoped Fenton wouldn't take them somewhere that they couldn't keep an eye on the cars. If he and Adam were going to continue their ruse, though, they had to cooperate.

Fenton led them along the tracks to a pile of ties. "One of my men got hurt earlier today when a tie slipped and fell and busted his foot. So I'm a man short on this crew. I reckon the two of you ought to be able to take the place of one man."

"Each of you grab one end of a tie, haul it up there to where it goes, and hand it off to the gents who'll put it down in place. Then come back here and get another one. Got that?"

Ki and Adam understood, all right. They also understood that they wouldn't be able to watch Abernathy's train very well from way up here along the tracks.

Ki nodded anyway. "We can do that, Mr. Fenton."

"Good. Have at it."

They grabbed one of the long, heavy railroad ties and joined the procession of men carrying them forward. Adam spoke under his breath.

"This is getting more fouled up by the minute."

"Play along for a while. We'll figure out something."

They toted the heavy ties along the tracks for an hour or so, until both men were drenched with sweat and their muscles were aching. Ki watched Abernathy's train as best he could while they were doing that but didn't see anything suspicious. He wanted to get a better look around the train, though.

So as they picked up yet another tie from the pile, he whispered a warning to Adam. "Be ready, and play along."

Then he dropped his end of the tie on his foot.

Actually, it just looked like he did. With the speed he'd developed over years of martial arts training, he whipped his foot out from under the falling beam at the last second. It missed by no more than an inch and slammed into the ground. Ki let out a yell of pain.

"Get it off! Get it off my foot!"

Adam did a good job, wrapping his arms around the tie and heaving it up into the air with a grunt of effort, as if he were freeing Ki's foot. Ki fell to the ground, moaning and clutching the supposedly injured member.

"What the hell?" Fenton rushed up, drawn by the cries. When he saw Ki writhing on the ground and holding his foot, the construction boss yanked his hat off and slapped it disgustedly against his leg. "Damn it, not again! I thought after I warned you about what happened earlier, you'd be careful!"

Adam knelt beside Ki with a worried expression on his face. "He was careful, the blamed thing just slipped. I reckon it must've busted his foot."

"All right, all right." Fenton waved a brawny arm at the other men who had seized the excuse to take a breather. "The rest of you get back to work." He reached down and took hold of Ki's arm. "Get his other arm, and let's get him on his feet. Then you can take him back to the caboose and let Mr. Delahunt take a look at that foot."

"Who's Delahunt?"

"Chief engineer for the project. He can do some doctorin', too, though. He'll decide if it's broken."

Adam nodded. He and Fenton lifted Ki, who kept his right foot limp and yelped whenever it touched the ground. Adam was on that side. He draped Ki's right arm over his shoulders, then slipped his own left arm around Ki's waist.

"I can handle him, Mr. Fenton. Thanks."

"You sure?"

"Yeah. We'll go see Mr. Delahunt, like you said."

They started off down the tracks, Ki hopping a little and Adam holding him up.

"Pretty good acting." Adam's voice was so low no one but Ki could hear it.

"Thanks. When we get to the caboose, we'll slip over to the other side of the train where Fenton can't see us."

It was late in the afternoon by now. In less than an hour

it would be dark. Ki had a hunch that they would soon
know what they wanted to find out.

They reached the caboose. "Is Fenton looking?"

Adam twisted his head around to check. "No, I don't
even see him."

"Let's go, then."

Ki put his foot down and Adam let go of him. Together, they darted through the space between the caboose
of the work train and the cowcatcher on the locomotive of
the private train. They moved quickly along the private
train, Ki bending to look underneath the cars and see if
anything suspicious was there.

He stopped short as he came to the fancy car Clayton
Abernathy used for traveling. His voice was grim as he
spoke.

"Adam, look at this."

Adam bent over to join him. They peered at the car's
undercarriage. Tied to it with strong cord was a bundle of
at least a dozen sticks of dynamite. Their fuses had been
braided together into a longer fuse that ran along the bottom of the car, evidently all the way to the rear end.

Adam let out a low whistle. "That's enough dynamite
to blow this whole car to kingdom come, and probably the
coal tender, too."

"It would make a big explosion, all right. All the mastermind has to do is seize the right moment to light the
fuse. It's long enough that he could simply walk off then
and be well away before the dynamite goes off."

"What are you going to do?"

Whatever idea Ki might have come up with to thwart
the plan, he didn't get a chance to put it into effect, because at that moment a voice rang out behind them.

"What the hell are you two doing? Step away from
there!"

They straightened and turned slowly to see a man standing there pointing a pistol at them. He was short, well dressed, and had dark hair, and Ki recognized his voice.

The last time he had seen the man, there had been a hood over his head, hiding those handsome features.

Adam took a step forward. "You don't understand. There's a bomb under there."

The man's face hardened.

Ki smiled faintly. "He understands, all right. He's the one who put it there. Morgan Delahunt, right?"

He saw the man's reaction and knew that he had landed a twin blow. He knew who Delahunt was, and knew that he was guilty as well.

Delahunt's mouth twisted in a snarl. "You're that Starbuck bitch's servant. Did she send you out here to snoop around?" His eyes moved to Adam. "And by God, you're Warfield! You're supposed to be dead."

"And you're supposed to be building a railroad line, not trying to stop it," Ki said.

Delahunt laughed. "There's more going on here than you know about, mister. More than you ever will know about. Because I'm going to kill you and tell everybody that I caught you trying to blow up Mr. Abernathy's private car."

"What will you do then? Your plans for tonight will be ruined."

Again Delahunt looked surprised at what Ki knew. But after a second he shrugged. "I'll just put the dynamite back later. The plan can still go on."

Ki knew he was right. He also knew that he and Adam were only seconds from death. The workers were all at the other end of the camp. No one was paying any attention to what was going on back here.

The only thing that could save them now was speed.

As they turned away from the bomb, Ki had flexed his right forearm so that the throwing knife in his sleeve had

slid down into his hand. When he moved now, it was with
blinding swiftness. He leaped in the air and kicked Adam
in the hip, pulling the force of the blow so that it wouldn't
break bone but would knock Adam off his feet. At the
same time, his arm whipped out and the knife flew across
the space between him and Delahunt.

The crooked engineer fired at the same time, trigger-
ing two fast shots. The bullets sizzled through the space
between Ki and Adam.

The knife blade sliced across the back of Delahunt's
hand and made him cry out in pain as he dropped the gun.
Instantly, though, he bent and snatched it up with his left
hand. By then, Adam had landed on the ground and rolled
over, and he pulled the Colt from the holster on his hip.
Lying on his stomach, he opened fire on Delahunt.

Delahunt returned that fire as he threw himself between
the private car and the coal tender. He yelled for help.
Those shouts and the gunshots would bring Fenton and the
rest of the railroad workers on the run.

Ki knew that he and Adam were still in a very bad
spot. Fenton and the others would believe Delahunt. Their
only chance was to reach their horses and get away. They
needed to find Longarm and let him know what was really
going on.

Delahunt's shots forced them to retreat under the private car. There was no other cover anywhere nearby. Ki
glanced up at the dynamite, all too aware that a stray bullet might detonate it and blow both him and Adam into a
million pieces. There wouldn't be enough left of them to
bury.

But then Delahunt stopped shooting as running footsteps
pounded up. "I chased them under the car! They were trying to sabotage it, I think!"

"Pull the bastards out of there!" The angry roar came

from Fenton. "I knew there was somethin' about those two I didn't like!"

Adam still had bullets in his gun, but the men reaching for them now were innocent laborers, ignorant of Delahunt's scheming. With a curse, Adam threw down the gun, rather than commit murder. Strong hands grabbed him and Ki and dragged them out into the open.

Fenton bent and looked under the car, then recoiled as if he'd just found himself face-to-face with a rattlesnake.

"There's a damn bomb under here! Must be a dozen sticks of dynamite!"

That made the men back away swiftly. Somebody cursed.

"They were gonna blow us up! The sons o' bitches!"

Ki saw a fist coming at him. He tried to get his head out of the way, but men were holding him too tightly. The punch landed and rocked his head back. Another fist slammed into his belly.

Suddenly the railroad workers turned into an angry, frightened mob. They kicked and pummeled Ki and Adam. Ki tried to break free and fight back, but there were too many opponents for even his superior skill to do any good. He and Adam were beaten to the ground, and Ki knew that the men might stomp them to death.

"Hold it! Hold it, damn it!" Shots roared out, punctuating Fenton's bellowing voice. "There ain't gonna be any murder in my camp!"

The punches and the kicks gradually stopped, and the workers pulled back. Fenton ordered that Ki and Adam be tied up.

"Riders comin', Boss!"

Ki was a little groggy from the beating, but his brain still worked well enough for him to wonder who the newcomers were and what was going to happen now. He saw the group part, saw a couple of riders come up in the fading light, heard Delahunt talking to somebody, then a man's voice replying. He couldn't quite make out the words because his ears were ringing from all the blows to the head . . .

Then Ki heard the newcomer's voice quite clearly.

". . . mad bombers you nabbed, old son?"

And for the first time in several minutes, he felt a surge of hope.

Longarm was here.

Chapter 28

"Step away from those men!" Longarm's voice was clear, powerful, commanding.

Fenton looked confused. "But Marshal, they were about to blow up Mr. Abernathy's train."

Adam looked over at Ki. "Marshal? Why do they keep calling him marshal?"

Ki laughed in relief. "It's a long story, Adam."

Moving carefully because of his wounded side, Longarm swung down from the saddle and strode forward. His eyes were cold and hard, and his right hand was ready to reach for his gun. He gestured with his left toward the prisoners.

"Untie 'em. I know those fellas, and they never tried to blow up this train."

Fenton was stubbornly angry. "I tell you, there's a bomb tied to the undercarriage! Take a look for yourself if you don't believe me, Marshal."

"Oh, I believe you, old son. I just don't believe that Ki and Warfield put it there."

Ki spoke up. "That's because we didn't. Morgan Dela-hunt did."

Delahunt opened his mouth to protest, but the lie died aborning as he found himself staring down the barrel of Longarm's .44.

"I already had my suspicions about you, Delahunt, and I reckon Ki just confirmed 'em. Last time I was here, you said something about me bein' in Rimfire. How'd you know where I was unless you had spies there in town keepin' an eye on the Warfields? And why would you need spies unless you had somethin' to do with all the trouble around here?"

Delahunt swallowed hard. "That's insane. I work for Mr. Abernathy. For God's sake, I wouldn't blow up his private car!"

"You work for somebody, but I got a hunch it ain't Abernathy." Longarm's eyes narrowed. "You're probably the one who sent that bushwhacker into town to try to kill Jessie Starbuck, too. You didn't want her helpin' the War-fields, and you knew she might complicate things with Abernathy, too. You said he's gone to town. I'll bet he went to talk to her."

Fenton frowned at Delahunt. "Morgan, I'm not fol-lowin' half of this, but the marshal's right about one thing, now that I think about it. You knew he'd been in Rimfire. How'd that happen?"

"Earl, you can't possibly believe—"

Fenton's voice was hard now. "I believe I want some straight answers." He looked around at Ki and Adam. "Somebody untie those men!"

As several of the workers followed Fenton's orders, Delahunt began to back away. He looked angry now.

"I can't believe any of you would take the word of some Chinaman over mine! I'm a loyal employee of this rail line! I shouldn't have to answer anything—"

Ki was on his feet now, rubbing his wrists where he had been tied roughly. "I'm half-Japanese, not Chinese. And you've just started having questions thrown at you, Delahunt. Why don't you start by explaining what you were doing up in the hills this morning, meeting with the gang of hired hard cases who have been attacking both the railroad and the stage line?"

Delahunt looked sick, while a grin spread across Longarm's weary face. "That's it! There was only one bunch of gun wolves. The whole thing's startin' to fall into place now."

Fenton glared at Delahunt. "You said you were scoutin' the route ahead this mornin', even though I'd told you not to ride out alone anymore. Son of a bitch! I'm startin' to believe what these fellas are sayin', Morgan, even though I don't want to."

Delahunt returned the glare. He fumbled a pipe and a tobacco pouch out of his pocket and put the pipe in his mouth, clamping his teeth on it tightly.

"I won't forget the way you turned on me without any proof, Earl." Delahunt started backing away again. "I'm hurt, I'm really hurt that you don't trust—"

He had taken a handful of lucifers from a pocket on the side of the pouch. Longarm's eyes widened as he realized what Delahunt was about to do.

"Grab the little bastard!"

Fenton reached for Delahunt, but the smaller man twisted away lithely. He snapped one of the matches alight with a thumbnail, and that ignited the others. With a lunge toward the private car, Delahunt threw the blazing lucifers at the bundle of dynamite.

Men yelled and scattered frantically.

As a diversion, it wasn't bad. Adam didn't panic, though. He launched himself in a diving tackle that drove Delahunt off his feet. Adam's big fist slammed down twice into Delahunt's face.

Meanwhile, Ki rolled under the car and looked up to see that while the burning matches hadn't hit the dynamite, they had ignited the fuse. It was sputtering and sizzling, only inches from the greasy red cylinders of death.

Calmly, Ki reached up and pinched out the fuse before it could ignite the dynamite.

By the time he climbed out from under the private car, Adam had a groggy, bloody Morgan Delahunt on his feet again, and Longarm was standing by with Fenton and a beautiful, pale-faced young woman with auburn hair.

She licked her lips nervously. "It almost blew up, didn't it?"

Longarm looked at Ki, who shrugged. "Almost doesn't really count, does it?"

Fenton looked at Delahunt and shook his head with a sigh that mingled anger and sadness. "I don't get it. If he's the head of the bunch that's been attackin' both the railroad and the stage line, then who's he really workin' for?"

Longarm fastened a hand on Delahunt's collar and jerked him toward the steps that led up into the private car. "That's what we're gonna find out." He paused. "Well . . . as soon as somebody gets that dynamite out from under there, I reckon. I'd feel a mite better with it gone."

Jessie saw the lights of the railroad camp up ahead in the twilight as she rode the buckskin alongside the horse that carried Clayton Abernathy. She had been mighty surprised when he showed up in Rimfire that afternoon on horseback, but as he'd explained to her, he had grown up on a farm and had ridden a great deal as a boy and a young man. It was something you never really forgot.

Seeing the buzzardlike Abernathy on a horse was just the first surprise. The second had come when he dismounted in front of the stagecoach company office, smiled at her, and actually asked for her help.

"I was surprised to hear that you were here in Rimfire, Miss Starbuck. I hope you came because you heard about my railroad line and realized this area is about to boom even more than it already is. You could do worse than invest here."

"I have invested." Jessie gestured at the sign over her head. "I'm part-owner of the Rimfire Stagecoach Company."

Abernathy's expression fell. "I was hoping that I could convince you to invest in the spur line."

Jessie took a deep, surprised breath. "You want me to partner up with you, Abernathy?" She wasn't trying to be polite anymore. The two of them had clashed in the past, and she wasn't going to pretend to be friendly.

"I'll be honest with you," he said.

"That would be a good idea."

"All the delays in completing the line have strained my finances. I may be forced to sell the entire thing at a loss . . . unless I can find someone willing to invest."

Jessie frowned. The keen business sense she had developed over the years was trying to tell her something. Longarm had told her that he hadn't been able to uncover any other suspects in the case. It appeared that no one had anything to gain by attacking the railroad except Adam and Rose Warfield.

But what Abernathy had just revealed indicated that someone else could have a motive for the attacks. Someone who wanted to make completing the spur line so difficult for Abernathy that he would be forced to sell out cheaply . . .

She needed to know more, and the best way to find out what she needed to know was to play along with the railroad baron for the time being.

"All right, I admit that I'm intrigued. Why don't I ride back out to the railroad camp with you and have a look at the operation?"

A look of relief appeared on Abernathy's face. "That would be excellent."

Rose must have been eavesdropping in the office, because she stepped out on the porch then with a furious glare on her face.

"Jessie! You . . . you're not actually going to throw in with this . . . this vulture, are you?"

Jessie turned to her. "I know what I'm doing, Rose. I know I agreed to help you and Adam, but, well, sometimes things change."

She didn't like upsetting Rose like this, but she wanted Abernathy to believe that she'd possibly had a change of heart.

"If you feel that way, maybe you'd better just get the hell out."

"We'll talk about later." Jessie came down the steps from the porch.

"There's nothing to talk about. When Adam gets back from Laramie and hears what a turncoat you are, you won't be welcome here any longer. We'll find some way to pay you for your share of the company."

Jessie shook her head. "The money hasn't actually changed hands yet. We just came to an agreement, that's all. So there's really nothing to pay back."

Rose just sniffed and went back inside. Jessie turned to Abernathy.

"Let me get my horse."

They hadn't reached end-of-track by dusk, but there was still enough light in the sky to let them follow the graded roadbed. And then when the lights of the camp came into view, they had those to guide them, too.

"You'll spend the night in my private car, of course. The accommodations are very comfortable. We can discuss the entire operation."

Abernathy's voice sounded strained, and Jessie got the sense that there was something he hadn't told her yet.

"What's wrong?"

Abernathy hesitated, and for a moment Jessie thought he wasn't going to answer. Then he sighed.

"My daughter Danielle is missing. No one has seen her since yesterday, and one of the saddle horses is gone. She must have ridden out for some reason, and I . . . I'm afraid something has happened to her."

Jessie heard genuine pain and fear in Abernathy's voice. She told herself that she shouldn't be surprised—the man was human, after all, and of course he loved his daughter—but she was used to thinking of him as nothing more than a cold, calculating business machine.

She was able to muster up a little sympathy for him. "I'm sure she's all right. She may have even turned up today while you were in Rimfire."

Abernathy sighed. "I hope so. It hasn't been easy raising her alone, you know. Her mother passed away when Danielle was quite young."

Sympathetic or not, Jessie didn't want to hear his life story. She changed the subject.

"We should be getting to the camp soon—"

The sound of shots drifted faintly through the night air, causing Jessie to stop short in what she was saying.

Abernathy heard it, too. "Good Lord! Is that gunfire?"

"It sure is. Come on!"

She leaned forward in the saddle and heeled the buckskin into a run. She had no idea what sort of trouble was going on up there, but whatever it was, she wanted to be in on it. A glance over her shoulder told her that Abernathy was following her, although the railroad baron was having to struggle to try to keep up. He bounced uncomfortably in the saddle.

Even at a gallop, it took several minutes for them to reach the railroad camp, and by the time they did, the shooting had stopped. A lot of men were gathered around the private car of Abernathy's train. A tall man stood on the steps leading up to the rear platform, and as Jessie rode closer, she felt a jolt of recognition go through her.

Longarm!

He raised a hand in greeting as she and Abernathy rode up, the crowd parting to let them through. He was wounded, bare from the waist up except for bandages wrapped around his torso, but he didn't seem to be badly injured.

Jessie felt an even greater shock as she recognized Ki and Adam, who were about to go up the steps to join Longarm on the platform. Adam had hold of a smaller man who was bruised and bloody from a beating. Ki and Adam looked pretty banged up themselves.

"Howdy, Jessie." Longarm's drawl held a hint of amusement. "I'll bet you're wonderin' what's goin' on here."

She stared at him. "You're right about that, Custis."

He motioned for her to join him. "Well, come on in, you and Abernathy both. We're about to find out."

Chapter 29

"I don't know who they are. I have my suspicions, but I was always paid in cash, through intermediaries. I was told to keep my identity a secret from the men I hired to carry out the plan. I suppose the men behind it didn't want any sort of trail leading back to them."

Morgan Delahunt's voice was dull and full of despair as he sat in a straight-backed chair in the middle of the opulent sitting room in Clayton Abernathy's private car. Around him were Longarm, Jessie, Ki, Adam Warfield, Earl Fenton, Danielle Abernathy, and her father, who had been tremendously relieved to see her. They hadn't really had to do much in the way of questioning Delahunt. The engineer was eager to spill his guts, now that his villainy had been revealed.

"The whole idea was to take advantage of the rivalry between the Warfields and Mr. Abernathy and keep things stirred up between them. My bosses didn't really care about the stage line, but they wanted somebody to blame for everything that slowed down the railroad. That way Mr. Abernathy would never suspect that they were behind it."

"The treacherous bastards." The words hissed a little with hatred as they leaked out between Abernathy's clenched teeth. "I have a pretty good idea who hired you to betray me, Delahunt. My so-called partners!"

Jessie nodded. "I said all along that so-called Railroad Ring was a mistake, Abernathy. The members have already started to turn on each other."

"The mistake was in thinking that they could get away with this. I'll find out exactly who's responsible, and they'll regret it. I'll see to that."

Longarm didn't care about the members of the Railroad Ring turning on each other. They could consume each other like a snake swallowing its own tail as far as he was concerned. What he cared about at the moment, he thought, was that there was still a gang of ruthless killers out there in the night that had fallen while they were questioning Delahunt.

Abernathy glared at the engineer. "You've worked for me before, Delahunt. What made you turn on me now? Was it just the money?"

"*Just* the money?" Delahunt laughed. "They offered me twice as much as I've made on all your other projects combined. I was promised a good job with them, too. They appreciate my skill as an engineer."

Longarm doubted that. As ruthless as the members of the Railroad Ring were, he suspected that if Delahunt had succeeded in his assignment, sooner or later he would have wound up dead in some sort of "accident," just to be sure he couldn't ever implicate his true employers. Railroading was dangerous work. An accident like that wouldn't be hard to arrange.

Longarm raised his concern. "Accordin' to what Ki told us, those killers are out there waiting for an explosion as the signal to attack the camp. I think we should give 'em what they're waitin' for."

The others looked at him, puzzled by the statement. But after a moment, Jessie nodded.

"They're still a threat, and we need to deal with them."

Longarm nodded. "Yep, that's the way I see it."

"How do we do that?"

Longarm tugged on his earlobe, then scraped his thumbnail down the rugged line of his jaw. "If they see a big explosion in the dark, they won't be able to tell exactly where it came from. I think we should take that dynamite out a ways from the train and set it off."

"And the blast will signal the gang to attack." Ki nodded. "Only when they do, we'll have well-armed men in both trains waiting for them. A good plan, Marshal."

Adam looked at Longarm. "I still can't get over the fact that you're a lawman. You lied to us, Parker. I mean . . . What is your name, anyway?"

"Custis Long. And I'm sorry about pullin' the wool over your eyes, Adam, and Rose's, too. But I thought that would give me the best chance of findin' out what was really goin' on around here."

Adam shrugged. "I don't suppose I can argue with the results. And for what it's worth, I think your plan is a good one, too."

"Let's get to it, then. Fenton, you're in charge of passin' out guns to your men and getting them in the trains. Think you can handle that?"

The construction boss nodded. "Damn right I can, Marshal." He looked at Jessie and Danielle. "Beggin' your pardon for my language, ladies."

Jessie smiled. "Don't worry about that, Mr. Fenton. Just get a nice warm reception ready for those hired guns."

"Yes, ma'am! It'll be downright hot." Longarm crouched in the darkness next to the end of the fuse. The bundle of dynamite was about a hundred yards west of the tracks, lined up with where Clayton Abernathy's train was parked behind the work train. If the killers were out there listening, and Longarm was convinced they were, they wouldn't be able to tell that the blast hadn't destroyed the train.

Ki had re-rigged the fuse so that it was shorter and then had offered to light it himself, but Longarm claimed that chore. The wound in his side had been cleaned and re-bandaged, and Earl Fenton had loaned him a shirt. He felt pretty good, considering all he had been through. Now there was just one more job to take care of . . .

He had lit a cheroot before walking out here from the train. He puffed on it now to get the coal at the end glowing orange, and when he was satisfied it was hot enough, he took it out of his mouth and held it to the end of the fuse. Sparks jumped in the air as the fuse caught and began to burn.

Longarm stood up, turned, and ran toward the train.

Ki had done a good job on the fuse. Longarm had just bounded up the steps to the rear platform of Abernathy's private car when the dynamite went up with a huge blast that shook the earth. Longarm felt the vibration in his feet as he turned to look at the ball of fire lighting up the night. It lasted only for a second.

Ki had placed the dynamite in a cleared area so the explosion couldn't throw any debris around. Even so, dirt and gravel pelted the train cars and forced Longarm to duck inside. He picked up a rifle that was waiting for him and joined Jessie, Ki, Adam, and Fenton at the open windows. All the lights in both trains had been extinguished so that the hired guns wouldn't be able to see that they were still intact. The cars of both trains were packed with railroad workers armed with rifles and six-guns. All they had to do now was wait for the gang to come charging in.

They didn't have to wait long, either. As the echoes from the blast rolled away over the Wyoming plains, the rumble of hoofbeats took its place. The gang of killers must have been fairly close by. They swept in, guns blazing, ready to wipe out the railroad workers and put an end to Clayton Abernathy's goal of building a spur line to Rimfire.

Instead, the men in the railroad cars waited patiently as the muzzle flashes came closer like a swarm of deadly fireflies. They held their fire until Longarm squeezed off the first shot, which would be the signal to open the ball. Longarm knelt by one of the windows in Abernathy's private car, cheek nestled against the smooth stock of a Winchester. A little closer, a little closer . . .

His finger took up the slack on the trigger, and the rifle cracked as it kicked back against his shoulder. An instant later, all along the line of both trains, flame jetted from the barrels of the rifles and pistols that were thrust through the open windows. Men who lay atop the piles of coal in the tenders opened fire as well, as did men who crouched inside the cabs of the two locomotives. A brutal death storm of lead swept across the prairie, mowing down the outlaws and their horses like they were so much wheat before the scythe.

Then, with angry shouts, the railroad workers poured from the trains to finish the job, anywhere it needed finishing. Billy Vail might not be too happy with him for orchestrating a slaughter like this, Longarm thought as he stepped out onto the car's rear platform, but when a deputy was out in the field, he had to do what he thought was best. He had eliminated any further threat from those gun wolves, that was for sure.

Clayton Abernathy stepped out onto the platform with Longarm. "I've ordered my crew to get steam up, Marshal. I'm going back to Laramie tonight."

Longarm frowned. "You're in that big a hurry?"

"I'm going to be there to start sending wires first thing

in the morning. If those other bastards in the Ring want war, then it's war I'll give them. This was just the opening move."

"Well, better you fightin' that war than me. I'm done with this job."

Abernathy smiled. "Marshal, from now on, the war will be fought at much higher levels than the one you occupy."

That comment didn't really surprise Longarm. Abernathy might not have been to blame for the attacks on the stage-coach company, but Longarm still didn't like him. Not one little bit.

Jessie came out onto the platform, too. Abernathy turned to her, still wearing an oily smile. "Miss Starbuck, I'd still like to persuade you to join forces with me, as we discussed earlier."

"You discussed that, Abernathy. I still don't want any part of you or your Railroad Ring."

Abernathy's expression tightened with anger. "I hope you don't have reason to regret feeling like that someday, Miss Starbuck."

"Try to rope me into your mess, and you'll be the one with regrets."

Abernathy didn't say anything else. He went to order his train crew to get ready to travel. Longarm and Jessie stood side by side on the platform, holding the iron railing that ran around it.

"Seems like fate keeps pulling us back together, Custis."

"I ain't one to argue with fate."

"The only problem is that Rose Warfield is a mite sweet on you herself."

Longarm shrugged. "I seem to be powerful attractive to women."

That brought a laugh from Jessie. "And you're not the least bit swelled-headed about it, are you?"

"A man is what he is. No use in fightin' it."

"Well, I'm going to stay around Rimfire for a while. I think I might have a proposition for Adam."

Longarm looked at her and cocked an eyebrow.

"Adam's a stagecoach man, and the day of the stage-coach is just about done in these parts. But I was thinking, Custis . . . there are other places in the West where the railroads haven't reached yet. Places where the railroads may never reach. There's still a need for stage lines, and there may be for a long time to come."

"So you're thinkin' about starting up a new one with the Warfields?"

"Several, actually. The Starbuck holdings have always liked to invest in transportation."

Longarm nodded. "Sounds like a good idea to me."

"What about you?"

"I was thinkin' that I'd head back to Laramie tonight with Abernathy and take Delahunt with us. I can turn him over to the law there and then get back to Denver. Knowin' Billy Vail, he's already got some new job lined up for me."

"I wouldn't be a bit surprised. Rose will be disappointed that she didn't get to say good-bye to you."

"That's a shame, but maybe it's for the best. You'll tell her so long for me, won't you?"

Jessie sighed. "Of course. Are you ever going to stop moving on and leaving heartbroken women behind, Custis?"

"Oh, I reckon I probably will, one of these days. If I live long enough." Longarm grinned. "But that day ain't yet."

Chapter 30

Live by the gun, die by the gun . . . It was as true on this night as it had ever been. All of the hired killers working for Delahunt—and by extension, for Delahunt's employers back East—were dead, either killed outright or mortally wounded in the tremendous volley from the trains that had met them when they came charging in. Delahunt was the only one of the bunch left alive, and he was tied up in a storage room in Abernathy's private car.

Longarm stood near the locomotive of the work train, talking to Jessie, Ki, Adam Warfield, and Earl Fenton. An uneasy truce existed between Adam and the construction boss. They had blamed each other for their troubles for so long that it was hard for them to trust each other.

The other locomotive chuffed softly. Its steam was up, and Abernathy would be leaving soon, taking Longarm with him. Longarm hoped that Danielle would behave herself during the trip back to Laramie. Otherwise things might get awkward. Maybe he could claim his wound was hurting him . . .

He shook hands with Adam, who said, "So long, Marshal. Sorry if I treated you like a common shotgun guard."

"I'm glad you did. Shows what I did was workin'." Longarm grew more solemn. "Take care of your sister."

"Of course. Will we see you again?"

"Probably. One of these days." Longarm glanced at Jessie. He knew she hadn't discussed her plans with Adam yet, but once she did, if he agreed to go into business with her somewhere else, it was entirely possible Longarm would see him and Rose again. As Jessie had said about fate, it took a powerful delight in putting the two of them together every now and then.

Longarm shook hands with Fenton next, the railroad man thanking him for everything he had done. Then he clasped Ki's hand, the two of them knowing it was only a matter of time until they saw each other again.

He saved hugging Jessie for last and enjoyed the feel of her warm, strong body in his arms. He planted a kiss on her forehead.

"Try to stay out of trouble."

She laughed. "Don't I always?"

Longarm didn't answer that. He knew better.

He was about to step away from the group when the sound of the locomotive suddenly changed, growing louder as steam was fed to the engine. The drivers clattered and clanked as they engaged. Longarm turned with a frown to peer back along the work train.

"What in blazes? They ain't supposed to leave without me."

"Custis, what's going on?"

Longarm didn't take the time to answer Jessie's question. Instead, he broke into a run alongside the work train. The other locomotive was picking up speed and backing away from the railroad construction camp.

An unsteady figure loomed up out of the shadows. "Marshal! Marshal Long!"

Longarm caught hold of the man's arm, recognizing him in the dim light as the engineer who drove Abernathy's train. "What the hell's going on?"

"It's Delahunt! He got free somehow and climbed up to the cab. He hit me with his pistol and threw me off the train, then I reckon he must've forced my fireman to shovel coal at gunpoint. He's stealin' the damn train with Mr. Abernathy and his daughter on it!"

"Son of a—"

He didn't waste any more time cussing but again took off at a run after the private train. As he saw the locomotive picking up speed, he felt his heart sink. There was no way he could outrun a train, and he knew it.

But then he saw the small group of the outlaws' horses that had survived the barrage. They had been brought into the camp and penned up with the other horses, and they still wore their saddles. Longarm raced over to the rope corral and yanked the gate open. He grabbed the bridle of the nearest saddled horse.

By that time, Jessie and Ki were with him. Jessie grabbed a horse, too.

"We're coming with you, Custis!"

He didn't argue with them. He just threw himself into the saddle and took off at a pounding run after the stolen train.

Clearly, Delahunt knew how to handle a locomotive. That was no surprise since he had worked around railroads for a while. He had the train moving fast, especially considering the fact that it was backing away from the camp in the dark. As Longarm leaned forward in the saddle, he saw sparks rising into the night from the diamond-shaped stack of the locomotive.

The horse he had picked was a little faster than the ones

ridden by Jessie and Ki. When he looked back, he saw that he was pulling away from them, even though they were urging all the speed they could from their mounts.

Unfortunately, the train was faster than all of them. The initial spurt of speed from Longarm's horse had brought it almost even with the locomotive, but Longarm knew that wasn't going to last. Within seconds, the train would pull away, and he'd have no chance of catching it.

"Give it all you got, old son!"

The ringing shout of encouragement made the horse strain for every last bit of speed it possessed, and Longarm drew even with the front of the retreating train. He glanced over at the cowcatcher, told himself that he was even crazier than when he'd jumped from his horse to that stagecoach, and then said to hell with it.

He had never cottoned to the idea of dying in bed.

He left the saddle in a powerful leap that had all his strength behind it. As he sailed through the air, he stretched his arms out as far as they would go. He came down on the cowcatcher that extended five or six feet in front of the engine and grabbed on to it desperately.

His feet dragged on the roadbed for a second before he pulled them up, just in time to avoid having them slam into a cross tie. Pain throbbed in his side, and he knew that he had probably broken open the wound again.

But he was on the train. He hauled himself higher on the cowcatcher. When he could stand up, he did so, balancing carefully. There were narrow ledges on both sides of the engine leading back to the cab. If Delahunt was at the throttle, as seemed likely, he would be on the right-hand side of the cab. Longarm began working his way along the ledge on the left side of the engine.

The train was rocketing along now, going much too fast for the circumstances. Longarm felt it swaying a little on the rails. Luckily, this stretch was straight and fairly

level. If there had been any sharp curves, the train probably would have derailed by taking them at this speed.

Delahunt just wanted to put as much distance as he
could between himself and his pursuers, thought Longarm.
He was willing to take the chance of wrecking the train.

Longarm took his time working his way toward the cab.
One misstep could be fatal, and if he was dead, there
wouldn't be anybody to stop Delahunt. It was possible that
the renegade engineer might even kill Abernathy and Danielle, if he hadn't already.

Longarm could see into the cab now, but he didn't spot
Delahunt. That confirmed his hunch about Delahunt being
at the throttle. A new worry prodded its way into Longarm's brain. At the speed they were going, it wouldn't
take them long to reach the spot on the main line where
the spur branched off. If the train was still going this fast
when it got there, it wouldn't stay on the rails where they
made the big curve to form a siding next to the main line.

As he pulled himself closer along the ledge, Longarm
caught a glimpse of the fireman through the cab window.
The man clutched his shovel in both hands, and something
about his stance told Longarm that he was about to try
something. Before Longarm could do anything else, the
man raised the shovel like a weapon and leaped out of
sight. Delahunt must have turned his back, and the fireman
was seizing his chance to fight back.

A gun blasted, and the fireman reeled into view again.
He had dropped the shovel, and he used both hands to
paw at the blood-welling hole in his chest. Delahunt had
whipped around in time to shoot the man before the blow
with the shovel could fall.

The fireman's attack was a distraction Longarm could
use, though, so the man's sacrifice wouldn't be in vain. As
the fireman crumpled onto the floor of the cab, Longarm
grabbed the edge of the window and swung around through

the opening. He landed in the cab and saw Morgan Delahunt standing next to the throttle, wild-eyed, smoke curling from the barrel of the gun in his hand.

Delahunt's surprise at seeing Longarm lasted only a split second before he fired again. That hesitation was enough to give Longarm a chance to dive under the barrel of the gun as it roared. He crashed into Delahunt and drove the smaller man back against the side of the cab.

Longarm was bigger than Delahunt, but he was wounded and had been through more of an ordeal during the past few days. Also, Delahunt fought with the crazed strength of desperation. He slammed the gun against Longarm's head. The blow sent fireworks cascading through the lawman's brain and caused him to sag toward the floor. Before Delahunt could shoot him or wallop him again, Longarm grabbed his legs and jerked them out from under him.

Delahunt screamed as he fell so that his face was right in front of the open door of the firebox. The fierce heat made him jerk away. Longarm grabbed him and shoved him toward the firebox again. Delahunt's face went right into the opening this time, and he shrieked as his skin began to blister.

Longarm couldn't stand being that close to the heat, either. He had to let go of Delahunt and roll away. As he did, he saw that Delahunt had dropped his gun. Longarm looked around but didn't see the weapon. It must have slid out of the cab, he thought.

Delahunt snatched up the shovel the fireman had dropped and swung it at Longarm's head. Longarm rolled aside. The shovel clanged into the floor of the cab. Longarm brought a booted foot up into Delahunt's belly. That caused Delahunt to double over in pain, but he didn't drop the shovel. Instead he chopped at Longarm's face with the blade. Longarm jerked his head aside just in time. He reached up, grabbed the handle of the shovel, and heaved.

Delahunt wouldn't let go. He flew over Longarm's head, screaming again as he crashed into the front wall of the cab. As Longarm twisted over, he saw that Delahunt's head had gone completely through the open door of the firebox this time. With a lunge, Longarm grabbed the door and forced it against Delahunt's back and shoulders, pinning him there. Delahunt screamed and screamed as he flailed, his arms and legs flopping around like insane things. Longarm gritted his teeth and held the door in place, though, fighting back the pain in his side, the heat that washed over him, and the sickness that roiled in his stomach as he smelled Delahunt's head cooking.

Finally, Delahunt lay still. Longarm let go of the firebox door and sprawled on the floor of the cab, sick and exhausted. He grabbed Delahunt's legs and pulled the man away from the firebox. The flesh had been completely burned off Delahunt's head, leaving only a grinning skull.

Longarm lay there for a few seconds, catching his breath and feeling his heart slugging madly in his chest, before he realized that the train wasn't out of danger yet. Without the fireman to stoke the flames, the steam would gradually die and the train would slow down. As much speed as it had built up, though, that would take a while. Longarm wondered how close they were to the main line. The train was going at least a mile a minute, and it had taken him at least ten minutes to climb back here to the cab from the cowcatcher and then deal with Delahunt.

He pulled himself upright and staggered over to the window to lean out and look behind the fast-moving train. He spotted a light off to the west and frowned at it for a second before he realized that it was moving, too.

It was the headlight of an eastbound train. The runaway was almost back to the main line.

Longarm lunged to the throttle and disengaged it, then

hauled on the brake lever as hard as he could. The horrible, high-pitched squeal of metal on metal filled the night as the brakes tried to catch. The train slowed slightly, but not enough.

Longarm needed to get to the top of the caboose so he could work the brake there. Gritting his teeth against the pain that filled him, he left Delahunt's body and climbed the iron rungs to the top of the tender. From there he scrambled over the pile of coal and dropped to the platform on the front of Abernathy's private car.

He jerked the door open, ran through a short corridor with compartments on both sides, and burst out into the sitting room. Abernathy lay on a divan, blood on his head where Delahunt must have struck him with his pistol. Danielle knelt at her father's side, her face ashen with fear as she tried to wipe away the blood.

"Custis!" She sprang to her feet. "Oh, God, Custis, I can't believe you're here! Delahunt's loose! He—"

"He's dead." Longarm rushed past her. "Got to get to the caboose! Got to slow down the train!"

Danielle hurried after him. "There's a brake wheel on top of this car, too! I'll get it."

He didn't argue with her. If Danielle could help, that would increase their chances of slowing down enough in time to prevent a wreck.

He came out onto the rear platform, reached across the gap to the grab irons bolted to the caboose, and began climbing. When he glanced over his shoulder, he saw Danielle climbing to the top of the passenger car. Her long skirts didn't seem to hinder her.

When they reached the top, Longarm came to his feet and ran toward the brake wheel at the rear of the caboose. The car swayed and threatened to pitch him off a couple of times, but he managed to keep his balance. When he got to the wheel, he grabbed it and began to twist it. Looking

back at the private car, he saw that Danielle was turning
that wheel, too.

The brakes screamed as they fought against the incredi-
ble hurtling weight of the train. Longarm looked toward the
main line again. The eastbound train had almost reached
the spot where the spur line curved in. Even if he and Danielle slowed the runaway enough to keep it from derailing
when it reached the curve, they might not be able to stop it
before it clattered over the siding and rammed right into the
side of the passing eastbound. That would cause both trains
to crash in a hellacious tangle.

But if the next few seconds were in fact the last few
seconds of Longarm's life, at least they had boiled down
an amazing clarity and simplicity. All he could do was
haul as hard as he could on that brake wheel.

That, and pray.

The train slowed, slowed . . . It reached the beginning of
the curve and didn't derail, although Longarm felt it sway
and tilt dangerously underneath him. The eastbound was
passing by on the main line now, clattering at full speed
through the darkness. Longarm looked for the end of it,
hoping against hope that it wasn't a really long train. He
saw passenger cars, freight cars, baggage cars, then . . . the
caboose! He saw the red lantern swaying on the caboose's
rear platform. There was a chance the eastbound would
clear the siding before the runaway jolted from it onto the
main tracks.

That was now their *only* hope, Longarm realized, because the train he was on wasn't going to stop in time. He
leaned on the wheel anyway, trying to slow it as much as
he could.

Suddenly they were on the siding, the runaway's caboose leading the way as it raced along beside the caboose
of the eastbound. Longarm caught a glimpse of the other
train's conductor staring goggle-eyed from a window at

the train that had appeared apparently out of nowhere and seemed intent on outracing the eastbound to the end of the siding. Gritting his teeth, Longarm hung on to the brake wheel and braced himself for the horrible, grinding impact.

The collision didn't come. With inches to spare, the eastbound's caboose roared on past the siding, and the runaway jolted onto the main tracks right behind it. Longarm sagged to the roof of the caboose and whooped in relief. The conductor of the other train rushed out onto his caboose's rear platform and stared at the caboose following about ten feet behind, with Longarm riding the roof of it. Longarm lifted a weary hand and waved as the gap between the trains began to grow. Inertia was finally taking over. The private train slowed even more, and the eastbound pulled away from it.

Longarm wasn't sure how long it took before the train finally shuddered to a halt. But then Jessie and Ki were there, having followed all the way from the construction camp. Ki practically had to pry Longarm's hands off the brake wheel. Somehow they got him to the ground and into the private car, where soft, warm arms went around his neck and Danielle's voice whispered in his ear.

"You did it, Custis, you did it. You saved us all. And now I'm going to take care of you. I'll help you recuperate from everything you've gone through."

Longarm sighed and sank back into the cushions of the divan where Ki had placed him. As he fought off oblivion for a moment, he wondered how soon Billy Vail would have another job for him. He wasn't quite sure what to hope for.

Chasing outlaws might not be as tiring as all the "recuperating" Danielle probably had in mind!

LONGARM

GIANT-SIZED ADVENTURE FROM AVENGING ANGEL LONGARM.

BY TABOR EVANS

penguin.com/actionwesterns

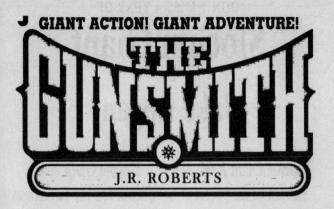

GIANT ACTION! GIANT ADVENTURE!

THE GUNSMITH

J.R. ROBERTS

DON'T MISS A YEAR OF

Slocum Giant
by
Jake Logan

penguin.com/actionwesterns

M457AS0510